THE DISCLOSURE

MEL TAYLOR

Severn River Publishing
www.SevernRiverBooks.com

This is a work of fiction. Names, characters, businesses, places, events and incidents are either the products of the author's imagination or used in a fictitious manner. Any resemblance to actual persons, living or dead, or actual events is purely coincidental.

ISBN: 978-1-64875-634-4 (Paperback)

ALSO BY MEL TAYLOR

Booker Johnson Thrillers

The Exclusive

The Arrangement

The Disclosure

The Frank Tower Mystery Series

Investigation Con

Investigation Wrath

Investigation Greed

Investigation Envy

To find out more, visit

severnriverbooks.com

For teacher Catherine Wright, who inspired me to write.

1

Seconds after she turned into the curved gravel driveway, everything looked wrong. Strong gut feelings told her to turn around and leave. She got out of the car and took a quick survey. A line of trees along the back of the lot and no outside lights kept the property blanketed in shadow. Sunset was an hour ago, and the lack of a moon didn't help. The place also had no garage light on so the front and side yards were cloaked in shadow. The house had two stories, with several windows top and bottom. There was a wrap-around porch, rare for South Florida. The nearest neighbor was a quarter mile away. She squinted into the darkness and finally spotted a single light coming from within the depths of the house, a dim yellow seen through a giant front window. She stopped and looked for movement. There was nothing.

The house was so far from the road, the one dimly lit streetlight was almost useless. Two banyan trees and a few short palms blocked any view of the back yard. A powerful sense of being alone surged through her.

She could taste the fear in her now dry mouth. Her right hand was less than steady. Turning back now, though, was not an option. The information she could receive was far too valuable to ignore. She kept telling herself this had to be done. Months of work might fall right into place with the things she could learn tonight. Her right foot crunched in the dirty gravel, cracking the near silence. A dozen more steps and she was up the three stairs of the porch. Now, she thought, just knock on the door. She turned around and made a mental note of the distance and time back to her car in case she had to make a run from the place. The gravel might slow her down.

Her fingers squeezed tight into a ball, ready to knock. The first knuckle tap on the wood gave her a surprise. The door creaked open on the jamb, swinging to the left and revealing a look inside the last house on Willdrift Lane.

"Hello," she announced. "I followed the directions. I'm ready to talk."

Another survey, left to right. The weak light came from the kitchen, directly ahead. She stood in the living room, with a wall unit full of old books on one side. Off to her right rested a worn-down L-shaped leather couch. She stepped inside, her shoes quiet on the thick area rug. She took three more steps to the wall, flipped the on-off switch and got nothing. No light. Someone wanted the place as dark as possible.

"Is anyone here?" Her voice was louder this time.

Still no answer. She mustered up the will to walk toward the dim kitchen since maybe no one heard her. This had to be done, she kept thinking. Just get the giant end-all bundle of information so her questions would be addressed. There would be some answers. Finally.

Just as she was about to enter the kitchen when she heard the front door slam shut. She whipped around and saw no one there, yet someone made sure the door was closed. The hallway near the door was dark as midnight.

Answers aside, she ran to the front door and turned the knob. The door was locked. Panic replaced reason. She banged on the door, shook and yanked on the knob, and got no movement. When she turned around and leaned against the door, the assessment of the room was now different. She looked for anything to protect herself with or to offer an escape. When she pulled her cell phone out of her purse, a gloved hand pulled the cell away and pushed her to the floor. Did she still have mace in the purse? Quickly, she got to her feet and looked for the person in the room. Again, she was seemingly alone. There was no time to dig for the mace and instead she ran toward the kitchen. Two steps away from the kitchen entrance, someone turned out the light.

Her eyes raked the room again, looking for another room so she could hide and push her five-foot-six-inch frame against the door. What she discovered sent fear tremors through her body. The doors to the two rooms off the kitchen were removed. She felt the entire house closing in on her with escape options disappearing by the second. Her hands dug deep into the purse for the mace, then she stopped when she heard a noise coming from the kitchen. In her hand were her car and house keys. She placed the longest key, for the house, in between her fingers, making the key protrude out so she could poke someone in the face.

She yelled, "Let's stop playing games. C'mon out. I just want to talk." She held the key ready for the person to return. The house held its own form of quiet. Rug runners in the hallway and throughout would let anyone get around in near silence with relative ease.

She stood there weighing what to do next.

An object moved fast through the air, an angular metal something, catching ripples of light and shadow, picking up speed in a sweeping rip-like motion somewhere near her left side. Everything was so fast, she hardly recognized what happened. The person must have been wearing all black. A moment later, the hurt came. Her left hand jammed against her side in an effort to stop the growing fire of pain searing across her hip and stomach. She pulled back her hand, now dripping with blood, droplets spotting the rug. There was no time to check the wound. She had to turn and seek a way out through the kitchen. Now. Four steps in, she dropped to the floor. She knew the weapon must have been a knife. Hurriedly, she checked her body and could tell the cut through her clothes and skin was deep. More blood seeped through her fingers with each breath. The house keys fell to the floor. There was only one objective; just get away from her attacker. Now she was all the way down to the linoleum, her right cheek just barely off the floor, spittle dripping from her mouth.

After moving her head around looking for help, she estimated the kitchen exit door was perhaps twenty feet from her. When she moved, weakness started to replace natural energy as she lost more and more blood. Another thought came to her and while she crawled to the door, she made sure to put her blood, her DNA, on everything possible. She ran streaks of crimson across the tile, a chair leg, and a cabinet kickplate. Three more pushes along the floor and she was now just yards from the door. Still, there was the task of getting up and actually walking. If she could just reach the doorknob, maybe she could pull herself up.

Everything before her became a blur. Objects looked in multiples. There was someone near her feet. Vision was difficult in the dark, so identifying the assailant was almost impossible. The blade, however, was back and just above her. The long-edged weapon moved through the gray-black air, catching the slightest glint on the steel. A hard slicing motion moved until the blade found its soft target. She wailed in pain then gave in to the repeated darting, sweeping motions assailing her body. There were words being shouted down to her in the form of a question. The words were repeated, again and again. She couldn't answer with the pain erupting through her body, shutting down the ability or will to say anything. Her hands raised up instinctively in a defense posture to protect herself from the incoming stabs. She held out until the cries stopped and a growing red pool formed around her body, arms, and legs. The very last house on Willdrift Lane was once again quiet.

2

Four Years Later

When Booker Johnson entered the Channel 27 newsroom, he was met by smells of Cuban coffee, bits of laughter-chatter and reporter desks with small plastic plates filled with donuts. Other reporters were biting into pastelitos, the delicious tiny pies of pastry stuffed with various fillings. Breakfast in a newsroom was always on-the-go. People were making last-minute preparations to leave. Monday was in full swing.

"You're late, Booker." Claire Stanley ran the assignment desk. In reality, she ran everything. All new or old information flowed through her with the precision of a person who had seen everything in more than twenty years in the so-called news business.

Booker moved past his cubicle and walked across the raised floor, heading for the assignment desk area. The floor was actually a platform where underneath was a maze of wires and intricate connections, part of the makeup of a building designed to take in video and audio feeds to a large number of people.

"Sorry I'm late. I see the meeting is over." Booker prepared himself for his designated story to cover, since he wasn't in the morning meeting where he could have proposed a story idea of his own.

"Just sent you the email." Stanley's jaw was working a piece of gum. Her eyes never came up to meet Booker's and she kept staring at the list of story assignments on her computer. "We gotcha lined up with a woman who catches pythons."

Booker tried to sound intrigued. "There's lots of python hunters. Florida is always looking for them. Like, so what?"

Finally, Stanley stared directly toward Booker. "The 'what' Booker is this woman is ninety years old. She lives with no air-conditioning, only uses water from her well, stays off the grid, and loves the stench of python musk." The gum chews were in high-speed motion. "I'm just thankful she has a cell phone."

"Loves python musk. Wonderful. Pythons only put out musk—"

Stanley finished the sentence. "When they're fighting a predator. This woman is tough as Alligator Alley. And she holds the record for the second largest python caught in the state. And she's not much taller than two stacked beer barrels."

"Okay. I'm sold. I'm in. Who am I working with?"

"Coffee."

"Perfect." Booker turned toward his desk, but didn't get far.

"Just one thing, Book. The boss is keeping track of you being late. Your evaluation response was due two weeks ago and you almost missed a story deadline for the third time this month. Just passing it on."

"No problem." He walked off, knowing full well missing slot, or missing a designated story deadline was a critical news screwup. Missing slot might mess up an entire newscast. And three times? He shook it off for now. What Booker wanted to do was check in on a number of matters, any one of which might turn into a decent story. The python lady was a nice distraction.

Junice Coffee turned the corner and locked eyes with Booker, her signal that she was packed up with her camera and ready to go. Coffee always wanted people to address her by her last name. Two years ago, she was pinned down, caught in between a bank robber and police, bullets flying past her, with just her camera for protection. She stayed down, prone position, in a ditch, calmly videotaping a gun battle just yards from her until the man gave himself up to a S.W.A.T team. She caught all the action, finally standing up when the suspect was in the patrol car. The story earned her a spot news Emmy Award. A wicked smile etched across her face when she approached Booker. "Ya ready to catch a python?"

"Doubt if we find anything in the daytime."

Booker grabbed an old-style reporter pad, making sure he had his phone and earpiece before leaving the room.

"Book! Don't leave." The voice was Stanley. "You got a call coming your way. Will only speak to you."

Booker sat down and waited for the call to be transferred. "Booker Johnson. Can I help you?"

"I hope so. Not sure where to begin." The male voice sounded distant.

Booker pulled out his pad. "Where you calling from?"

"Let's just say I'm calling from another country."

"Okay. Go on."

The man paused, as if gathering together exactly what he was about to convey. "I don't know if you remember me, but I definitely remember you since you were at the courthouse a lot. My name is Judge William Rocker. Let me correct that. Former judge."

Booker waved his hand at Coffee, directing her to look at what he was writing down on his notepad. Booker wrote the words GET YOUR CAMERA.

Without hesitation, Coffee turned and retreated to the side doors where her SUV was parked. Before she stepped out of the newsroom, she motioned to Claire Stanley to immediately go to Booker's desk, something was up.

When Stanley got to Booker, he motioned to her and others to be quiet. He wanted to make sure he could hear the man. Booker wrote down more words, this time for Stanley to read: JUDGE ROCKER ON THE PHONE.

Booker started a series of questions. "I want to be clear about this. You say this is William Rocker, who disappeared after his wife was found murdered?"

"Booker, we've spoken on several occasions. You know my voice. I'm not some imposter. Yes, I'm the person you speak of. I..." His voice trailed off.

"Judge, where are you now? That was what?"

"Four years ago. She was killed four years ago. I hate to say it, but I took off."

"Judge, is it okay if I record this conversation or we can do a video call? Or I'll put it on speaker and we can continue to talk. Is that okay?"

"I'm going to call back in one hour. Give you time to do whatever you guys do and we will talk. I promise, I'll call back. But no video."

"Okay, just audio."

"Booker, I'll give you a hint that it's me. Remember what we used to laugh about? About why I kept the courtroom so cold during a trial?"

"You said it was so the jury—"

Rocker jumped in. "So, the jury wouldn't fall asleep. I'll call back." Silence.

"Judge..."

He was gone. Booker looked up to see Coffee hustling in with her camera gear. "Set up in the conference room. He's going to call back."

Stanley's jaw was moving hard, up and down. "Book, did it sound like the real judge?"

"It did. There was no phone number that came up?"

"Far as I know, it was unknown. Did he say where he was?"

"No. Just that he was going to call back."

Booker's fingers typed up a computer query in Channel 27's bank of past news stories and found several. All of them from four years ago, with an anniversary story three years ago including interviews with police about the case and the missing judge. Stanley was up and doing four things at one time. For a quick few minutes, she went in and spoke with the news director. When she came out, another reporter, Merilee Yang was assigned to gathering all the past stories on the murder and would do a background piece. Booker would do the main news story if the judge called back. Another reporter was given the assignment of the python woman.

Coffee set up two cameras in the conference room. One would be aimed at Booker. A second camera pointed toward the speaker on the office phone. Coffee's arms bulged slightly from the years of hauling camera gear, tripods and light box cases all over South Florida. Stanley had more questions for Booker. "Did it sound like he would do a video phone call?"

"He said no."

Booker knew the look. Stanley was in deep thought, as if connecting story angles with reporters, blocking out what should be covered and what should be teased for upcoming newscasts and even into late-night assignments. Her expression and questions were all indicators of a person with a stern tenacity to grip and develop a news story.

Booker read her some of the information from his computer. "So, they found Shanice Rocker in a home on Willdrift Lane after a phone tip. Apparently, she was stabbed multiple times. Deep cuts. Really gruesome scene. We did a big to-do on it at the time especially since this was the wife of a judge. He claimed he was away at the time but wasn't clear on his alibi. Looks like police were about to name him as their person of interest when the judge just disappeared. He's been on the police radar ever since."

"Until now." Stanley's gum chewing stopped. "Did he say why he contacted you?"

"No. I expect to find out more when he calls back."

"You expect that to happen?"

"I do."

Stanley kept the questions coming. "And he sounds legit? Not some clown trying to be a fake judge?"

"As he said on the phone, we've talked many times. I know his voice. I'm convinced it's him. He talked to reporters just after his wife was found. And let me check." Booker typed in a new query. "No interview done with her, ever. Just some photographs given to us when she died."

Coffee was done setting up the gear. "And you didn't cover the murder?"

"No, I was busy on another story. I got to know the judge during a couple of trials in his courtroom."

Stanley's expression was worrisome. "Is this guy using us? I mean, he comes to us, who knows what he might say. Say he killed her, hid, and now he's using Booker Johnson as a way to deflect his guilt?"

Booker settled into a chair next to the phones. "I thought about that. I just want to see what he has to say first. Then, we'll adjust."

Stanley left to attend a whirlwind of other stories and issues. Booker and Coffee sat ready. Twenty minutes went by. Then an hour. Three times Stanley walked past the conference room.

Booker turned to Coffee. "She thinks we're being played. I don't think so."

Exactly two minutes later, the phone rang.

3

"Booker."

"I'm here." The former judge sounded like he had moved to another phone. The voice was clearer than before. Coffee was already recording with both cameras.

"Judge, before we start, I have to let you know this conversation is being recorded. Is that alright with you?"

"Yes. I give you permission to record my voice as this is a phone conversation."

"First, judge, why did you contact me?"

"Booker, I want to tell you that I'm returning to South Florida. I'm coming back because I want to find the person who killed my wife. And in doing so, make sure the public knows I had nothing to do with her death."

"Why did you leave? You made yourself look guilty. And now you're saying you had no involvement in her death?"

"After consulting with a few people at the time, it seemed to me I was being singled out for something I did not do. Let me tell you a few things that were not released at the time this happened." Booker and Coffee heard a rustling sound like he was moving papers around.

"Booker, let me check. Yes, when this happened the public was not told that they found a knife at the scene of my wife's murder. A knife I was told had my fingerprints on it and no one else's. Just mine."

"Did police let you see the knife? This evidence?"

"I saw a photograph and, yes, this is a knife that was in my collection. But let me stop you there and get back to the reason I am calling. I want to come back. A return. I want to clear some things up and I want to bring some justice to my wife's murder."

"Can you explain how your prints were on the knife?"

"Booker, here's what we're going to do. I'll let you and your station decide on what you want to do about this, but I don't want a circus when I return. So, I want to keep this part between us, otherwise I will consider a different way to do this."

"Go ahead." Booker was taking notes.

"First, I want you to meet me in Chicago. You will meet me there and together, me, you and your crew, we'll do a sit-down interview and then we will fly back to South Florida. I won't speak to anyone else. We'll fly in and go directly to the police station. Are you still there?"

Booker stopped writing. "I'm still here. What makes you so sure things haven't changed? You still might be a person of interest. No other arrests have been made since you left."

"Things have changed. I will tell you all that on camera in Chicago. I just have one thing to ask and I won't deviate from it. Please do not broadcast when we will be arriving. I don't want fifty cameras in my face when I go to the police. Just one station. Yours. Do you understand, Booker?"

"We can keep it quiet until we get back. When do you want to do this?"

"Tomorrow morning."

"Tomorrow? Okay. We'll be there. You have a spot where we will meet?"

"Yes. Have you heard of The Bean? Famous sculpture in Chicago?"

"Yes. Been there."

"Good. We will meet at The Bean at exactly nine a.m. We meet, we talk at the hotel I picked, and we fly out in the afternoon. That means you probably have to leave today. Are we good with all that?"

"No problem. Mr. Rocker, what about a phone number? Is there a way I can call you?"

"No phone. And the details on the hotel will come when we meet. Blind faith Booker. Just plain blind faith. I will be there. If I don't see you at that spot at the appropriate time, I will find another way to go in. Is that clear?"

"Very clear."

"Good. See you tomorrow."

The conversation was over. Coffee turned off the row of portable studio lights. While she broke down the gear, the tripods and two cameras, Booker headed into a meeting with Claire Stanley and the news director.

Octavio Acevedo had spent years writing newscasts for the eleven p.m. newscast before becoming executive producer, then finally news director of Channel 27 eighteen months ago. Before Booker had a chance to sit down, he had to answer some questions.

"So, Booker, all this is a way of getting out of doing your evaluation?" Acevedo smiled.

Booker was all business. "I don't like the fact he's so vague. Once we meet him, we do the interview where? No phone number, We're not even sure where he's calling from. I say we go, but all that is up to you."

From his past actions, Acevedo always relied on his staff to decide most matters. A kind of put-good-people-in-position-to-do-good-things strategy. "Claire, what do you think?"

"I agree with Booker. Why is he being so evasive?"

"There's a lot we don't know. The last time we checked, there is no warrant for his arrest."

Acevedo leaned back in his chair. "We're going to Chicago. We'll book a flight and you can stay there tonight. Meet Mr. Rocker and check in right away. Also, we don't put anything on television just yet. Hold on to the telephone interview. Let's get the real judge sitting down before a real camera and then we'll make another judgement call, pardon the pun."

Booker got up from his chair. "Sure. Okay if Coffee goes?"

Stanley's gum chewing began in earnest. "Already figured it that way. Just remember, he says he's not guilty. But you could be meeting a killer."

4

Booker entered his apartment, opening the door to the sounds of someone on the phone, speaking loudly. These days, Misha Falone was working at home as a sales rep who did almost all of her work on the phone. She could be anywhere in the world and sell computer hardware.

Her voice was still elevated. "No, no. It's Misha, like Me-Sha. Hard on the me. Yeah, yeah, Misha. And the last name is Fa-Lone. That's right Fa-Lone. Thanks, I'll wait." She looked up from the two computer monitors set up in the small living room. "I'm on hold. Whatcha doing here?"

"I'm leaving. Headed for Chicago."

Now she was extremely interested. "Chi? My hometown? Okay, Booker. What's up?"

"Can't talk about it. Just throwing a bag together. Got to get to the airport in an hour."

"Take me with you. I can visit my mother."

"No time, I gotta go." In the bedroom he pulled out the small carry-on he used for short trips. Two dress shirts went into the bag along with a sweater, socks and underwear. He heard Falone's voice from the other room. "This is September. It's hot as blazes here, but September in Chicago could be tricky."

He heeded the warning and reached deep into the closet and pulled out a light jacket. Something he wore maybe twice a year in South Florida. Now the bag was full. He closed up the carry-on and stopped immediately when he reached Falone's makeshift desk. Her eyes were soft brown, what Booker called bedroom brown, sunlight highlighting the tops of her cheeks. On the phone or in person, she always had the ability to speak with a smile. And with no makeup, she still looked ready for a magazine cover. He was about to take her up on her suggestion and find a way to take her with him.

"I should be back sometime tomorrow." He looked around the room for anything missing. He sped past the glass case with four gleaming Emmy Awards inside. She had on too much gear with the wrap-around microphone hanging off her left ear, so he kissed her on the forehead.

She looked playfully annoyed. "A forehead kiss. Great."

"I'll call tonight."

"You better. Tell me everything you can." And she was back talking to a customer. During the drive to the airport Booker had Misha Falone in his thoughts. They dated hard for a year, then broke up. She was caught up in finding the right job and accused Booker of not listening to her continued conversations about terrible jobs. And he was convinced she never paid any attention to any story he ever covered. She left town, he stayed. They got back together, made adjustments, and she moved into his apartment. More than a year in, things were okay as long as there were compromises.

When he got to the airport, Coffee was already in the check-in line explaining to the person behind the counter that the news station had purchased a seat just for her camera. Booker heard Coffee tell the airline clerk the camera never left her side.

———

Even though Chicago was a big Midwestern city, there was nothing in-the-middle about its inhabitants. People took up a side and rallied strong. Chicagoans were either a Northsider or a Southsider. Dedicated Cubs fan or White Sox fanatic. And all of Chicago loved the Bears. Seemingly afraid of nothing, city dwellers, if pushed, could be tough as a Chicago winter.

The flight into Midway Airport took more than two hours, arriving around 1:45 p.m. They had plenty of time to check into the hotel and get the interview in the morning before flying back to Florida. Stepping off the plane, the air was fresh with a coolness not seen right now in Florida. The Chicago temp was sixty-eight degrees. There was no need for a walk to baggage pickup since they were carrying everything they needed. Literally minutes after they got the rental car, Claire Stanley called Booker.

"A meeting at the Bean tomorrow morning is out. Everything's changed. Rocker called. You don't have time. He's meeting you today, like right now, at a hotel just two miles from Midway on Cicero Avenue. I just texted you the address. And then you all fly back tonight. Call me when you can."

"Thanks." Booker ended the call and checked for the address. Stanley sent the location to both of them. The drive was only minutes. They got out of the rental and Booker carried the tripod case while Coffee had her big bag of equipment and the camera in her hand. They walked directly to the second floor without taking the elevator and avoided curious eyes and questions about their TV gear. Room 226 was halfway down the hallway. Booker took a breath and knocked. He noticed the door had a book wedged so the door would not close.

"Hello. It's Booker Johnson. Judge, you in there?"

He pushed the door open and walked inside. There was a piece of paper on the bed: COME ON IN BOOKER.

Coffee rolled her eyes like the whole thing was strange and followed Booker into the room. "Judge?" Still no answer.

They both turned to the door when he walked inside. Former judge William Rocker was all of six-two. Maybe six-three. He had that slight forward tilt some taller people do as if making themselves smaller for others. What struck Booker was the hair. He was now all gray with a matching short-cropped gray-black beard. When he was on the bench, he was always clean-shaven. His ebony fingers looked like the hands of someone who worked hard and moved things around.

The deep voice however was not changed. "I had to check you out from the hallway. Sorry for the spy shit. Just wanted to make sure it was you."

Booker wasn't sure about a handshake. For all Booker knew, this just might be the person who deftly wielded a knife, leaving his wife cut open and calling out for mercy. Booker bypassed the handshake and simply directed him to a chair. "If you can sit over here, Coffee will put a micro-phone on you."

"Coffee?" Rocker smiled as he sat down.

"Yep. I just go by Coffee. And so you know, I hate coffee, just drink tea." She told him to slide the lavalier microphone up through his button-down shirt. After he did that, she clipped the mic to the shirt material. The lights setup took longer. In order to get it just right, photographers always took more time to set up lights than anything else. The subject had to be perfectly lit with no shadow, especially around the face, making sure to avoid what Coffee called "raccoon eyes." Finished, she stood behind the camera mounted on the tripod. Thirty seconds later, she nodded, meaning she was recording.

Booker had his own microphone. "Let's start."

5

"Before you ask me anything, let me just say one thing." Rocker straightened up in his chair. "I did not kill my wife. Let me repeat that and I want to be clear. I did not kill my wife."

Booker stared directly toward Rocker. "Then, why did you take off? And where have you been?"

"I was directed to leave, from those around me who could see I was about to be falsely charged with a crime I did not commit. My professional life was on a path to maybe move to a federal judge post. I left that scenario and spent the last four years in Vietnam."

Booker said, "Currently, a country with no extradition policy with the United States. We have not heard anything from you in those four years. Didn't you think leaving like that made you look guilty?"

"Yeah, I thought about that. I had no choice. The police did not report this publicly, but I can tell you they found a knife next to my wife's body. A knife with my prints on it. Mine. And no one has reported this. Something only the police and the killer know about. But please, let me get back to the point. I did not do this. I did not kill my wife."

Booker waited and did not ask a question, letting the judge work through his thoughts. When he said the word wife, a small tear welled in his right eye. "I loved my wife, Booker. No one can dispute that. We never had any arguments, public or private. I dare anyone to say otherwise. One reason I am back is to find out who killed Shanice."

"Judge. Where were you the night Shanice Rocker was killed?"

"I don't want to get into that right now."

"The police will be asking that as soon as you return to South Florida."

"I know. I have my reasons. But I can't answer that just yet."

"You sound like you have some confidence about your case. Has anything changed?"

"Yes. A major change." Rocker ran a finger across his wet eye, pressing tear drops into his dark skin. "People are about to come forward and change statements made to police four years ago. Statements that will clear me. That's the other reason I want to return. There will be some disclosures that will shake this case wide open. I have to be there for that."

Booker saw Coffee's hands on the camera controls, probably zooming in tight on Rocker's face. "Why do you think she was targeted? Did she have any enemies?"

"Everyone loved Shanice. She was involved in two charity causes. Those charities were her whole life. I can't imagine why anyone would hurt her. But I'll find out."

"What did you do those four years living in Vietnam?"

"Well, at first I bounced around. I found a job as an assistant bar manager since there were so many American tourists. My English came in handy. I had to learn how to cross the street with so many mopeds. Thousands of them. And the place is booming. Companies moving their business there, away from China."

While he listened to Rocker, the main question for Booker was simple: was he telling the truth? In his years of reporting, Booker had always relied on his gut feelings to direct him on where to take his story. And there was usually a focused determination on whether the person on the other side of the microphone was truthful. In Rocker's case, Booker wasn't convinced either way.

"Judge, county records show the house where your wife was found belonged to a shell company. Efforts to find out who exactly owns the property have been difficult and the place has remained empty and abandoned. Do you have any idea why she was there?"

"Well, I know, if possible, the police want it to stay untouched since it's still considered a crime scene. I've never been there but I've asked myself that same question. Why would Shanice enter that house? I tried all kinds of angles and ideas, but I have no idea. And she never mentioned that place prior to her death."

For Booker, approaching a family member about the murder of a loved one was always the hardest thing a reporter could do. He made their privacy a priority and if anyone did not want to speak, he made a quick exit. If family did want to talk, Booker let them discuss, if they wanted, something about the victim.

"Judge, for those of us who did not know Shanice. You have many reasons why you loved her. For the rest of us, let us know. What were the great things you remember about her?"

"Shanice took time for others. She really cared about her charity work, the kids in the neighborhood. There was a special quality about her that made you like her right away. I miss her every day."

Booker checked his watch. "We're done for now. We're headed back to the airport. You have a way there?"

"I'll be fine. I think we're all on the 5 p.m. flight. I'll see you at the airport. I promise."

Coffee unsnapped the camera from the tripod. "And then?"

The tall man stood up, staring at Coffee. "And then, I'll ride with you to the police station. I don't want to contact them until we are on the way. I only want one camera there. Yours."

Just as Booker was about to leave, Rocker got his attention. "One other thing. And I didn't want to say this on camera. Maybe you can look into it. Twice now, someone has broken into my own house. Obviously, they are looking for something. What it is, I don't know. I checked around and I couldn't find anything. I want to give you written permission to check out my house when we get back. I'll give you the keys."

"You're not going to stay at your house?"

"No. I can't go there just yet. I found a place to stay."

On the flight back, Coffee was a bit nervous. The flight was full and there was no seat for her camera. The valuable piece of equipment was in the overhead bin. She kept staring up.

"It'll be okay." Booker and Coffee sat midsection. Rocker was six rows ahead of them. Coffee leaned into Booker. "What does your bullshit meter tell you?"

"Is he telling the truth? I can't tell. He sounded sincere, but I've seen BS artists before. This is murder. I really don't know just yet."

Coffee sat back in her seat. "I can't even sleep with him up there, knowing what he might be capable of. I'll sleep later."

They arrived in South Florida at 8:25 p.m. The plan was that Rocker would ride with them in the news SUV. They both unbuckled their seatbelts. Coffee was up and moving before anyone could disturb her camera. She smiled back at Booker. "Let's go."

6

William Rocker insisted on sitting in the back of the Channel 27 SUV. He said he wanted to be there, a self-imposed insurance measure he would stay true to his word and let Booker accompany him to police HQ. Coffee showed her discomfort with the arrangement by staying quiet the entire time to the building. Rocker had just one last thing for Booker. "When I come out of the building, there is something very important I want to tell you. It's important, I promise."

Booker broke himself away from the others to call Claire Stanley. The play was all set up. On the news, there would be no tease or mention of Rocker going to police. Booker would be the top story of the eleven p.m. newscast. There were crossed fingers in the Channel 27 ranks because they didn't want another TV station to show up and somehow steal some of the story's impact.

When Coffee pulled up, she got out and, within seconds, she had the camera on her shoulder and in position some twenty yards away for what the news biz called "the walkback." Coffee was very familiar with the long sidewalk leading to the front glass doors of the police station. The familiarity meant she could walk backwards with the camera with confidence she had a clear path and wouldn't bump into something. Since they had an interview already recorded, there was no reason to ask anything else.

Booker and Coffee waited for the judge to emerge from the SUV. There were no other TV crews around. Rocker looked like a man ready to address his future. He walked directly in Coffee's direction, not looking down, eyes forward, somewhere between angry and unyielding.

Forty steps in, Rocker almost looked like he wanted to say something. Booker held out a microphone, yet the former circuit court judge remained on his mission.

Five steps from the entrance, a person opened the tall glass door. Brielle Jensen, homicide detective, part time P.I.O., or Public Information Officer, let Rocker inside the building. From where he was standing, Jensen appeared to show Rocker where to proceed. When they were completely out of camera range, Coffee took a deep sigh. "Okay, that part is over. You ready to put this together?"

The word 'together' meant Booker writing a short script and recording his voice in the closed SUV. Coffee worked the laptop editing equipment with flying fingers. They did not want to use all of the interview, just a few questions, saving more for a day-two story.

Just after 11 p.m., Booker stood alone in front of the police department. The world was about to find out about

William Rocker. Coffee's story was fed into the station, and now she did last-minute adjustments to the three portable lights. Their brightness heated up the South Florida night and Booker yearned for some Chicago cool air. He stood in front of her tripod and listened to the lead-in coming through his earpiece.

"We begin tonight with a story that is exclusive to Channel 27. It was four years ago, we first told you about the murder of Shanice Rocker, wife of Judge William Rocker. She was found brutally stabbed to death. Days later, her husband disappeared. Tonight, there is a major break in this case. William Rocker has returned to South Florida and only one station was there when Rocker went directly to police. Our Booker Johnson was there when Rocker arrived. Booker…"

"Early this morning William Rocker, former judge, called Channel 27 saying he wanted to come back, return from his place of hiding, and look for the person who killed his wife. He also wanted to face the scrutiny of possibly being implicated in his own wife's murder."

For the next one minute and thirty seconds, South Florida saw part of the interview Booker recorded in Chicago. There were the video clips of Rocker saying he did not kill his wife, but Booker did not use the bulk of the interview. The entire time, Coffee kept a hard look on Booker and the front door in case Rocker walked out. Once Booker heard the end of his taped package, or roll-cue, he started talking again.

"More than anything, Rocker says he wants to cooperate with police. We will have much more on William Rocker's comments to us, tomorrow. For now, this is Booker Johnson, Channel 27 news, live outside police head-quarters."

When Booker heard the 'all clear,' in his ear, he moved back into posi-tion to wait for the judge to come out. The response from the South Florida news community did not take long. Exactly sixteen minutes after the story aired, two news SUV's pulled up hard, tires screeching, TV crews pulling out gear and running to where Booker and Coffee were standing. There were the usual comments to Booker. How did he get the story? When did Rocker go inside the building? Was he still in there?

Booker politely answered most of the questions, just telling them Rocker was, as far as he knew, still in with detectives.

Coffee spoke up. "He's coming out." She focused on the front door. The two other crews also aimed cameras toward the glass outer door. They could see figures and a few officers near the entrance.

Booker did not expect what was about to happen.

7

When Rocker stepped out of the building, there was a woman walking in front of him. Booker guessed she was around five-ten, wearing a dark blue skirt and white blouse. Her glasses were large and black-framed.

Booker always sized up a person with a few glances and stored information into his memory. She had a real confidence in her walk, like she was about to control everything in front of her.

She stopped in front of the arc of three reporters and cameras. "Evening. My name is Serenity Hart. I represent Mr. Rocker in this matter. From this moment on, please direct all of your questions to me and no one else. Do not contact Mr. Rocker. I can tell you we had a brief meeting with detectives, just letting them know William Rocker is here and ready to cooperate and do whatever it takes to find the person who killed his wife. We will not entertain any questions tonight."

Reporters from the two arriving stations yelled questions anyway. They asked where he had been, why did he come back? Hart remained silent.

She handed out business cards and stepped back into position like she was about to undergo an inspection. She repeated her declaration of no questions sounding so final, no one uttered another one. Besides, her face glared like someone daring just one fool to even think about violating her directive. She started walking, with Rocker following along. Her heels and loud steps echoed off the building. Rocker did not turn around, and the promised follow-up of something important was not offered. For now, there was nothing more to share with Booker.

Coffee stayed focused on the pair until they reached an all-black Cadillac SUV with a driver. The man got out and opened the door for Hart and Rocker, and once all were inside, the car drove off into the silence of the evening.

Once they were gone, one reporter exclaimed, "And who was that?"

Booker admitted to himself he had never seen her before. He studied the business card, which had a Jacksonville address. Once Coffee put away her gear, she took Booker aside. "Book, I know who she is 'cause I knew her when I worked in Jacksonville."

"And?"

"Her name might be Serenity Hart. But don't go by the name. Hart, my ass. Woman has no heart." Coffee tossed cables and wires around in the SUV. "And serene? Never. I've seen her destroy people on the witness stand. She's beautiful and all, but she'll flatten you like a new paved road."

"I see. I've never seen her before. We kinda got blindsided on this, but I'll check her out." Booker reached for his phone, but before he got a chance to speak to someone on the night desk, he got a call from Stanley.

"Nice job Booker."

"Thanks. We have a new player in this. Someone named Serenity Hart."

"Yeah, heard of her. Jacksonville. Only takes on high status clients with a million-dollar retainer. Haven't seen her down here, but up in Jax, I don't think she ever lost a case."

On the drive back to the station, Coffee's words sounded like someone ready to spew out her thoughts. "This guy is playin' us Book. He tells you he's got some important stuff to say, then says nothing. He walks in the place and lawyers up, what, while he was in with detectives? She must have been there already, waiting for him."

Booker finished sending in a Rocker story for the Channel 27 website and closed up his laptop. "I know. He didn't mention a lawyer."

She pounded her right hand on the steering wheel. "Suddenly, I trust him less and less."

"We'll see how it plays out." Booker leaned back in the car seat. He looked over at the still very agitated photographer. "Thanks for your help today. It was a long day."

"I keep thinking about Chicago. I heard and read about those great pizzas. And I was this close to eating a slice." She pinched up two fingers. "This close! We passed up a couple of pizza places and I didn't even get a chance to sniff a pizza or a hot dog."

"Ya gotta plan a return trip to Chi."

"Right now, I just want to find a late-night restaurant and eat myself into oblivion. I'm starving."

Booker tried to keep his eyes open. "You go right ahead. We got more to do tomorrow."

Forty minutes later, Booker was in front of his apartment complex. Misha's last text said she would stay up and wait for him no matter how late. He parked behind a moving truck and went inside. Two minutes later, he walked into the embrace of one Misha Falone.

"Tell me all about it. I saw the newscast. Welcome back."

"Thanks. I'm beat."

She pulled out a package from the fridge and reheated a chicken piccata dinner from his favorite restaurant. He sat down. "It's what, past one a.m? It's late. I shouldn't be eating this." Then he cut into the meal anyway and chewed.

She kissed him on the forehead. "I'm returning your forehead kiss." Falone eased into a chair and propped up her arms to support her head. "Okay. I'm all ears. Talk."

"The story? Well, he called me this morning."

"This guy? Judge Rocker? Wow. And?"

Booker paused to take in another helping of chicken smothered in butter sauce with capers. "Yep. Wanted to come back to South Florida. We watched him walk into the police department."

Misha was also consumed by something on her nearby laptop. "You're rubbing off on me."

Booker was about to drag more chicken through the sauce. "Rubbing off on you?"

"Yeah, you're making me a nosey-body. This security camera app from the complex is great. Been watching who just moved in. I went back and pulled up some security video."

The last piece of chicken gone, Booker moved to the small pile of mixed vegetables. "Yep. Nosey sounds about right. You're spending too much time looking at basically nothing."

She stopped the video feed and stared hard at the laptop. "Booker..."

He dabbed a cloth to his lips and got up to put his dirty plate in the dishwasher. "I'm tired Mish. Gotta git up early. Lots to do."

"Booker, you have to see this."

"Going to bed. You're better off watching Netflix."

"Booker! Come see this right now."

Booker walked up behind her and leaned down, staring into the laptop monitor. Misha had frozen the video on a single person walking into the building. Booker shouted at the computer. "Ya gotta be kidding."

"I didn't see him earlier. I've never seen him in person but isn't that—"

"William Rocker. Walking right into our building."

Misha moved out of the way, letting Booker sit down at the laptop. He tapped more keys. "Damn, that's him alright. Must be the new tenant. He said he found a place."

"Right next to us?"

Booker's mind was a whirlwind of thoughts. He again weighed all of the comments said to him by Rocker in the past twenty-four hours. There had to be a reason why Rocker wanted to be within yards of him. The time-stamp said 12:10 a.m.

Misha had her own opinion. "He wants to be right under your nose. Show you he's not guilty."

"Finding where I live wouldn't be hard." Booker got up and walked to the door.

Misha pushed her fingers through her curly locks. "Where you going?"

"Thinking about knocking on his door."

"Now? Booker get some sleep."

Too late. He opened the door with the enthusiasm of someone on a mission. Before he took a step into the hallway, he saw an envelope on the floor. The large white envelope was apparently stuck under the door. Booker picked it up and found his name on the front. He ripped open the envelope and found a notarized letter. Booker read the two pages and turned back to Misha. "He wants me to search his home. Doesn't give me a timeline. Just says I have his permission." Booker pulled out a set of keys.

"Search his house for what? And why?"

"I have no real idea. He says the place has been broken into twice. Someone probably looking for something."

"Ya gonna do it?"

"I've got to run this by Claire at the station. Uncharted stuff for a reporter. If I find something, then what?"

Misha looked confused. "He's staying here rather than his own home?"

"I brought up the same thing. Doesn't want to go near the place."

Booker walked back toward the laptop and checked the live video coming through the feed. A person was leaving the building. Booker ran to the kitchen and looked out the window at the view of the street. He knew the man leaving the complex.

Judge William Rocker.

For a hot second, Booker thought about getting down two floors to the ground and running out to confront Rocker. Instead, he watched from the window. Rocker got into a white Honda SUV and drove off. He tucked the house keys back inside the envelope. Booker noted the time. 1:20 a.m.

8

Ken Capilon was the king of not trusting anyone or anything. He had stayed at the bar too long downing beers, chased with whisky, using the so-called depth-charges to soothe his brain over the decision he had made. Four years was a long time to hold onto a lie. His distrust of most things transcended to his car and home, which he once had checked for recording bugs. All of this because he found a tracker stuck to his car. He changed passwords more often than he washed his hair. Used text messages for important exchanges rather than emails. That's what the king of distrusting did. He kept all of these quirks to himself and did not openly discuss his habits at work or any social gathering. When he drank at the bar, he drank alone. The thoughts on what to do consumed him. The lie had to be vanquished. The appointment with homicide detectives was set. Now, it was just a matter of following through. However, doubt kept tearing at him. Three or four drinks, he reasoned, would help him lock in his decision.

He kept thinking about his next move during the short drive to the house. He sat in his car in front of his beautiful home for ten minutes, fighting with his thoughts.

Then the phone calls started.

He did not answer them. For one, they were from an unknown caller. And if he did answer, the call would not be taken in the house. One who distrusted everything like Ken Capilon would not do that very thing. No cell phone conversations inside. Weird, but he kept by his convictions. Cell phone calls were only done outside. He walked along the side of his house, down past the newly installed impact windows, into the grand expanse of his back yard. He wanted to be away from any possible bug devices, preferring the open air. The calls kept coming. On the sixth call, he answered.

He jammed the phone up against his ear and listened. He knew the voice. "Yeah, I saw him on the news. He said all the things I expected him to say." Capilon stood there, staring off into the thick branches of southern maple, black darts of shadows cutting through. Finally, he stopped talking and ignored the caller. The yard was devoid of any noise. If he wasn't so tired and definitely drunk, he could just stand there among nature. There was comfort in the plants surrounding him.

Then, his own words cut into the silence. "I know you don't agree, but I made up my mind. I'm keeping the appointment. No one is going to talk me out of it." He ended the conversation and pushed the phone into his pocket, defiantly. Capilon liked the peace. This was why he spent the money to move to the edge of the city.

He stood there, three a.m., just him and his irregular arrangement of plants that required little watering. Just regular rainfalls. He had rows of red Ti plants, a section of Fox Tails, and a row of thirty-foot-tall Birds of Paradise. The only thing he hated about them was the ants also loved the birds as much as he did. For now, he was more than satisfied with just him and the stillness. He looked up and thought to himself it was so quiet he could hear the clouds move.

He rubbed his eyes and decided it was time to head inside.

There was some movement off to his right. He directed his attention to the sound interrupting his late-night, early morning viewing of his enormous back yard.

He had an occasional coyote, an intruder now more and more common in South Florida. There was the noise again, like something moved in the distance. He stopped, trying to zero in on the location of the sounds. Capilon turned to his patio, ready to go inside and give the quiet back to the animals.

Something was now moving fast directly toward him. He whipped around looking all over and was not able to find the source of the noise. Just three steps from the brick edge of his patio, someone knocked him to the ground. The push was hard. When he looked for the assailant, the pain took over and he pushed both hands down to his stomach and side. The movement was so fast, he didn't notice he was hurt until he was down on the grass. Blood was seeping heavily from his sweatshirt. He looked around again for the attacker, seeing nothing, then he heard a few footsteps behind him before there was another quick slash, this time on his right side. He screamed in pain. If he got up and moved, could he make the twenty yards to the back door?

A foot stepped down hard on his neck, pinning him into the St. Augustine grass. Rivulets of pain shocked his system and made him close his eyes. He felt someone over him, in full control of what was about to happen next. The figure seemed to have a covered face. Capilon was not able to mount a defense, just barely eking out some words. "Why...why are you doing this?"

The figure again stepped down on his neck, and breathing became a difficult chore for Capilon. A voice came at him, yet he couldn't make out if the attacker was male or female.

"You know why. And where is it?"

The foot was removed from his throat. Capilon looked up for the attacker and only saw the rounded clouds against a charcoal sky. If he could just sit up and somehow stand, maybe there would be a moment to reason, or even beg. "I won't do anything. I know what this is about. I promise I won't talk. Just let me live."

For several seconds, there was nothing. He could feel himself losing his life connections. Breathing was harder. The blood was coming from an untold number of slashes to his midsection. He was getting weaker.

Someone straddled him, blocking out the clouds and sky. The long-bladed knife dangled above him like a tantalizing method of death. The sharp edge was waved about in a gloved hand. Capilon made one last attempt to convince his attacker he would not say anything, speaking as best he could. "Won't go to the appointment. I won't."

The blade didn't care. A swipe just missed his body. Capilon channeled all his energy into the single effort that might save his life. His options to do something were now down to just milliseconds. Somehow, he needed to duck from another slash, stand up and fight back or run. He winced when he used the strength he had left to try and lift himself up. For all of his efforts, he was not quick enough. The knife came down and across again and again with angled slashes like the claws of some prehistoric imagination, with rapier-like thrusts finding skin, bone and muscle, until finally there was nothing left except the predawn buildup of dew mixed with spewing blood on the grass.

9

It took a warm hard kiss from Misha to awaken Booker Johnson. He opened his eyes to her smile and warm laugh. "You slept right through the alarm. Book, you got to get moving."

Booker agreed with her. He was twenty minutes past his schedule to shower, eat a quick bite and get to the office. Booker snapped through his Tuesday morning routine, even ignoring a study of the morning newscasts. A wave of his hand to Misha and he was out the door. When he reached the outside front entrance to the complex, someone was walking toward him.

"Judge Rocker?"

Rocker looked like someone in a big rush. And one giant mess. His white hair needed a good comb and he was wearing the same clothes he had on the day before. One shoe was untied, laces dragging on the sidewalk. "Sorry Booker. Hope you got my note and the key."

"Yeah, but..."

Rocker was sidestepping him and dodging any possible questions. The former judge moved quickly inside the small lobby and the wall of mailboxes. Over his shoulder the judge shouted, "Didn't have time to tell you, I'm upstairs from you. Can't say much. My lawyer is tight on me." And with that, Rocker was up the stairs, two at a time, rather than waiting for an elevator. Four flights. Booker shook his head. Booker never had a chance to bring up the letter and the house key. He had them safely in his briefcase. There was one more surprise.

"Yo, half-bruh." A man opened the driver's side door and emerged from a perfectly painted blue antique car. The man was Booker's half-brother, Demetrious Moreland.

"What are you doing here? And where did you get that car?"

Moreland was a bit taller than Booker by two inches. He had just about the same almond skin and they shared the same mother.

Moreland pointed to the car and smiled. "A 1968 Chevy Super Sport 396. Mag wheels, four-on-the-floor shift, and black bucket seats. Muscle car."

"First, it's good to see you. But you never call first. You just show up. You need a place to stay?"

"Naw, got a place. Just wanted to see my half-bruh. I missed you."

Booker checked his watch. "I'm running late. Call me."

Moreland still had a streetwise lilt to his voice. Each word painted with a heavy inner-city hue. He looked toned up like he was spending a lot of time in the weight room. He wore jeans and a cream white shirt with a pattern of green palm fronds, triceps well rounded. "Whatcha think of my ride?"

"Like I said, where did you get the car?"

"Part of my new part-time gig."

While Moreland's words were bathed in big-city toughness, all of Booker's streetwise dialect was gone, wiped away by hours and hours of college classes on newsroom announcing. Booker arrived in college with a hard rip to his words, slurred consonants and dropped word endings. Now, each word had a distinctive clarity of its own and he graduated with the smooth rounded voice tones of an extremely polished television journalist. "New gig?"

"I'll tell ya about it later. But that's not why I came lookin' for you."

"What's up?"

"My father called me. Wants to connect."

For Booker, the person he called father, the man responsible for Demetrious coming into the world, never deserved one ounce of respect for the word father. Booker was direct. "You mean the drug dealer?"

"He's not dealin' I think. At least not right now."

Booker put down the briefcase. "That's because he took off, ran from police. There's still a warrant out for his arrest. He's a wanted thug."

"I know. Trust me Book, I don't want anything to do with him. But I just want to hear him out."

"There's nothing to hear! He ran drugs, had a big operation. Police shut it down and he took off. People around him died. Not much to hear."

Moreland edged closer to the driver's door. He stared at Booker with the same brown eyes they shared from their mother. "Book, I didn't want to talk about this over the phone. Only in person. Text me when you have a minute. We can talk. Okay?" He got into the Super Sport and turned on the key. The hard rumble of the engine revving to perfection sounded like something out of a movie.

"Okay, we'll talk."

The car roared off down the street. Booker got into his near quiet BMW and slowly pulled out into traffic.

Booker already had a story slated for the day with his day-two follow-up on Rocker. He still had plenty to share with the public about the knife, something he did not release the night before. Since he was already penciled in for the Rocker story, he bypassed the morning meeting and went straight to his desk. When he opened his computer, he saw all the emails about a murder overnight. Merilee Yang was the reporter assigned to the story.

The newsroom was only partly filled with reporters probably already on the street covering various stories. Coffee was in an edit booth looking over video from the Chicago trip and the police station. The pleasant aroma of Cuban coffee was in the air. A new reporter was in the room, ready to leave. Lacie Grandhouse. Just two short years ago, she was an intern, going out on news stories with reporters, learning first-hand. Now she was back, a fresh-out-of-college reporter on the sometimes-tough streets of South Florida. Not very tall, Grandhouse was impressive in her investigative skills. Still, there were some surprised looks and conversations when she was hired. Grandhouse skipped the normal route of working in smaller markets like Tallahassee or Mobile, Alabama, before a major market like South Florida.

Booker walked to the assignment desk and waited until Claire Stanley got off the phone.

"Morning, Booker." Her mouth was unusually absent of gum.

"We're working a murder?"

She checked her notes. "Yang is down there. We don't have much. Our traffic copter spotted it. Unreal. They were done doing traffic video reports, headed back to the barn, looked down and found this guy sprawled out in his back yard. We couldn't air the original video. This guy was cut open like a fresh caught fish. Blood all over the grass."

"So, the police found out about this from us?"

"Yep. Isn't that something? And then they promptly kicked us out of the airspace."

Booker looked over Stanley's shoulder, reading information on her computer screen. "They say when we can put the helicopter back over the scene?"

"Not yet. They want some privacy for their crime tech guys. I get it. But we were the ones who alerted them." She tucked a piece of gum in her mouth and started the chewing. "You running with the knife information today?"

"Yes. We still haven't heard a word from police. There is one other thing."

"One other thing?" The gum chewing stopped.

"Rocker gave me the keys to his house. He is convinced there is some evidence there that he and everyone has missed."

"The keys? To his house?"

"And before you say anything, I haven't moved anywhere in that direction. I know we want to talk about it first. I'm not going into Rocker's house until we have a meeting."

Stanley's voice struck loud on the next three words. "Got that right." Her phone rang, and Booker turned toward his desk. Stanley shouted to his back. "We'll set up a meeting later."

Stanley always looked like a person stewing on a multitude of facts, all at once. She could look right at you, yet she was probably weighing seventeen different decisions, from placement of news crews, whether to add a second reporter on any given story and what to do to stay ahead of the two other TV news stations. What always amazed Booker was her capacity to make the right decisions, every time.

Three seconds after Booker sat down to write and contact Coffee, Stanley's voice boomed over the newsroom. "Call coming your way, Booker."

He answered. "Booker."

"Hey Booker, it's Merilee."

"Sure. What's up?"

"I know you're busy with day-two of the judge story, but I think you better get down here."

"To your murder scene?"

"Yeah, Book. Trust me, I think you need to get down here now."

10

Police had blocked off both ends of the street so there was no access to set up directly in front of the murder house. Homes here were expansive with multi-acre lots, rimmed with trees with thick branches and occasional wildlife. The area was not gated. For now, the only good view was perhaps three hundred feet from the front door. And Yang was still awaiting an okay from police to put the helicopter back over the scene.

The last time Booker was anywhere near this neighborhood, there was a round-up of sorts for a stray horse that got away. This was a community known for horse riding and very low crime. Until today. The home in question was the only two-story. There was a natural barrier between the homes with cherry hedges and tall ficus, all trimmed and neat. Booker always imagined this would be a place for him to buy once he pooled enough for the downpayment. There were absolutely no gawkers out staring. And perhaps no one wanting to venture anywhere near a camera and microphone. A line of reporters and photographers stood waiting for police to update them.

Booker and Coffee pulled up and parked. They could spend one to two hours helping Yang before they had to get back to the station and prepare Booker's five p.m. news story. He waited until Yang acknowledged him. Immediately, she pointed to two unmarked cars.

"See them?"

Booker stared hard. "So, what are they doing here?"

Yang followed Booker's gaze. He walked all the way up to the yellow crime tape. She followed. Booker was looking at Brielle Jensen. "Now I understand why you called. The detectives from the Shanice Rocker murder are here. Could it be they are taking on this case as well? Just working hard?"

Yang kept her voice down from nearby reporters. "I'm hearing, and please know I have not confirmed this, but I'm hearing this just might be related somehow to the Rocker case."

Booker was more than intrigued. He looked back and Coffee was already getting video of just about everything that moved. "Is the Public Information Officer coming over soon?" Booker took out his pad.

"They keep telling us ten minutes, but nothing so far."

"What do you have on this place?"

"Well, the assignment desk worked up a short profile." She looked through notes compiled on her cell phone. Often just called 'the desk', Claire Stanley and the few people around her were extremely helpful.

Yang studied the mix of crime techs and police while she spoke. "Records from the property appraiser show the home belongs to a Ken Capilon. If the victim is Capilon, we found no arrests for him. No liens on the property. Other records show he is forty-seven years old, not married. He bought the place four years ago. I looked it up." Yang's fast fingers brought up a realtor's website. "The pictures of the inside of the house are still online for when it was on sale."

Booker scanned and swiped right on the more than twenty photographs. The Capilon home had five bedrooms, three baths and no pool. The walls had chair rails, upscale crown molding and marble floors. The home was immaculate.

Yang said, "This guy was really busy on social media platforms until about five years ago. After that, not much. But for a while, he was every-where online. He was all over the place. Not sure yet where he worked. If we find out, Claire wants to send a crew. But for the moment, police haven't confirmed anything."

Yang again went to her phone, this time for video files. She eased the cell toward Booker and Coffee to see. "We obviously can't put this on air, but this is what the helicopter found."

Booker examined the video. The helicopter camera zoomed in on a male figure, face up, midsection covered in blood. Upon inspection, Booker could see the slashes. He froze the video and took out his own cell phone. Booker clicked off three or four pictures. When he widened the photo and examined some more, Booker had a question for Yang.

"Take a look at this. What do you think that is?" He showed Yang the photo.

"I see it but what is that?"

"I think that's a knife." Booker clicked another photo. "No wonder police wanted us to move back. There's a lot to process here."

Yang was staring at the frozen piece of video. "Good catch. I didn't notice that at first."

A police officer walked to the gathering of reporters and waved everybody off, meaning he was not about to speak. He did say a police P.I.O. would be out in ten minutes. Guaranteed this time.

There were two crime scene tech vans parked near the front of the house. Men and women dressed in white gear and booties entered and came out of the house carrying evidence bags. From what Booker could see, no one went down the sides of the house, probably entering the back yard through the patio. Booker made a mental note and wrote down in his pad *why was the side path so important?*

Since they were so far from the front, there was little to no chance of getting home surveillance video. Police had that whole aspect locked down.

Another SUV pulled up and Lacie Grandhouse got out, along with photographer Luis Alvarez. With three crews now at the murder home, Alvarez stood by his car, looking like he wasn't sure what he was supposed to do. Grandhouse joined Booker and Yang.

Yang looked around again toward the houses down the road. "I will stay here and have Grandhouse knock on doors farther down the street and see if anyone saw or heard anything and ask for doorbell camera video."

Booker nodded in agreement.

Booker understood. Home surveillance video was becoming one of the best methods for police to help put together cases. Home burglary video, store break-ins, porch thieves, people looking for open car doors, all provided valuable information. Years before, surveillance video mainly came from bank robberies or convenience stores. Now, just about everyone had door cams and home cams recording anything and everything that moved. Millions of private cameras sold and installed. News reporters used videos from homeowners and stores eager to find a resolution to crime. Even in black and white, the value of surveillance video had grown tremendously. Today, just about every newscast included the vids.

Grandhouse joined the group. "Claire Stanley sent me. I'm backing up Yang. Booker, she wants you to call her. I think she wants you back to work on your judge story."

Booker stepped back so she could survey the house. "Okay. I thought you had a feature story?"

Grandhouse cocked her chin to one side, like she was disappointed. "I was all set to do a feature on a really neat job. Had it all lined up. Get this, they hire a few people to drive around really expensive classic cars. Just drive them. It was all set and then just as we were about to leave, the company cancelled."

Booker got ready to call Stanley. "There will be other features."

"I know. The guy I was supposed to interview says he knows you. Now, it won't happen."

"The guy? His name?"

"He claims he knows all about you. Said his name was Demetrious Moreland."

11

Booker stopped, his face showing surprise. "Demetrious?"

"Yeah. Sounded like he really knew you. That he just got to town."

"Demetrious Moreland is my brother. Half-brother, but he's my brother." Booker was torn. He wanted to stay and pose questions to Grandhouse on what Demetrious was doing since Booker had no idea himself. And he had to leave and get back to the station. "Lacie, what exactly do these drivers do? I never had a chance to talk to him about it."

"Older cars, and some antique cars, just can't sit there. They have to be driven every now and then or some mechanical issues can come up. So, Demetrious is part of a company that has drivers take these cars on short trips. What a great job."

"I had no idea."

Grandhouse shook her head. "Only they cancelled on me. Not sure why. I loved the story."

Booker peeled off and got into the SUV with Coffee just as the police spokesperson stepped up to reporters. A device called a Lenny Stand held all the microphones in place. Coffee pulled away from the scene. Grandhouse and her photographer walked off in search of a home with surveillance video.

Booker pulled up the Channel 27 website on his cell phone and tapped the screen to watch the live feed. He saw Detective Brielle Jensen, the P.I.O., speaking.

"Everyone ready? At approximately six-ten this morning, we got a call from a traffic helicopter of a person in the back yard at this location. We arrived and found a deceased male in the back yard, who we can say died from multiple stab wounds. We have no name on the deceased victim as we are still contacting next of kin. We also found a possible weapon at the scene. At this time, it is too early to tell if this is the weapon in question. All of the evidence is being gathered by crime scene technicians and we will update you after an autopsy has been conducted. We want to add, if anyone saw anything overnight, or heard anything, please call police or you can use the tipline." Jenson paused.

Yang jumped in first with a question. "Can you say if the weapon you found is a knife?"

"We understand there is some video of the scene prior to our arrival on scene. The weapon we found was a knife. Again, we have to make sure this particular weapon was the one involved in this homicide."

Another reporter asked, "Any suspects or suspect description at this time?"

Jensen pressed her fingers back across her blonde locks pulled back into a bun. "We do not have a person description or a vehicle, but, again, we are asking the public, if they saw anything, to contact us."

Yang again, "Do you have a tentative time on when this happened?"

"From everything we have so far, we believe he was attacked sometime after two a.m. We are documenting his timeline before he arrived at home. It does appear someone broke into the victim's home, either before or after he was attacked. If we have anything else later, we will update you with an email news release. That's all we have for now. Thank you." Jensen was gone, walking back to detectives.

Driving the car, Coffee was almost back to the station. She looked over at Booker. "I know we didn't release anything yesterday about this, but a knife was found at the scene of Shanice Rocker's murder. A possible knife this morning. I'm just bringing it up, Book."

Booker put his phone away. "That's a long, long shot. Shanice was killed four years ago. Currently, we have absolutely no connection between her and this guy, except knives were involved. But I have to admit, I thought about it."

"Gotcha."

They parked and went inside the newsroom. The noon newscast was still more than an hour away. Before he had a chance to sit down, Claire Stanley cornered him. "We waited until you got back. We got a meeting with the boss." Stanley nodded her head in the direction of the news director's office. Booker followed her into the large glass-encased office. Octavio Acevedo ushered them to sit while tapping buttons on his phone. "Leonard, can you hear us? Are you there?"

"I'm here."

Booker had only spoken to Leonard Doff, the Channel 27 attorney on six occasions, all of them dealing with news coverage situations.

Acevedo took out a sheet of paper. "Leonard, I think you know everyone here. I've got Claire and Booker with me. I asked Len to listen in. Booker, why don't you tell us what you have?"

Booker explained the situation of finding out the judge was just two stories above his own and about the envelope tucked under his door with the note and house key.

Doff spoke first. "Booker how did you want to proceed?"

"The invitation to go into the judge's home brings up all kinds of problems. As a reporter, I very much want to explore all avenues to this story. But on a purely practical point, what if we find something? What if we find real evidence? Then what? The police will say we broke the chain of evidence and it would hurt their case. We're not the police."

Stanley cut in. "What if we find something but it was planted there for us to find? I like the fact we were invited in, but we should be cautious."

Acevedo said, "Leonard, what do you think?"

"I understand you want to be aggressive but at what cost? What if a neighbor sees someone in the home and calls police? Then what? Will that flimsy little notarized note save you? This is a tricky question, but being cautious just might be the right answer."

Stanley's gaze swept past the two others in the room. "Technically, Rocker's lawyer doesn't need us to go into that room. She has an investigator. They could do it without us?"

Doff agreed with her. "Booker, does the lawyer even know about this?"

"I don't think so."

Doff's voice kicked up in volume. "No? So, if she found out and didn't like this whole arrangement, there might be a problem?"

Booker responded. "I have no idea what she might do. Rocker does things his own way, regardless of her."

Acevedo looked like a judge ready to give an order. "Okay, this rests with me. For now, we do nothing with the note and the key. There's too many sticky issues with this right now. If there comes a time when this could advance this story, we will address it again but for now, no entry into the house. We clear Booker?"

"Perfectly clear. I'll lock the key in my desk."

Acevedo smiled. "Thanks. And where do we stand on the Rocker murder anyway?"

"We've teased the story all day, and on the web," Booker advised. "But Yang found out the detectives from the Rocker case were out at the murder scene today. That's why she called me."

Acevedo's eyes moved from Booker to the bank of televisions bolted onto the wall. "Anything there?"

"Nothing yet. If she gets a chance, she's going to pull someone aside from the police and ask."

"Good. I'll see you on the news." Now, his full attention was on the TV monitors and what the two other stations in the marker were about to report for the top story at noon.

Stanley and Booker went out into the newsroom. He entered the edit booth where Coffee was going through the interview video. When Stanley got to her space on the assignment desk, she read an incoming email, stood up and shouted to the gathered room of producers. "The police just confirmed the victim as Ken Capilon."

12

The decision was made in the morning meeting to hold Booker's Rocker story until the five p.m. newscast, and so no reports from him in the noon. He had a moment to see how much the other stations could catch up to his story on Judge Rocker and what the stations were reporting on the Capilon murder.

Booker stood in front of yet another set of TV monitors in the newsroom. What always fascinated Booker was how people were always concerned about turning off their televisions at home. Yet, in a newsroom, the many televisions were turned on and left on for years. They were never turned off.

On TV, he saw Yang standing near the Capilon house, close to the crime tape. Her voice was smooth and calming, something that aided her during hurricane storm coverage. Her vocal tones were appealing and seemed to keep viewers focused on what she was presenting rather than alarming them. Booker turned up the volume.

Yang said, "Police say they got a call this morning from our news helicopter after flying over the house." The station ran her edited video story which included the police interview and a short comment from the helicopter pilot who first spotted the body. Booker did not see any surveillance video from a neighbor, nor did any other station have vid. All three stations had the same story, name of victim, interviews, and a promise the police investigation was continuing. Booker turned down the volume and went back to his desk.

He had a script ready for Coffee when she returned from a short lunch break. While he waited for Coffee, he made the usual checks, calling police for an update, checking in with Hart, Rocker's attorney and reading several websites all dealing with the death of Shanice Rocker. The police assured him there were no updates, although he was certain they would be watching to see what Rocker had to say. Hart's office never returned a phone call, and the websites were mostly all older accounts and nothing new.

Unless something changed by five p.m., Channel 27 was prepared to say Booker's interview with Rocker about the knife was still an exclusive. Four hours later, after leaving a two-minute-ten-second story behind, Booker and Coffee drove toward the police department's main building. Three minutes into the drive, Booker was determined about something.

"Head to Rocker's house."

"Now?"

Booker glanced at his watch. "We have time. You know where it is, right?"

"Booker, we don't have time. We have to be set up and ready to go."

"Just a quick drive to his house. I want to see it."

"Can't it wait?"

"Please, Coffee. Just drive there for a few seconds. We have time."

Coffee made a left turn and drove in the direction of the home of William Rocker. "You know sometimes you push things too far. You're the only reporter I've worked with who came so close to missing slot."

"You said close. I have never missed a deadline. Close yes, but always there."

"And how many times are you late in the morning?"

"Okay, late to work, yes. But never late for making slot."

Exactly seven minutes later, Coffee was in front of the Rocker place. Booker got out, but Coffee stayed in the SUV, poised and ready to leave. From memory, Booker knew the home was three bedroom, two bath, no pool, small front and back yards. There was nothing special about the home. Booker walked to the side and looked into the back yard. The front had three small palm trees and little landscaping. The one plus for the home was the closeness to the ocean. Booker could smell the mix of salt air and brine. A developer might suggest knocking down the home and building a two story with a two-million-dollar price tag. For now, the place was abandoned. Booker tried to look through the windows, made difficult by the dark layer of tinted film meant to protect the inside from the sun. He walked in the direction of the door. Coffee bolted out of the SUV.

"You've got the key, don't you?"

"You're good at reading my mind."

Coffee made another couple of steps, closing in on him. "We can't go in there and we don't have the time. You're pushing it. We have to go."

Booker Johnson backed down. He turned around, walked back to the car, and got in. Coffee made a U-turn and pushed on the gas pedal. She gave him that look. The Coffee look.

"Stop staring at me. I want to know what someone could be looking for in that house."

"That's fine, Book. But not now. We've got work to do. And if we miss our assigned slot time, it'll be a bitch to explain to Stanley. You up for that?"

"No."

"I didn't think so. Let's get over there and we'll talk about this later."

"No problem."

Coffee pulled up in front of the police station and parked. They had just under twenty minutes to get set up. Once parked, next came the parade of equipment. Camera, tripod, and maybe lights.

Coffee looked at the front door of the police HQ. "When this story airs, it's gonna put a lot of pressure on the police to say something."

Booker kept checking his cell phone for any updates on his and the story on Capilon. "When the public hears him talk about the knife and that it was his, then yes, the phone calls to the attorney and police will intensify."

Something else also intensified. A scenario that was never reported on television. Input from the public. When Booker's first story aired the night before, going to the noon newscast and beyond, people called with their opinion on whether the judge was guilty. Not a lot of calls, yet a light steady flow of callers. Most, according to Stanley, were mixed. The calls were not limited to the former judge. In a newsroom, people called to speak about what the news anchors were wearing, both positive and negative. They would call about the hairstyle of the person doing the weather, even the color of shoes worn. When a favorite TV anchor was on vacation, people called inquiring why they weren't on the six p.m. newscast. Viewers just wanted to question and vent. News stations let them. Anyone on the assignment desk was always instructed to listen as long as possible. Viewers were treated as loyal customers and TV stations valued each one of them.

Booker made another attempt with Brielle Jensen, the Detective and P.I.O., to ask for any update and was told there was none.

Just after five p.m., Booker stood before Coffee's camera. In his ear, he heard the intro to his story. "Tonight at five, we have an update to the story we brought you exclusively last night on Channel 27. We were there when former Judge William Rocker walked into a police station to cooperate with the investigation in the brutal murder of his wife, Shanice. Booker Johnson has more on the story. Booker..."

"We sat down with William Rocker before he spoke with detectives. He repeated many times he did not kill his wife Shanice. Police have not named him as a person of interest, but the investigation will certainly move forward now that Rocker has returned after staying out of the country for four years. He had this to say about the murder itself and what police told him."

Booker waited and, through an earpiece, listened to the sound clips of Rocker explaining a knife was found next to his wife's body. A knife, Rocker stated, that had his own fingerprints. The story also included the sound bite of why he left South Florida and where he'd been living. And again used the part with Rocker saying he did not murder Shanice.

Booker wrapped up his live comments. "We called and, right now, there is no update today from police. As soon as we know more, we will pass it on to you. For now, live outside police headquarters, Booker Johnson, Channel 27 news."

He waited until he heard an 'all clear' in his earpiece. He pulled off the microphone and handed it back to Coffee. Before he had a chance to move to the SUV, he got a phone call from Lacie Grandhouse.

"Hi, Booker, I wanted to catch you before I leave."

"What's up?"

"I did some poking around. Remember the car story that got cancelled? The one involving your brother?"

"Yeah. You find something?"

Grandhouse said, "I think so. At least this might be the reason they don't want to do the story. Just over five years ago, one of their employees, a woman, was found dead. She was a driver for this company for just three months."

"Details on the death?"

"Only that she was found inside her apartment. The death was ruled an overdose, but it remains an open case because some things about it were suspicious."

Booker slid into the passenger seat of the SUV. "Suspicious. That could be a lot of things."

"At the time, the reports from police say they found drug paraphernalia near the body. With her blood work, definitely an overdose."

"Okay, Lacie, what do you think?"

"There's not much to go on. Stanley says there's almost no story here since there's nothing new and if police don't want to talk, that's it. Story over. But in the morning she's going to let me do some more digging."

"If you need any help from me, let me know."

Booker ended the conversation and leaned back in the car seat, eyes focused on the HQ front doors. The phone rang again. He thought the call was again from Grandhouse with a follow-up question.

"Hello."

"Booker, it's me."

"Misha, anything wrong?" There was worry in her voice.

"Book, you better get over here."

"The apartment?"

"Booker, there are four police cars out front. An officer came to the door and told me to stay inside for now. I think they're up there at Judge Rocker's apartment. I'm not sure but I think they're serving a search warrant."

"I'm on the way."

13

An intense Florida sun was working its way downward, reflecting orange hues off the windows of the Banyan Apartments. Booker got out of his car and took in everything he could in just seconds. There was one police car parked out front, routine for any search warrant. Booker took note the S.W.A.T. team was not there. An officer was outside the door of the complex checking people coming inside, probably to make sure they lived at this address. Coffee, given overtime permission, arrived three minutes later, got out, and immediately started to video activity. Booker also saw what looked like the unmarked SUV of Brielle Jensen. He called Claire Stanley.

"Whatcha got, Book?"

"I'm going upstairs. They won't let me get past my own apartment but at least I can get near there. If they have a search warrant, police won't say squat. Not why they're here, nothing. And it will be weeks before the warrant itself is filed with the clerk's office."

"How do you plan to work this?"

"Coffee is outside. I'll go in, see what I can see and go from there. I can only report on what I see. If they take out bags of evidence, we'll get it."

"Any other stations there?"

"Yeah, I saw Clendon Davis and his photographer. Channel 74 out of Miami."

"They came up to Apton County? Okay, no one else?"

"Not right now. Let me check this out and I'll call you back."

"Book, if this is anything, you'll be the lead at eleven."

"Got it."

From the street, Booker saw curtains pulled back and curious faces stretching to see the activity below. Beyond the hellos and good-byes, the building was full of young up-and-comers, hard-working singles and couples doing everything they could to save enough to move into the next level. A home. The few conversations Booker had with his fellow apartment dwellers all ended with vast descriptions of what kind of home they would buy and where. The motivation was simple: work, save and move out.

Booker walked past an officer who let him go inside. Once he showed a driver's license and said he lived there, Booker was allowed entry. When he got off the elevator, Booker went to his apartment, closed the door and started for the apartment surveillance video.

"They stopped the feed." Misha looked deflated. "I heard them though. They have to be at Rocker's apartment."

"So there's no video..."

"No video of police coming in. Nothing. I think they must have called first. I'm guessing you're still working."

"Correct. Maybe police asked for the surveillance video. Pinpoint when Rocker left the apartment." Booker weighed every option he had available to him. He could shoot a bit of video with his cell phone and decided against the idea since he would be limited to his floor where nothing was going on.

He stopped and took another look at Misha. She was wearing shorts, reminding him of her long legs, with a yellow blouse, top button open. Booker stepped close and leaned down toward her face.

Her voice was just above a whisper. "Are you on the clock?"

"Does that matter?"

"Well, can you kiss me while you're still on the clock?"

"Our place, my rules." The kiss brought him to places and images of where they first met, her always-lilac smell and exotic eyes. He headed for the door.

"Where you going?"

"To Rocker's floor."

"Will you get very far?"

"I'll go until they tell me to stop, then I will do exactly what they tell me to do and go outside."

Misha posed the question. "I have to ask. Is she up there?"

"She?"

"You know. That detective. You almost had a thing with her."

"There was never any 'thing'. Trust me. Where did you hear that anyway?"

"Book, you're not the only one with sources." A grin etched across her face.

"The only person I want to be with is you." He was out the door and taking the stairs up two more flights to the fourth floor. When he walked out onto the floor, the hallway was filled with people. Two crime techs in their white Tyvek gear were stationed just inside the door of Rocker's place. He saw the back of a detective and five seconds later recognized the blonde hair bun of Detective Brielle Jensen. The 'she' Misha was talking about. Jensen was talking to someone. He could not make out the words, just the feeling the conversation from the other person was not cordial. Still, knowing Jensen, she was very professional.

An officer saw Booker and was just about to head toward him when a woman bolted out of the apartment.

What Booker saw was quiet, very controlled anger. Her lips were a flat line, eyes flickering from police to the inside of the apartment and back to Jensen. No yelling, just the hard-nosed scrutiny of a person checking every single movement from the tech team and detectives, making sure every-thing was done right. The woman stared at Booker Johnson. This was the attorney Serenity Hart.

Her tone was level, showing almost no emotion. She was speaking toward those working the case, yet clearly loud enough for Booker to hear. "You know you're not going to find anything. Just wasting our time." She clutched some papers close to her chest. "We've been cooperating every single step." When Hart saw Booker a second time, she lowered the temperature more. The voice was now calm as a Florida sunrise. Hart marched in Booker's direction, and without him asking a question, she blurted, "I can confirm they are serving a search warrant. Can't say more right now, but we are cooperating."

When Hart turned to look again at the apartment door, she dropped the papers held so closely to her body. She immediately snatched them up.

Jensen came out of the apartment. "Booker what are you doing up here?" Jensen pointed a finger toward him. "Officer."

The mere mention of officer meant Booker had to leave right away. He did as he was directed, walking toward the stairs. Hart caught him before he entered the stairwell and followed him. "I understand you live here too. That ends tonight. I'm moving him out of here. No contact with the judge." Her words echoed in the stairwell.

"Is he here?"

"The judge is inside."

"I think the judge and your office will confirm that, when I called, I have only asked for you, not the judge."

"Well, one more thing before you go, and I won't say this on camera, but you know that man they found murdered?"

"Ken Capilon?"

She was still calm, but firm. "Mr. Capilon. Well, guess what, Mr. Booker Johnson? That very same Ken Capilon was supposed to meet with detectives in two days and help clear my client. He was going to change an earlier statement. Now, he's dead. Can you explain that to me, Mr. Reporter? A witness who could clear a devoted husband and judge of murder and now that witness is dead and where are police right now? Inside my client's apartment. As if he had something to do with the death of the very man who could free him from all this. Explain that on the news."

Booker was staring at a very pointed finger just inches from pushing him in the chest. "And you won't say anything on camera?"

"Not a word. It's not time. But everything I told you is on the record. Every word. Capilon was cooperating. And somebody killed him." She turned so quickly Booker was ready for her papers to come flying again.

Booker went all the way downstairs and connected with Junice Coffee. "Were you up there?"

"I was there. I think they're about to come out soon."

Coffee adjusted the camera on her shoulder. "I'm ready."

"Got to call Stanley. One, the attorney confirmed the Capilon murder from overnight is directly tied to Rocker's case. He was about to give testimony backing Rocker. And two, I caught a quick glance at what I think is a copy of the search warrant. The attorney says she's not talking on camera, but I'll try and confirm it, I hope, when she comes out. The part of the warrant I saw said they were looking for Rocker's shoes and also a set of knives."

14

Outside, beside Clendon Davis, a third reporter and crew were also set up and shooting video. These were the moments never mentioned by a reporter: the wait. Once Booker had stood outside the federal courthouse for almost four hours waiting for a man charged to show up with his attorney. The wait consisted of standing and searching a door, a street, a courthouse exit, anywhere a person of note would leave or enter. Tonight, he waited for the tech team to come out. Or Detective Jensen, Hart, or Rocker himself. He briefly thought about asking for a second crew in case several people left the building at once. Then he remembered this was the night shift. The other crews would be out and busy.

The crime techs emerged first. Two people walked to a van, each carrying one bag of evidence. They looked at the evidence, probably checking to make sure everything was logged, closed up the van, and left.

Next came Detective Brielle Jensen, lips tight, looking straight ahead, impervious to the couple of questions yelled her way. She got into her SUV and drove off.

Coffee got video of everything that moved. The wait now continued for Hart. Twenty minutes went by, and thoughts were swirling for Booker. He could call the assignment desk and risk missing her coming out so that idea was tabled. The time was 10:20 p.m. He was able to send off a text, letting them know he had a hard update from the earlier news. Booker also knew he needed time to feed back video and set up for the eleven p.m. newscast.

More waiting. The other crews looked nervous and Booker thought the reason was they had almost no information. Just people coming and going.

10:45 p.m. The window to do several things was getting smaller. Still no sign of Hart or Rocker. They could easily wait out the crews and stay inside the building until two a.m. if they wanted. Booker took a chance and broke away from the row of waiting reporters to retrieve Coffee's tripod and equipment for a live feed.

10:50 p.m. The newscast was just ten minutes away. Booker got a text message: he was the top story in the eleven p.m. newscast. No matter what, he had to be ready.

10:55 p.m. Coffee changed her mind. No tripod. She wanted to be mobile in case Hart walked outside. Mobile and live at the same time.

11:00 p.m. In his ear, Booker first heard the producer say standby. Then he heard the anchor announce the lead-in to Booker. "We continue to update you in the case of former Judge William Rocker whose wife was murdered four years ago. Tonight, we've learned police served a search warrant on his apartment. And there's one major update. Channel 27's Booker Johnson is live outside the apartment. Booker..."

"Police arrived here just before six p.m. We watched crime techs bringing out bags of evidence, however police are not saying anything yet about what they have found. There is one other development. Earlier today, we told you about the murder of Ken Capilon. He was found murdered in his back yard. Tonight, Channel 27 has learned the Capilon murder is directly connected to the murder of the former judge's wife, Shanice. William Rocker fled the country, telling me he was about to be arrested. Rocker came back to South Florida and was staying in this apartment complex. His attorney, Serenity Hart, told me Capilon was just about to give a statement to detectives, changing testimony from four years ago. This time, Capilon was expected to help clear Rocker of any wrongdoing. Yet, tonight, police searched Rocker's apartment."

Booker saw Coffee move away from him and pointed toward the front door. Booker turned around toward the door and kept talking. "You're looking at a live picture of Rocker's attorney Serenity Hart coming out of the complex." As he was talking, Booker and the two other stations tried to converge and ask Hart a question. She kept her head turned away from the crews, got into a car, and closed the door. All three reporters tossed questions her way, and Hart ignored all of them. She turned the car around and drove up until she was directly in front of the complex. Booker was still live and talking. When Hart parked, William Rocker ran from the front door to her car, swung open the passenger side, and her car sped away. Booker wrapped up his report while Coffee's live camera captured the scene. "Rocker, as you watched, emerged from the building and left with his attorney. We will have more on all of this tomorrow. For now, this is Booker Johnson reporting live. Back to you."

After an all clear, Coffee and Booker started to pack up the camera gear. She stopped what she was doing and looked at Clendon Davis, who was talking on the phone, hands and arms animated, his voice shouting back at someone. Finally, he ended the conversation, eyelids bent in anger and lasered a death stare toward Booker Johnson.

Coffee spoke down toward the ground, words only Booker could hear. "I think he's getting yelled at because he didn't have the same information you did."

"I had an advantage. I live here. That's all."

"Well, Book, I think he's cooking up some of that RR for you bud."

"RR?"

"Yeah. A little reporter revenge."

"We'll see."

Booker then walked the shortest distance he'd ever experienced going from a news story to home.

Demetrious Moreland looked down at his phone. No email messages from his half-brother Booker. Not even a text. He shook his head like a thought had just woke up his memories. He was supposed to call Booker, not the other way around. Moreland sat outside in a chair removed from the one-bedroom, on the second floor of the When Ready motel, near the Florida Everglades and U.S. 27, about five miles from no place and seven miles from nowhere. From what he could tell, most of the rooms were unoccupied. The one bright spot was the upper floor was a perfect spot to watch the sun going down in the Glades. No buildings in the Glades, just the green-black water and home of pythons and thousands of alligators. Moreland was just about to go back inside the forty-five dollar a night bed bug trap when he heard a noise coming from down below. Since the motel was so close to the Glades, he half expected any critter to wander up to the door. He put his hand on the doorknob.

"You gonna leave this beautiful view?"

Moreland stopped. "Whatchou doin' here?"

"Can't say hello to your father?"

"What I need is for you to stay away from me. Far away. Why are you here?"

The tall man with almond skin, perfectly cut hair and business shirt, unbuttoned at the top, sleeves rolled up, started to approach. His shoes were immaculate and buffed to a nice shine. Roland Caston studied his son. Caston had the same large shoulders, height, and big hands like Demetrious. Caston's words were smooth as blackstrap molasses dripping off the end of a table. "I just wanted to see my man. The son I never get to see on a regular basis."

"You should be in prison. There's still a warrant out for you."

"I won't be here long. Just came to make you an offer." He smiled when he spoke, like a well-oiled sales job with the most evil intentions. Moreland always figured the soft candy-coated words trapped his mother years ago into a coupling that produced the baby Demetrious.

"You might be my father, but I don't want anything to do with you. It's two a.m. I gotta get some sleep."

He stepped closer to Demetrious, always charming, spewing words low and easy that would make a snake proud. "I want to start up again. I got the capital, and I can get the product. I just need a few more people I can trust."

"The drug business? How big of a dumbass are you? Your old business cost people their lives. You can peddle that shit somewhere else. Now git, before I throw you off this floor."

"Those deaths weren't on me. Someone stepped on my stuff too hard with the wrong things. You know I wouldn't hurt anybody."

"I didn't learn about your meth lab until police shut it down, but it could have exploded."

"But it didn't."

"Your twenty employees spread poison all over South Florida."

"Just drugs, man. Just drugs."

Moreland pointed a finger at Caston. "You still have your right-hand man? What's his name, Strap?"

"Yeah, Strap stayed with me. All the rest took off after that dustup."

"Dustup? You ran a criminal enterprise, took over a section of an apartment building and lived there, your group sold drugs to anyone with the money. And you were just about ready to expand when this so-called dustup blew up in your face."

"That's why I need you. To start over. With you and Strap, I can move a lot of product. Just say yes and I'll show you how we can make a ton of money."

Demetrious recognized the look on Caston's face. The look of a man who loved to give orders and never got blood on his hands when he could just tell others to do the bad things for him.

Moreland's voice was loud. "Let me repeat this so listen good. Real good. I don't want anything to do with you. Nothing! Just back away and disappear."

"Okay for now. I get it. But I'll be around for a while, just checking on you. Just think about what I told you. C'mon and get this offer Demetrious, while it's hot."

"Go."

The man with the permanent smile backed away, until he was swallowed by the shadows. Moreland then typed a text to Booker: Coming to see you in the AM before you go to work.

15

Booker pushed a plate of eggs in front of Demetrious Moreland. "And he actually wanted you to sell drugs with him?"

Moreland grabbed the fork. "Now you see why I changed my last name. I didn't want to be a Caston."

Booker looked at the bedroom door one more time, making sure it was closed. Misha was still sleeping. "Please tell him for me, if I see him, I'm calling police. He shouldn't be on the street."

"I thought about calling them, but by the time police got there, he would be long gone." Moreland dabbed a paper napkin to his mouth. "He said he's gonna stay around for a while."

"What does that mean?"

Moreland finished up the eggs and sipped on a bottle of water. "That means he's gonna find a way to poke into my life. I won't know when or where but he's coming."

"Nice." Booker pulled up his own plate of eggs and a piece of wheat toast. "Maybe you should just call and tell police he's in the area."

"You don't understand, Book. He's my bio."

"He may be your biological father but he's still a wanted thug. Calling police would be a huge favor to the community."

"I guess you're right. I'll think about it."

"Tell me more about this job. Driving around antique cars. I love it."

Moreland's eyes aimed down toward the floor. "It's gone. They fired me."

"Why?"

"I thought it would be a great feature for your station and for my company. I called Channel 27, and they were all set to come out."

Booker bit on the toast. "Yep. Lacie Grandhouse was going to do the story."

"Well, when they found out a TV crew was coming, they freaked out. Yelled at me to cancel, so I did."

For the next two minutes, Booker downed the rest of the toast and eggs. His mind shifted to a reporter's curiosity and the various reasons why they would get so upset over an interview. Just about every reporter knew actions like that could be from a number of very legitimate reasons for cancelling. Some companies were so private they didn't want any coverage on the inner workings of the firm. Others had strict company policies about not contacting the media. And there was the other reason. They could be hiding something.

"Did you know about the employee, a female driver, who was found dead?"

Demetrious placed his plate in the sink. "One other driver, he mentioned something. That she overdosed on drugs five years ago. That could be the reason they wanted me to back off."

"What are you doing now?"

"For a job? I'm back at the Internet Café. Working full time. Driving the cars was just going to be every so often. Nothing full time. They hired me because I can work on cars."

"Didn't know that."

"Yep. Can take apart and put a car back together. If one of these antiques ever broke down, at least I could try and fix it."

Booker heard some movement coming from the bedroom. "You want to do dinner tonight?"

"Maybe." Moreland pushed the chair under the table. "You know what? I'm gonna look into the girl's death."

"Be careful. People sue."

"Booker c'mon. You can't sue for poking around. I still know a few people with the company. And I have access to some computer files. I'm not locked out just yet."

"Okay. Not asking you to do anything."

"I know. I'll get back to you."

Booker took another risk at poking into Moreland's private life and asked anyway. "Where are you staying?"

"I'm out at the When Ready motel."

"That dump out by the Everglades?"

"Thanks for the beatdown. It's not perfect but I like the quiet. It's peaceful out there."

Booker looked around for his cell phone and wallet. "I'll walk you out. But I've got to find you a better place to stay."

Booker was in the Channel 27 newsroom early enough to grab a remaining donut. The room was abuzz with tiny conversations, talk about a sports game last night, the latest celebrity gossip, and wails of laughter coming from the gathering near the Cuban coffee machine.

"Morning, Booker." Lacie Grandhouse sounded like someone or something had just taken the magic out of her morning. "Can I pass something on to you?"

"Sure, Lacie. What's up?"

"A couple of years ago, one of the greatest things about that summer was working with you as an intern."

"Thanks."

"One moment really stood out for me, Book. No matter what, you always went with your gut feeling about a story, even if no one believed there was a story there. You never gave up on it. And you showed people there was a big story there."

"I try. Not always right, but I try to follow my gut instincts. But I gotta tell ya, sometimes my gut gets me in trouble."

"I know. I saw some of that trouble firsthand." She handed Booker a small stack of papers. "I emailed you a bunch more stuff. Take a look at it. See what you think."

Booker glanced at the pile of papers in his hand. "And this is?"

"That's everything I have on the girl's death. The young woman who was driving antique cars. It's about her death."

"You're not working on it?"

"Nope. Claire Stanley made it very clear I was moving on to other stories and that girl's death is very old news. Five-year old story, cold case, overdose death, no new angles. I thought maybe you could carry it forward."

"Sure, Lacie. If I can pull you back into the story, I will. This was your baby."

"Thanks." Grandhouse left, headed straight for the door. From the in-house emails, Booker knew she was going to a three-car crash. Live at noon. Booker put the remains of the donut on his desk. Stanley approached him.

"I saw you talking with Lacie. I'm not the wicked witch. We need her on today stories, not a whim from years past. That is, unless there's something new. Anything new?"

"No, not yet. No problem, Claire. It's under my wing."

"So I'm headed into the meeting. You are permanently assigned to the Shanice Rocker murder story. Especially since the lawyer gave you that edge last night. You and Coffee. Just tell me later what we can expect for the newscasts."

Before Booker had a chance to respond, she was off to the morning meeting. A parade of producers and reporters filed into the meeting room.

Booker had one immediate Wednesday mission: Find out all he could about Ken Capilon—where he worked, any relatives who might talk, his neighbors, anything to advance the story.

Coffee pulled up in front of a business called Find-A-Way Relocation Services. "So, this is where Capilon worked?"

"Yes. The owner agreed to an interview."

"Okay. Let's go."

In less than forty seconds, Coffee was unpacked and moving toward the front door.

"Welcome. I'm Branson Landale."

Coffee walked through the business and out the back door to a patio area, where she set up two chairs. Once the tripod was in place, she would be ready to go.

Landale was much shorter than Booker, sandy-blond hair, muscular, wearing a polo shirt with the company name on the front. Booker asked, "I read about this place online but what do you do here?"

Landale smiled. "We help businesses all over the country by helping their newly hired employees move to South Florida. We know the neighborhoods, the schools and what condos, homes or apartments are available. Then we set up the moving companies, get them moved and resettled. Kinda like one-stop shopping. We do it all."

"And Ken was a part of that?"

"Of course. He worked here almost nine years now. We were sad about what happened. Murdered?" As he spoke, Landale moved out into the patio where Coffee directed him to a chair. When he sat down, she attached a microphone to his shirt.

Booker took up the other chair. Coffee liked shooting interviews outside since, most of the time, she didn't need to set up lights. Once Coffee nodded, Booker started.

"For those of us who did not know Ken, can you explain who he was?"

"Ken was a hardworking person who did whatever he could to help a client. I still can't believe he's gone. He worked hard, always ready to do overtime, if needed, to get someone moved in. He did charity work, and he was never, I mean never, late."

"Did he ever speak to you about the William Rocker case?"

"Me? Very little. Just like everyone, when we first heard about it, we spoke about the case, but nothing since."

Every single person Booker ever interviewed was measured by the BS meter. The reaction from the questions were lodged into Booker's memory and captured by the lens of Coffee's camera. "When was the last time you spoke with him?"

"Oh, a couple of days ago. But he was working from home at the time and I was just checking in."

"Thank you, Mr. Landale. And thanks for your time."

"No problem."

Interview over, Coffee moved around the office getting video of the plaques on the wall, Capilon's desk, and video of Booker and Landale walking around the office.

Even though just the three of them were in the office, Landale lowered his voice. "Ya know, Ken was kind of weird."

"Really? How so?"

"He got really paranoid of his own house. Started talking on the phone out in the yard, had the place screened for listening devices. He got really out there." Landale's arms made big sweeping motions. "All of a sudden, he didn't trust anyone."

Booker took note. "Did he tell you he was about to be interviewed by police?"

"No. Not a word. First I heard about it was from you, on the news."

"When Shanice Rocker was killed four years ago, did police talk to you at the time?"

"No. I didn't know anything about it."

Coffee was finished getting video and she was out the door with her camera and tripod. Booker followed her to the SUV. It was time to check in with Claire Stanley. Booker waited until 12:20 p.m. to call her. Right at noon, she would be busy watching all of the TV news stations to see if there was a story Channel 27 had missed.

"Claire, can you talk?"

"I can now. The other stations still don't have your angle about Capilon getting ready to speak with detectives. And so far, police aren't saying anything. So, for the moment, that angle just belongs to us. How is it going?"

Booker explained the interview he got with Landale and admitted he didn't have much for a day three news story. He was coming close to his own three-day rule. By the third day, if there wasn't a good fresh top on a news story, it was time to move on. "What I think I'll do, Claire, is make one more run to the police. If they're not talking, we might have to bust this story down to just one minute tonight."

"Understood." Claire ended the conversation.

Coffee headed to a fast-food restaurant. They both ordered burgers and bottled water and parked under a shade tree overlooking the Atlantic Ocean.

The beach was full of retirees, scores of tourists, and a line of roller skaters wearing string bikinis. While Coffee sipped her water, Booker re-examined the findings of the young woman found overdosed. The one who drove antique cars. Booker did more research on the girl. Her name was Fila Mackee, age twenty-six. From Booker's research, developed mostly from Lacie Grandhouse, Mackee lived alone in an apartment on Birkston Street.

"Your lunch hour done?" Booker caught Coffee staring at a body-builder type flexing his muscles.

"I was just admiring the beach."

"Sure you were. You ready to go?"

Coffee gripped the wheel. "Where we going?"

"To an apartment complex on Birkston Street."

Coffee wheeled the SUV through the sand-filled parking lot. "I'm guessing this has nothing to do with our story?"

"I'm just checking something out."

"No problem. Let's go."

The complex was protected from the sun by a row of Live Oak trees. In front of the large entrance, another eight crape myrtle trees and a couple of bottlebrushes offered a shady walk.

Booker turned to Coffee. "Stay here. If I need you, I'll call."

"Gotcha."

Booker examined the layout of the place. There was no front lobby, meaning the onsite manager probably lived in one of the apartments. He looked for security cameras and didn't see any. He walked to the second floor, apartment 206, and knocked. Nearly a minute passed and no answer. Booker knocked again, and this time he also pulled out two business cards. He slipped one card in the door jamb and the other he tried to slip under the door. Just when he turned to leave, a woman's voice stopped him.

"She's not home. Must be at work. She'll be back sometime tonight."

"I'm Booker Johnson, Channel 27. I'm trying to find anyone who remembers Fila Mackee."

"Fila? Of course. It was sad."

Booker took out another business card, extending it to the woman who just emerged from 210. She took the card in her hand. "Booker Johnson, eh? I think I've seen you on TV."

"I'm just following up on her death. You knew her?"

"I was here when the police removed her body. Yes, I knew her. I'm sorry, my name is Rona Bascomb. A lot of people who knew her moved out. Like any complex, people come and go."

"You say you were here that day?"

Bascomb's blue eyes turned somber. Her hair was being blown around by the breeze. Both her arms were tanned and one side of her face was always turned up in a half-smile. She had two empty cloth shopping bags and appeared to be headed to the grocery store. "I had just got home and found two police units. The crime unit was also here. I didn't know her that well. But you need to talk to her roommate."

"The one who will be here later?"

"Yes. She's a flight attendant. Works all kinds of hours. I think she would be likely to speak with you. Just one thing. Your phone might not work that great around here. We're in a dead zone. Sometimes it works, sometimes it doesn't."

"Well, thank you for your time." Booker took the stairs rather than the elevator. When he got to the SUV, Coffee had that familiar face like Booker had messed up again. "Are we back on our story?"

Booker answered, "Yes. Before I forget, let's check out Capilon's neighborhood."

"Both Yang and Grandhouse checked it out. No interviews, no surveillance. Nothing. Going back, isn't that a waste of time?"

"Let's just check it one last time."

"Okay."

Fourteen minutes later, in front of Capilon's residence, all the police tape was gone. However, one piece of red tape was over the front door jamb. Booker got out and again requested Coffee stay ready, he would knock on doors alone. He checked seven homes near the murder house and got nothing. Booker crossed the street and knocked on the door of the home directly across the street from Capilon. A distinguished man around seventy answered the door.

"Can I help you?" He had an Irish accent, high forehead and a face full of wrinkles.

"I'm Booker Johnson, Channel 27. Not sure if you heard about the incident that happened across the street. Mr. Capilon's home?"

"Ken? Sad story. I just got back in town. Been to a conference. Missed what happened. Rory Madigan is the name."

For the next few minutes Booker told Madigan what happened while he was away. In that time, the homeowner brought up the surveillance video for the time period of the murder. Madigan stopped when they saw what looked like Capilon pulling up in his car. Since the car might have elements connected to the case, the car was towed away the morning the body was discovered.

Madigan pointed to the computer monitor. "See, that's Ken getting out of his car." Both men watched Capilon on video. He walked down the side of his house, entered the back yard, and was gone.

Booker got out his phone and called Coffee. "Get your gear. C'mon in, the door will be open."

Once inside, Coffee set up camera and tripod. She knew exactly what to do. All three stayed quiet while Coffee recorded the surveillance video. The vid was time stamped. When she stopped recording, Booker turned to the man with the full head of white hair. "Have the police seen this yet?"

"You're the first."

"This is up to you and it's your video, but you might want to contact Detective Jensen at police."

"I can do that. You want the video emailed to you?"

"That would be great."

While Coffee stood ready, Booker and Madigan searched forward on the recorded video. They did not see anyone follow Capilon into the back yard. The video kept going up until police arrived.

"That enough?" Madigan looked a bit tired.

"Just one last thing. We've seen all the video after midnight. What about an hour or so before Capilon got home?"

"You sure we'll find anything?"

"Since we're here, if it's okay, let's check."

From the time Capilon arrived in the video, they searched backward. They kept going until a car pulled up. A white Honda SUV. For almost six minutes the man in the car just watched the front door. Twice he looked around as if checking to see if anyone was watching him.

Then he got out.

Booker just had to look over toward Coffee. She was focused and recording the surveillance video.

The three of them watched the man get out and he started walking toward the front door. After a few seconds, he stopped, turned around and looked again down the street. Then he got back into the SUV and drove off.

A minute later, Coffee stopped recording again.

Booker said, "You get all that?"

"Yes."

Booker looked at his phone and unmuted the cell. Three calls from Claire Stanley. He called her. "Yes."

"Been trying to reach you."

"We're ready. What's up?"

"Serenity Hart has called a news conference. You got ten minutes to get there. I sent Grandhouse ahead just in case you're running late."

"Thanks. We're on the way." Booker put away the phone.

Madigan reached for his now cold tea. "Booker, that man in the video, the one who got out of the car. I noticed you staring at him real hard. You recognize him?"

"We sure do."

16

The South Florida office of Serenity Hart had plenty of room for four TV crews. Booker and Coffee found Grandhouse had secured a nice spot in the middle of the arc of cameras. Coffee put her tripod in the place where Grandhouse and her photographer had a tripod set up. Coffee snapped her camera into the top of the tripod. "Thanks, Lacie, for saving us a spot."

Grandhouse and her photographer moved toward the way out. "No problem."

Next to Coffee was reporter Clendon Davis and a photographer. Two other crews made up the mix. They all waited another sixteen minutes before Hart and William Rocker sat down in front of the four microphones.

"I'm Serenity Hart and I represent William Rocker. We got a lot of phone calls after Mr. Rocker's apartment was served with a search warrant. I didn't speak that night, but I wanted to address a couple of things now. Please know, Mr. Rocker will not be answering questions."

Booker checked his muted phone and read a text message from Stanley. The live feed to the website was good.

Hart adjusted her glasses. "Mr. Ken Capilon was all set to speak with detectives and was about to change some of his testimony. Information that would further clear Mr. Rocker of any suspicion in his wife's death."

Booker raised his hand to ask a question and Hart ignored him.

"There is one other matter I wanted to let the public know. And it's best to get it out there so there is no confusion. As you probably saw, the interview Mr. Rocker gave with Channel 27 indicated the knife that killed Shanice belonged to him. I can confirm the knife also had Mr. Rocker's prints on it. The new element today is the knife found next to the body of Ken Capilon also belonged to William Rocker." Hart waited for some kind of response, however among the small group of reporters, there was no reaction just yet. "That knife belonged to a set of four knives all belonging to my client. That set was stolen and the theft was reported to police. So, it's not a big surprise for us that his prints were found on them." She paused.

Booker jumped in. "What information was Ken Capilon about to say that would clear William Rocker?"

"I'm going to leave that part up to police. I just know Capilon was about to change his statement, which I will not disclose right now. It was testimony that harmed my client's case before but now was about to add a lot of clarity."

Before anyone had a chance, Booker asked another question. "With the missing knives, there's still two missing?"

Hart answered reluctantly. "Yes. Two more in the set. These knives were highly valued. And now they are being used to wrongfully implicate William. I hope everyone understands that."

For the next seven minutes, other reporters asked when Rocker would again talk with police? She remained unclear, saying they were still finding a date and time.

This would be a moment where Booker had to decide if he wanted to disclose some information or wait just a bit. If he openly asked the question, everyone would know it and he would lose exclusivity. However, if he waited just a bit and asked Hart alone, he might maintain full control of the information. In order to do that he would have to stay behind somehow until he was the last reporter in the room.

Booker decided to speak up. "Can you or William Rocker explain why he was outside Ken Capilon's home just hours before he was murdered?"

Hart looked stunned. Rocker looked down at the floor, then over to his attorney who, for just a millisecond, glared at Rocker as if this was new information she was not prepared to answer. Her eyes bored into Booker. "Where are you getting your information?"

"Surveillance home video, of which I have a copy and, by now, police will also have a copy as well. So, again I ask, what was William Rocker doing outside the home of Ken Capilon just before he was killed?"

"I was just going…" Rocker started to speak. Hart's hand came up fast, like a basketball player blocking a shot. She stared down Rocker and kept her hand up over his face. "We're not going to answer that right now. I have not seen this video you speak of, and for now, and until we do, we'll withhold any comment. Thank you all for coming." She got up, gestured to Rocker to move and the both of them retreated into the inner offices.

Coffee got video of the two of them walking past reporters. There was also a slight stunned look on the three other reporters in the room. Davis and his photographer snatched up their camera gear and hurried for the door.

Coffee calmly put away the tripod. "By telling the whole world now about the video, aren't you concerned they'll also get a copy by five p.m.?"

"Well, while you were putting your gear away outside the neighbor's house, he told me as soon as he called the police and sent them the video, he was leaving town again. Won't be back until next week. So, unless police release it, which I don't think they will, I'm not going to call it an exclusive but I don't think Davis and the others can catch up."

Coffee waited until they got to the car for her next question. "And why do you think Rocker was outside Capilon's house?"

"I think he wanted to speak with him. Make sure he was really going to change his statement."

"Not to kill him?"

"Kill a person who might be ready to exonerate him? I don't think so."

Coffee was behind the wheel. "You keep forgetting that Rocker could still be guilty. Drive off, come back through a trail in the woods to the back yard, surprise Capilon and use one of the supposed stolen knives."

"I just don't see him killing off a chance for his freedom."

Twenty minutes later, Booker was in front of the Capilon home. There were now four TV crews there setting up to go live for the five p.m. newscast.

Just after five, Booker, the top story, started off his live stand-up. "There are several new developments in the murder case of Shanice Rocker, which has now expanded into the murder of Ken Capilon. We have home surveillance video of former judge William Rocker outside Capilon's home."

For the next one-minute-twenty seconds, Booker's story showed the video of Rocker getting out of the car and looking around and Rocker attempting to speak, only to be shut down by his attorney. There was also an explanation of Shanice Rocker's death, Capilon's death and the two knives coming from the same set. When the video portion was over, Booker again spoke live. "At some point, Rocker's attorney says he will again sit down with detectives. That date has not been set. Booker Johnson, reporting live."

He waited until he heard the all-clear words in his ear. Coffee looked over across the street. Madigan's home looked quiet. No lights on. Booker got a call from Claire Stanley.

"Nice move Booker. You had the only video of Rocker outside that house. The others talked about it, but they didn't have your surveillance. What made you go back to that house?"

"Just wanted to make one last check. Not sure for a follow for tomorrow. I'll talk to you in the morning."

"No problem." Conversation over.

One block from the Channel 27 news station, Booker got a phone call. "Booker."

"Are you the one who left the business card on my door?"

"Yes, it was me. Got a few minutes? Wanted to talk about Fila."

"I can do that. I don't want to talk on camera. Just with you."

"No problem."

Booker texted Misha he would be late, got into his own car and drove to the apartment complex. The woman who answered the door was a bit taller than Booker expected.

"Hello, Mr. Johnson."

"Just call me Booker."

She let him inside and extended her hand. "I'm B.B." Her hair was in long waves, with one thin line of silver off to the side. She was easily six-foot-one. B.B. kept curling one end of the silver streak away from her hazel eyes. Booker imagined she could have been a model.

B.B. led him to the kitchen table where she had several pieces of paper spread out on the counter. "I've been waiting five years for someone to take up her story."

"Why is that?" Booker tried to get comfortable on the stool without a back.

"Because she did not kill herself on drugs. I'm convinced of it." B.B.'s hand came down hard on the table causing one of the papers to fly off the counter. Booker picked it up.

The hazel eyes flickered with a bit of anger. "She was my roommate, okay? She lived with me for almost a year. Not once, not one time did I see her ever do any drugs."

"You tell that to police at the time?"

"Yes." B.B. stepped away from the table, arms flinging, then pointing to the couch. "They found her right there. On the couch. They said it was fentanyl. By the time they got to her, she was long gone. I was out of town. My neighbor thought something was wrong."

"They say if the door was tampered?"

"The door was locked. Windows secure." B.B. came back to the table and sat in a chair. She used both hands to keep her hair off her face. "I've gone through this a hundred times. Went over every detail. It has to be she let someone inside who forced the drug on her."

"But police aren't sure?"

"No. But they've called it an overdose. No drugs in her life and then this. Doesn't make any sense."

"When she was here what did she do for a living?"

"She worked down at the grocery store, in the bakery department. Fila could cook or bake just about anything. And the job driving cars was just perfect for her 'cause she loved old cars. Wait a second." B.B. left the table and went into a bedroom. Booker heard her pull something across the carpet. When she came back, B.B. was lugging a suitcase. "I kept all her stuff."

Booker took the case from her and placed the silver bag on the couch. B.B. opened the suitcase. "This is all I have left of her."

Inside the bag were several items including a box full of jewelry. There were some photographs of B.B. and Fila taken somewhere down in the Florida Keys. A left running shoe was in the case and when B.B. moved things around, a sock fell out of the shoe. A sock with an object inside. B.B. reached in and Booker only got a quick look at something that resembled a tiny window. B.B. stuffed the object back inside the sock. "It's her extra set of keys on that giant keyring."

There were also a few large manila envelopes which were sealed. Booker picked up one of them. "You ever open these?"

"I guess I should have but I didn't. I was going to send them to her parents."

"Where are they?"

"That's the thing. When they shipped her body, I couldn't get any information on where she was taken. I guess I'm not a reporter like you."

"I can do some digging." There were three empty boxes for surveillance cameras. "She set up any cameras around the apartment?"

"No. I really don't know what she was doing with these. They're just boxes. And I never found any cameras anywhere."

"Mind if I take a few pictures?"

"Go right ahead."

Booker took out his cell phone and started photographing everything in the suitcase. He had no idea how the items were connected to anything. Twenty-six photographs later, he stashed away his cell phone. "Was she scared about anyone? Anyone threaten her?"

"The police asked the same thing. No, as far as I know, she was happy." B.B. picked up one of the photographs. "I remember this trip. Big Pine Key. We had a great time. Guys kept trying to hit on her. They left me alone, I think, because I was taller than anyone in the bar." She smiled and kept the photograph. "I'm going to frame it."

"At least you have the memories."

B.B. pulled the picture up close and kissed it. "You know, and I forget exactly where we were in the Keys, but at a restaurant I started choking. She reacted immediately and did the maneuver." B.B. looked up at Booker, emotion almost took over. "She saved my life." She placed the photo back.

"I promised I wouldn't cry about this. Instead of crying, I want to stay angry. I want to find out what really happened to her."

"So do I."

"You know, when this happened there wasn't even a mention in a newspaper or on TV. It's like a junkie overdosed, so who cares. I'm not going to give up."

"Thank you for talking to me."

"Anything that will help, I'm willing to do."

"Do you know how this antique car job worked?"

"Book, all I know is she would get a text message on where to pick up the car. The route was always very short cause they didn't want anyone to risk someone hitting one of their babies. She only did this once in a while and kept her regular job."

"She ever mention a name on who hired her? Her contact or handler?"

"No. She somehow worked all that out."

For now, Booker had a story with no real conclusion. And he knew he couldn't spend much time on Fila Mackee since the station already deemed the case over long ago. "Look B.B. I'm gonna be honest with you. Just about everyone has moved on from her case, including my station. In my spare time I will continue to look into this. I promise. But you have to help me a bit. First, if you know anyone she was hanging out with at that time. Anyone she would feel comfortable opening the door for and let them in. Second, If you think of anything else to help me, please send me a text. I will follow up on it."

B.B. put her hand on her chin, as if deep in memories. "I just remember she said she was here to do something. That she came here to find something out."

"She say what?"

"No. I tried to pull it out of her, but she always shut down."

Booker started to check his cell phone. B.B. sounded less than hopeful. "Your phone might not work here. They keep promising to put up a new cell phone tower but we're still waiting."

Booker let himself out. "Thanks. I'll see what I can find out."

"Thanks, Book."

17

Booker Johnson considered himself lucky. He knew there wasn't a solid hard angle for a follow-up, so Stanley gave him Thursday to do some investigating on his own. This meant he would lose Coffee for the day unless he could find a good story line to follow. Coffee was matched up with Lacie Grandhouse. The two of them were sent to a three-car smash on the I-95 Expressway.

Booker spent forty minutes on the phone calling police. There was no update and no comment on the Rocker or Capilon murder cases. And nothing on the knife set taken from Rocker. Booker knew from past experience that when police shut down information to him, they were working hard. And when they got real quiet, they were usually about to make an arrest.

He also thought about Fila Mackee. Booker kept the short report about her death on the upper right side of his desk, where he would be reminded all the time.

After the phone calls, Booker went to an edit booth, where news stories were digitally put together. He pulled up the interview with Branson Landale, the man who worked with Capilon. He studied the interview. When that was done, he carefully examined the video taken by Coffee. There were the usual pieces of video, including a two shot—Booker and

Landale walking through the office. Booker took time to slow down the video and examine two certificates on the wall. One was for donating bicycles to an after-school program. The second certificate was from a charity. Booker remembered Landale stated Capilon worked, at times, for a charity.

The Gold Breakthrough Charity had given Capilon and Landale a certificate for volunteer work and donations given during the past year.

Booker went back to his desk and started a search on the charity. On its website, The Gold Breakthrough Charity helped young people through basketball programs, paid for horseback riding and summer camps.

What caught his attention was a short message about a deceased member of the board. The message said the charity would miss her tireless efforts and no one would be able to replace her.

The deceased former board member was Shanice Rocker.

Booker's thoughts turned to questions. First, he remembered from conversations with the judge that Shanice was involved in charity work. Maybe, thought Booker, Shanice knew Ken Capilon. A possible direct connection to her, and now Capilon was gone. Booker approached Claire Stanley.

"No, it's not anything to move on," Booker explained. "It's just an angle. I'd like to follow up on it. If you need me for breaking news, just call me. I'm ready to go."

She nodded yes and Booker gave her the information on where he was going.

Seventeen minutes later, Booker parked in front of an office building. In the lobby, the directory listed Gold Breakthrough on the eleventh floor. Booker took a chance someone would be there. The first two times he knocked no one answered. There was a phone number from the website and Booker was about to call the number when a tall Black man emerged. He looked like he was in a hurry.

"Can I help you with something?" He was almost Booker's height, black hair, wearing a blue business shirt and dark slacks.

"Yes, I'm Booker Johnson. Channel 27. I'm interested in your charity."

He looked at his watch like he was extremely late for something. "Well, I'm on my way out. Can this wait until tomorrow?" He quickly closed the door behind him. From the little Booker saw, there were no other employees in the place.

"I just had a few questions. If you want, I can go down the elevator with you. Won't take a minute."

"I don't know if I have time. What are you interested in? Making a donation? Doing some work with one of our groups?"

They both walked to the elevator, with the man punching the down button twice. "Again, I'm just asking some simple questions about the group. Can I get your name?"

"Are you doing some kind of story?"

"No, not really. I don't even have a camera crew with me. I'm just inquiring about Gold Breakthrough. Your name?"

"Look. I don't want to say anything until I can get some approval from the board. That's the way we do things."

"Fine. If I can just get your name." The elevator doors opened and the two went in. The man punched lobby and leaned back against the wall of the elevator. Down they went.

"Ray Aldon."

"Thanks, Ray. Can you tell me about Shanice Rocker? And her time on the board?"

"Why are you asking about her? She's been dead, what, four years?"

"I know. I know she is missed by this charity and I'm doing a follow-up on her death. What did she do for the charity?"

The doors opened and Aldon looked like he was being freed from prison. "I really can't get into that. Let me check with the board." Now, he was walking, faster with each step.

"What did she do for the charity?"

"That really is charity business. And I can't get into it right now. Have a good day Mr. Johnson." He literally ran from Booker once he got onto the street.

Booker got into his car and drove back to the station.

By the time Booker reached his desk, there were two messages for him, both from Aldon with the charity. Booker called him back.

"Ah, Mr. Johnson, I'm sorry but we got off the wrong way this morning. That's my fault."

"I only had a couple of questions. And call me Booker."

"Thanks Booker. Anytime you want to come back, please do so and I'll try to answer your questions. I didn't mean to brush you off."

"I understand. People and businesses can sometimes be protective of information. I'll try to stop by tomorrow."

"Thank you."

For the next hour Booker was again in an edit booth looking at video. He went over the crime scene video from the Capilon house. Since the photographers were so far away, it was difficult to see, yet he noticed crime techs checking locations within the house.

Claire Stanley opened the door to the booth. "Whatcha thinkin' Book? Anything new?"

"Going over some video and just trying to connect some dots. What if they broke into Capilon's home the same night he was murdered? And the judge said his home was broken into twice while he was out of the country."

"And?"

"Someone is looking for something. And as far as I can see, they still haven't found it yet. Maybe they took something from Capilon's home, I don't know. What I'm thinking is someone is desperately looking, and I don't think they're going to stop."

18

Her run was well past the usual time. She always liked to run when the sun was the lowest, taking advantage of the approaching evening cool air and leaving the park moments before the invasion of mosquitoes. Her timing was perfect. There was no one hiking and not one bicyclist. She would run now when most were preparing dinner. Her car was just a half mile away. The finish line. Her motions were smooth, running with few, if any, injuries to her feet. She passed the huge Banyan tree struck by lightning three years earlier. The tree was a landmark.

The path was her favorite. The old growth of trees provided shade. She ran beside stretches of Gumbo Limbo trees and Sabal Palms, ground cover of wild periwinkle. Giant-leafed variegated philodendron hugged tall southern maples. Light still made it through the trees and beamed soft sun darts toward her feet.

The running shoes were well worth the money, and she ran as if all the problems of the world were being trampled with each stride. She was in her zone, focused on her pure running style, oblivious to the demons plaguing others, because these were her moments. This was her path. She ran the two miles like her very existence was being lifted to its highest point, full of positivity. And when she ran in this manner, she smiled the entire distance.

Her car was just around the corner, where the running trail through the city park ended and reality was waiting. The sun was losing its brilliance and darkness was looming. She was usually done long before now. A gray-black blur came into her peripheral vision and made her look toward her right. Seeing nothing she continued to the parking lot. Once she reached her car, the routine then included a walk around and a cool-down to ease her body back from running strong to getting behind a wheel. Three laps around the parking lot, she realized her car was the only one there.

Finished, she bent over, putting one hand on her car, getting full control over her breathing and tucking away the memory of another great run through the woods.

A strong hand smashed her head against the car door and another hand held the blade of a knife angled down hard and just missing her face, the point slamming into the blue paint of her SUV. Unless she did something, the second attempt with the knife would hit somewhere on her body. She tried to do two things at once: look in the car window for a reflection of her attacker and also do anything to avoid being stabbed.

The face in the car window was a blur, possibly covered with a mask. His hands were gloved, and he wore a long-sleeved hoodie, so she couldn't see his skin color. With all her strength, she dropped down into a ball and actually rolled away from him. A second slash just missed her side and moved with such ferocity, she heard the noise the knife made slicing through the air. Without taking time to look for his face, she crawled under the SUV. The first swipe of the knife blade had almost creased her face. Now on the ground, she moved back and prepared for another stab. Three times, the blade ripped at her, just inches from her face and body. On the fourth swing, the blade scraped hard along the gravel, kicking up sparks with the miss. The attacker ran to the other side of the car and again made large slicing motions in her direction. She moved back and stayed clear of the knife.

There was no sound from the figure. He was now walking around the SUV measuring the steps, as if looking for a way to attack. Time was not in her favor, and her bottom lip trembled like she could only do this for a very short time before he would close in wielding the knife of around twelve inches long. She looked and searched around for answers.

She tried to get control of her breathing as she was preparing for one final escape, staying quiet as possible, not giving her position away. She made a move. In a loud gesture she moved to her right, purposely letting her crawl draw attention. The figure quickly moved around the front of the car toward the movement. This was her chance. She slid hard to the left and emerged from under the car and started running.

The man with the knife chased after her. All of the woods were now cloaked in shadow. He was closing in, using long strides, the glint of the knife catching what was left of any light. When he ran, the up and down movement of the knife in his hand caught the night reflections.

This was no longer a run for the enjoyment of using time and space. This was a run for her life.

She had the elements in her favor. She had run this path on a regular basis for years and knew each bend and twist, even in the dark. And could he keep up with a practiced runner? He got close enough to swing his armed fist in her direction, yet he was still a good yard behind her. If she was going to survive, the next move would be critical. She kicked up the pace, running as fast as she could, faster than anything in her time going down this same path. She zigzagged her run, moving left to right in quick bursts as if to avoid the knife being thrown toward her back. When she got a good twenty feet from him, another decision.

She left the path and darted through the trees. If he stopped to listen, there was a chance he might be able to track her down. Twenty yards into the run into the trees, she stopped and sat down. She leaned into the back of a tree, tried to make herself small and stayed silent.

If he found her, there was always the option of running again. She touched the stash pocket lined inside her running pants and found the car fob. Whenever she ran, in an effort to keep her run free and light, the cell phone, purse and wallet were left behind in the locked car.

She heard someone walking near the same path she took into the trees. Without looking out from her hiding spot, she relied on ears rather than eyes. He was perhaps twenty feet from her now. Then she saw the flashlight feature from his cell phone. The beam was only good for ten feet or so and the cell light jumped hard left to right and back. She dared not move. He stopped for a full twenty seconds as if listening for more steps.

Again, her quiet breathing techniques were paramount. The intake and breathing out of air were all directed toward the ground. Her face was down, hands pulled up tight on her chest. For a quick second, she reached out and carefully picked up a downed tree branch, pulling it over her head and back. She moved with almost no sound. Then there was more waiting. This was the hardest part, like she was just waiting to be discovered and face the point of a blade. For a short time she counted the seconds then gave up. Quiet was her best advantage. She listened and, for certain, his movements were more off in the distance.

He moved on, going a bit toward his left and away from her. Now, she chanced a look for her attacker. He was a good forty yards away. For her, another decision was coming, and she moved as if he would turn around and move in her direction. The time to go was now. Carefully, she walked as softly as possible back toward the running-hiking path. The farther she got from him, the quicker she picked up her pace. When she got within ten feet of the path, she ran. Full bore, legs pumping, heart aching, lungs near empty on air, pleading for her to stop. She kept going.

She heard a crash of movement and turned back to see a figure moving in her direction, picking up speed. Somehow, he looked smaller than before.

This time there was no cooldown. No time for a walk around the parking lot. In one fast motion, she reached down into her inner pocket, pulled out the fob and was smashing the open door feature on the car fob as hard as she could. Once inside, she locked the door, turned on the engine and put the car in reverse.

The hard thud of a human being landed on the hood and blocked most of the view of the windshield. He tried to hang on. She stepped hard on the gas, then stopped abruptly. He was still there. She mashed the gas pedal and turned the car in one giant circle and stopped again. The masked and hooded figure slid off the car and was sprawled out in front of her. She had a choice—run him over or keep going.

Once the car was in drive, she again floored the gas pedal and drove around the man on the ground. Three miles later, she kept going past her home, speeding through her neighborhood like a person leaving their past altogether. She did not stop driving until she was in another city, where then and only then she took a moment to calm her breathing so she could start to figure out what she would do next.

19

Friday, Booker Johnson remained fixed in his chair, head down, staring into a computer screen, considering whether the Shanice Rocker story might remain fallow for one to two days and he could work on something else. He ignored the morning subtleties around him, including the fantastic smell of Cuban coffee, and concentrated on the short list in front of him. Getting some word from police remained at the top. There were no relatives for Capilon as his only family were several states away and made it clear they did not want to comment. Serenity Hart managed to shut down William Rocker and, for now, they were not making any new statements. Claire Stanley gave him *the look*, meaning she was about to send him on a general assignment story in the next few minutes unless he had something to investigate. He admitted to himself she'd been extremely patient and let him follow every lead, staying out of his way.

This, however, was another news day.

"Damn Booker, you're trending." Merilee Yang held her phone close to Booker's face.

"Trending? Where?"

"Social media. You're big, Book. It's called Crummick. There are at least ten people on Crummick following each of your stories. They make their own posts, give short video clips of what you're doing. Some of these people are major content creators."

Booker took the phone from her and checked out what she was showing him. On the phone he saw one video post had received sixty thousand views. Another post had close to a million.

"Wow. Does Stanley know about this?"

Yang took back her phone. "She is the one who told me about it. They're making comments, following along, reposting your stories and all of them are getting big-time hits on the Net. Like millions of hits."

"I have to admit, I'm shocked."

Yang shook her head. "These days, anyone under fifty is getting all of their news from an app. Social media platforms are the main source for them. Not sitting in front of a TV waiting for the news to come on."

Booker agreed. "They look up information on their cell phones anytime they want. Instant news and a lot of cat videos."

Yang dropped the phone in her purse. "If there's nothing to follow, then there's nothing to follow, but man Book, a lot of people are waiting to hear what you say next. You're developing quite a following."

"Thanks."

He turned back to his list. He made the call to police P.I.O. Jensen and was told there was no update. Check one off the list. He could always check out the charity for a comment, but that angle was a low priority. He opened the drawer and stared at the house key given to him by William Rocker, then closed the drawer.

Someone shouted, "Booker, call coming your way."

He picked up his phone. "This is Booker. Good morning." He waited, and for the next ten seconds, there was no response. "Hello, this is Booker."

"We need to meet." Her voice sounded urgent. "This is Booker Johnson, right?"

"Yes. Can I ask who is calling?"

"No name just yet. Someone tried to kill me last night."

"Please, who is this? And exactly what happened?"

"Just listen for a second, Booker. I've been watching all the coverage. Someone tried to kill me after my evening run, and I know it has to do with Shanice."

"You knew Shanice Rocker?"

"She was a friend. I was supposed to go in and make a first contact with police about the case."

"The police were expecting you?"

"They don't know anything about me yet."

"If someone tried to kill you, what do police say?" Booker was writing notes as he spoke to her.

"I haven't called them."

"Haven't called them? Please, I really want to talk to you, but I am urging you, please call the police. They need to know about this, and you need to protect yourself."

"No police right now. Just you."

"And you won't give me your name?"

"Not yet. Very soon, I want to set up a meeting with you and get everything on video just like William did."

"You're friends with the Rockers?"

"I'm not saying anything more about them. I'm in a safe place and, right now, I don't trust anyone. Ken was about to speak to police, and look what happened to him."

"You knew Ken Capilon?"

"Yes."

"The attack. What happened?"

She started, "One man with..." she stopped. "No more information. I escaped. That's all that matters right now. And I want to speak to you on camera. No police until then."

"You're not giving me much information on quite honestly—"

"I know what you're thinking, Booker. This could be a hoax. There was a reason we all stayed quiet back then. We realized now we should come forward. The thing is police don't really know we exist yet. But we stayed quiet too long."

Booker thought of anything he could do to convince her to stay on the phone. He sensed a real fear in her voice, and someone with the will and strength to protect themselves—and that included Booker Johnson. He listened for any background noise to help determine where she was calling from and got nothing.

Booker pleaded, "We can meet today. Any place you want. I can make the arrangements."

"Trust me. I want everything to come out. Full disclosure. But not yet. This is a burner phone which I will destroy as soon as I hang up so don't try to contact me. For now, keep this just between us. No TV. I promise, I'll contact you."

"Okay, listen. I'm going to make one last plea. I can't say this strongly enough. You need to call police. That's critical right now. Just call them."

"Not yet. And this is our off-the-record secret until I meet you."

She was gone. Booker tried calling back and got nothing. She demanded to stay anonymous and, for now, he would honor that request. Besides, what would he tell police? Some mysterious woman who wouldn't leave her name claims she was attacked. He had absolutely no details. When he put the phone down, Claire Stanley was standing over him. "And what exactly was that?"

"I don't know what to make of it yet."

Booker explained the details of the cryptic phone call. "I don't have a name, where this happened, not even sure if this is real."

"How did she sound?"

"Like it was the real deal. I just don't have anything to report on. Without a person in front of me, just some voice on the phone, I really don't have much. But one thing she said has me wondering, and I have to contact Hart. This woman claims police don't know anything about her and possibly other witnesses as well. And she wants this off-the-record quiet. But what I do know is anyone who knows something about this case is in some real danger."

Booker and Coffee waited in the SUV outside the office of Serenity Hart. A TV crew arriving unannounced with no appointment might see the door and a hard goodbye in twenty seconds.

Using his phone, Booker checked for any reports of people being attacked that would match what the caller had described. He checked police reports and came up empty. Booker then checked the websites of other TV news stations and found nothing. Even the lauded Crummick app had no mention of a person attacked. Finally, he gave up.

"So, Book, what's the plan?" Coffee leaned back in the car's seat and had the SUV positioned so she could see the front door.

"I'm going in alone without you. See if I can find out something."

Coffee knotted her arms. "I'll be here if you need me."

Booker knew walking into an office, any office, without a proper appointment could end in several different ways, almost all of them not good. There was a youngish looking man, probably early twenties behind the desk. There were books near him and Booker guessed he might be a law student or someone about to take the LSAT, law school admissions test. He wore a blue shirt, green tie and no sport coat. His hair was cut close to the scalp and he looked clean and ready for the day.

"Excuse me, I'm..."

"Booker Johnson, I know. Ms. Hart isn't here right now. She's due back in about ten minutes if you want to wait."

Booker sat down on the wooden bench he swore felt like one stolen from a courthouse. The walls were lined with law school diplomas and photographs of Hart in court. The ten minutes turned into twenty. In that time, he watched and heard perhaps thirty or more calls into the office. The young man on the desk handled each one with the skilled approach and even-toned delivery of an office professional.

The door opened, and Hart clearly did not look happy when she saw Booker waiting. Her dour look turned into a smile. "So, a no comment doesn't mean anything to you, Mr. Johnson?"

"If you want me to leave, I'll do that. Thank you for your time." Booker headed for the door.

"Wait. Come into my office."

With no real reason to be there, Booker was resigned to their meeting being a feeling-out session. Both would attempt to cull information from the other without revealing too much.

Hart took a cleaning cloth and wiped down her glasses. Her brown eyes looked calculating. Like the rest of the office, her desk was clean, not even a knickknack. She slid the frames back into place on her face. "If you're trying to find my client, I have him in a discreet place with strict orders not to talk to you or any reporters." Her lips still held a smile for only another second, then she was back to the serious-looking Serenity Hart.

Time was too valuable for each of them. Booker got down to it. "The people who were set to talk to police, clearing Mr. Rocker, have they all come forward? Do you know exactly who they are?"

Hart looked at Booker like she was studying a test. There was no immediate answer, and the brown eyes bore into him. "Why do you ask that?"

"Just a question."

"Mr. Johnson, you seem to know more than you're telling me. Have you talked with police?"

"They're really not going to say anything. You, though, can say a definitive yes or no, depending on how it will help your client. If these witnesses are all known to police, William Rocker is that much closer to being taken off the suspect list."

She was about to answer when Booker's phone rang. He answered, "Booker." The caller was Stanley.

"We need you on breaking news. Head to the expressway."

20

The I-95 Expressway stretched more than three hundred and eighty miles through the state of Florida. Booker had been warned the expressway was backed up with drivers, and he had no idea of the situation until Coffee pulled up along a side road.

"Damn Booker, this is bad." Coffee only stopped for a moment to gauge the traffic. For as far as both of them could see, cars were lined bumper-to-bumper with absolutely no movement. "Like they're caught in quicksand."

Coffee got back onto the side road and traveled north. The side road itself was starting to fill up with disgruntled drivers moving off the expressway. She maneuvered around slower cars for another four miles until they found the situation.

A semi-truck was hanging over the edge of a flyover. All northbound traffic was stopped by Highway Patrol and fire trucks. Southbound traffic was at a crawl.

Coffee pulled out her tripod, moving fast to set it up. "Wow. Look at that! If you look close, you can see the driver is still trapped."

Somehow, the truck had managed to go up and over the concrete wall with the cab and wheels dangling precariously over the edge. Two fire-fighters were at the concrete wall barrier, and while Booker could not hear them, they seemed to be trying to calm the driver. Any movement the wrong way and the truck would topple over.

Booker and Coffee were not the main crew on the story. Lacie Grandhouse was a half-mile closer and was already in position. Channel 27 broke into programming and Grandhouse was reporting live, raising her voice over helicopter video. Above, the drone of the station helicopter made it harder to hear conversations on the ground. Beside the chopper video and the photographer working with Grandhouse, Coffee's camera was a third option for the directors. There was no need for Booker to speak. Coffee was set up with a live signal, earpiece in, ready for the station to go to her camera when needed.

Booker opened his laptop and watched the coverage live on the station website. He listened to Grandhouse. "Again, we are telling all drivers, please avoid the I-95 Expressway. All northbound lanes are stopped, and southbound traffic is slow because drivers are looking at what happened. Authorities say a driver had a blown tire while traveling up the flyover. His truck slammed into the concrete barrier, went up and almost over the edge. That is a ninety-foot drop to the expressway below. As you can see from our helicopter, firefighters are keeping the driver calm while they get their gear in place to get control of the truck and free him."

As she finished her sentence, everyone watching the video saw the truck had moved a bit. Some loose debris fell after working free from the enormous weight of the truck. A large chunk of concrete could be heard crashing on the vacant northbound lanes. The truck tipped forward slightly, evened up, and stayed in place.

Grandhouse described every detail. Her words were on point, smooth, and she stayed calm. The driver of the truck, however, was not. He started gesturing with his hands and moved around in the truck cabin. Clearly, he was moving around too much, as if panic was taking over. Viewers just barely heard the firefighters pleading with the driver to remain fixed and stop making any more sudden movements.

Booker watched the fire crews extend a fire truck's ladder out about fifteen feet above the truck cab. People on the expressway were now out of their cars, staring up at the life-or-death rescue.

The next portion of the work would take several minutes. Booker listened in again to Grandhouse. "So, the working plan is to get a firefighter out on that ladder, loaded with gear, who will then rappel down to the driver. That could take a while and they have to make sure everything is in place. And they will work slowly." For a few moments, Grandhouse stopped talking and let the live pictures tell the story. Booker could hear gasps from people watching on the ground.

The firefighter took his time, extending safety lines, moving closer to the end of the ladder. Booker saw him talking to the driver as if directing him on what would happen. When the firefighter got into place, Grandhouse again picked up the narration using video from the helicopter. "As you can see, a firefighter is just above the driver. With the firefighter saying something to him the whole time. And now very slowly the firefighter is letting himself down to the driver's side window."

Over the next ten to fifteen minutes, Booker watched live pictures of the rescuer lowering himself down. The truck driver was then fitted into a harness and lifted out of the cab, holding on to the firefighter. Then other members of the unit pulled the two of them to safety onto the flyover. The driver didn't seem like he wanted to let go and appeared to hold on until other firefighters urged him to a waiting truck to be checked out.

A roar of applause rose from the expressway, and drivers standing on the road were now applauding. Booker heard shouts of 'hero' coming from the roadway.

Traffic was still gridlocked. Even southbound was shut down during the last phases of the rescue. With the driver back, more connections were made to the truck cab to pull the truck back from the edge. In another twenty minutes, the whole ordeal would be over.

Booker looked down the side street. Traffic moved slow but steady. A car was near him, some two lanes away. The white Honda edged closer then moved past Coffee's SUV. Booker stared at the Honda and the driver. Coffee gestured to Booker, indicating she was free from the live coverage. She started to break down the tripod and followed Booker's gaze into the side traffic. Both of them looked at the driver of the Honda. Coffee loaded the camera into the car. "You see that car?"

Booker was still staring. "Yes. That's William Rocker." They saw him turn off and head down a street.

Coffee pulled out a towel and wiped down her brow in the September heat. "You know where he's going?"

"No. But I think we can find out."

21

Once Booker and Coffee were able to move, they drove down Wepner Street, the same street Rocker traveled. The Honda was long gone and they didn't see where he went. There was no indication if or where Rocker might have stopped. The next option was a trip back to the station. During the entire time, Booker kept thinking about the phone call and the woman who was attacked. Booker was beating himself up because he could not convince her to contact police. His phone was set to the loudest level, yet there was no call from her.

There *was* a phone call, this time from Stanley. "Booker, you talked with Hart today?"

"Briefly."

"You somehow lit a fire under her, and she's determined you know something, meaning you know more than she knows."

"And she doesn't like it."

"Bingo."

Booker relayed what happened during the short visit. "I didn't tell her anything, I just asked or proposed a scenario. Then we got the call from you."

"And the woman hasn't called back?"

"No."

Booker could just picture Claire Stanley thinking and gnawing on some gum. "Booker, when it comes to Hart, be careful."

"I'm fine. I won't have a story for you today. Unless you put us on something else."

"We're fine. But if another breaker comes up—"

"I know, we're at the top of the go-to list. No problem."

Conversation over, Booker had Coffee head to someplace to get a bite. It was just past two p.m., and Coffee was well past her breaktime. Booker stayed in the SUV while Coffee went inside a fast-food place. She agreed to bring him back a burger while Booker sat checking his phone for another call from the mysterious woman and checked the Crummick app.

He saw a text come in from his brother Demetrious. The text said he had an update on the woman who overdosed and he would see him that night. Booker texted back *okay*. When Coffee came back with the burger, Booker wanted to ride instead of eat. "Go back to the road again."

"The one Rocker took?"

"Yes. Wepner. Thanks."

Within minutes, they were again on Wepner street breaking off from the side road. There were warehouses and a plant nursery. There was a large facility, home to a company building pools in South Florida. There was nothing seemingly connected to Rocker.

"Stop here."

Coffee pulled over in the SUV. She scanned the area. "Booker, you sure about this?"

"No, but I'll be right back. Playing out a hunch."

Booker went inside, and when he came back a full sixteen minutes later, he wasn't surprised that Coffee gave him a hard stare and asked, "And?"

"I'll hold onto what I found out for now and speak to Rocker directly when I see him."

"You don't want to tell me?"

"Not yet. I will, I promise."

Booker reached for the bag and ate his cold burger in silence on the way back to the TV station. He kept his cell phone out in front of him, resting on his lap because he did not want to miss a call from the woman who was attacked. By the time they got back, there was still nothing. Booker headed home that night without a story for the newscasts. Half-way to the apartment, though, he decided to make one stop.

Ray Aldon, the director of the Gold Breakthrough Charity agreed to meet with Booker. This time, Aldon had plenty of time and was all smiles. The inside of the charity office was full of photographs, all of teens enjoying a basketball game or doing things outside.

Aldon himself was almost as tall as Booker. He had long ebony fingers and wore a black tie over a blue business shirt. The smile seemed genuine, and the handshake was firm.

"Thanks for coming. Booker, is it?"

"Yes. You have a lot of programs going?"

Aldon stood back and pointed to the wall of photographs. "We don't have a building of our own, but we have contracts with schools and other facilities to conduct basketball games, computer classes and summer camps. We even have a class on everyday skills like opening up a savings account."

"And Shanice Rocker was a part of that?"

"Very much so. She did a lot of the fundraising events. Without her help and the help of others, we couldn't do the programs I just mentioned."

Booker walked through the office, not wanting to look like he was inspecting. "Big staff?"

"Not many. We can't afford a weekly staff. We just ended our summer programs and everyone is back in school. In about a month, we'll start computer classes in the afternoon. We hire on an as-needed basis."

"I understand."

Booker looked for any signs of employees, a set of family photos at a desk, a sweater left on a chair. He just found the arrangement of six desks, computers and nothing else. Aldon seemed to notice Booker's interest in the empty desks. "Again, our budget is so tight, we just don't have the money for people year-round. I'm a paid director but I do the work of seven people."

Aldon moved back behind his own desk and pulled out a stack of papers and several photographs. "I know why you're here. You're interested in the work Shanice did." He pushed a stack of papers in Booker's direction. "Take a look at what she was able to accomplish. Now, she wasn't alone but the input was important."

Booker looked over the papers. He read down a list and found one charity event listing costs for the night and the bottom line on the contribution to Gold Breakthrough. Aldon's voice boomed across the office. "We raised seventy-five thousand that night, after expenses. Not bad. We had three more fund raisers during the year, all of which brought in more money than that one figure."

Aldon's smile was broad. He slid more papers toward Booker. "I was hoping, once you saw all this, that maybe we could convince you to do a story on us. Either now or the night of a charity."

Aldon took out a small towel from the desk and wiped his forehead. Since he'd first stood in front of a camera, Booker had always practiced memorizing every aspect of a person he met for the first time. In Aldon's case, he was constantly perspiring. Booker made mental notes. Aldon was right-handed, yet used his left a lot of the time. His watch hung loose on the wrist, so the thing slid up and down his forearm. If shoes were an indication of how he might take care of himself, Aldon failed. His black shoes were worn and desperately needed a good shine. When he walked around, Aldon's rear pocket had the outline of a wallet probably stuffed with too many business and credit cards. All of these facts were filed into Booker's memory like so many flash cards.

Booker had four photographs in front of him. One showed Shanice behind a microphone like she was asking for donations. In another, she was in a greeting line meeting people at the door. In another, a group photo of people involved in the charity. "Can I take photos of these?" Aldon looked like he was considering the request. "Sure. Go ahead."

Booker took out his phone and snapped a pic of each one on the desk. "Thank you. I'll bring your story idea to my station."

He pushed the entire stack of papers and pictures back to Aldon. "Did Shanice seem to have any enemies? Someone who might mean harm to her? Any arguments?"

"No. Far as I know, everybody loved her. Her work for this organization can't be measured. Years later, we are still working to fill the void she left."

Booker got up to leave. He was at the door when Aldon made one last comment. "I'm sorry I was so rude with you before. That won't happen again. I hope your station will consider my story idea."

"I'll pass it on."

With Misha out running errands, Booker was alone in the apartment when Demetrious knocked on the door. "I've got a surprise for you," Booker said as he ushered Demetrious inside and they sat down in the apartment-sized small living room.

"What's up, Book?"

"There's a vacant apartment upstairs. I checked, and I think it's yours, if you want it."

"You don't mind me living so close."

"Close? Not too long ago, you were living here, remember? I don't mind."

"I'll think about it." Demetrious looked over his brother like someone going through a checklist of emotions. "Something's bothering you, Book. I can tell."

For almost twenty seconds, Booker Johnson sat quiet, finally rubbing his face with his hands and not responding, all thoughts deep down a rabbit hole worrying about the woman who called him. The one who wanted her near-death experience kept a secret.

Demetrious watched him. "Okay, so it's something you can't talk about. Job stuff, I get it. Don't let it eat you up."

"You hungry?"

"Just ate. So, here's what I found out about Fila Mackee. She came here with one purpose. To find something."

Booker was interested and fully engaged, and this matched what Fila's roommate had told him. "Find something? What?"

"Well, that's it. I'm not sure what exactly she was looking for, but the guy

I spoke to said for sure, she moved down here with some information to find this thing."

"It's a start. Thanks."

"That's all I have to contribute. The guy who gave me the information got fired and now the business itself of driving cars is shut down."

Booker looked worried. "Because of your questions?"

"They claimed it's because of increased insurance rates for us to drive the cars, but I think it's because I started poking around."

"Again, who owns this business?"

"To tell you the truth, I don't know. I can give you a name but I think it's a shell company."

Now Booker was more than intrigued. "It's interesting they would entrust you with these expensive antiques and not be more forward."

"Book, I think something happened some years back. They were more involved back then, they tell me, and then everything changed."

"Thanks. That helps."

"No problem. When I picked up the car, the keys were always in a designated lockbox with a code that we'd get. I drove the car around and dropped off the keys."

"Gotcha." Booker watched Demetrious walk into the kitchen. "Have you seen him again?"

"My father? No. Nothing so far."

"Hope he stays away."

Demetrious pulled the curtain apart and stared down to the street. "I think someone's following me."

"You sure?"

"Yeah, it's the same car. Saw it earlier. He or she is down there now."

"What model?"

"Looks like a Caddy SUV. All black."

Booker started to join him at the window, then stopped. "You positive about this?"

"Has to be the car. Same one was parked outside the café, and now here. Yep. The same one."

"Stay in the window so they can see you." Booker walked to the door, entered the hallway and bolted down the stairs two at a time. He kept landing hard on each floor until he reached the lobby. He ran out into the street, cell phone up and already recording video. The caddy's windows were dark as midnight. Booker took two steps toward the car and the Caddy tore away from the parking spot, tires squealing, spitting rocks. Booker tried but couldn't get a good fix on the license plate. The car made a right turn, screeching off and out of sight.

Booker moved toward his own car, then changed his mind. He ran a few feet and realized that car was gone and there was no point chasing it.

Forty feet behind Booker, someone in another car was watching the entire thing. The figure sat there and made no movements, but observed the Caddy casing the building, Booker running out, and the SUV driving off fast. Now, the person just stared at Booker. The one behind the wheel pulled on black gloves, then patted the SIG resting in the passenger seat. The figure first ducked down when Booker ran out into the street and only now rose up from the hidden position.

Booker went back inside and back up to his apartment. He was a bit out of breath. "You piss off someone at that company?"

"Maybe. You get anything?"

"I'll send you the video. Maybe you can make some sense of it. But from now on, you've got to be careful."

"If they want to find me, I'm at the Internet Café. All I do is help people. We even give free computer access to people looking for a job. I'm not afraid."

"Well, starting tonight, maybe you should be."

22

On Saturday morning, Booker sat at his desk, watching a blank screen, oblivious to the a.m. routine surrounding him. He had checked out his cell phone video several times and no matter how many times he squeezed the video, he could not make out the driver of the Caddy. And when he looked for the license plate, there was none. No driver and no plates. There was one option; he could check out a few stores along the route and see if any business owners had outside cameras for surveillance. He gave up on that idea since his cell video was probably better than anything he would find.

Booker asked for and was granted permission to keep working beyond his five-day shift to wait for the mysterious woman to call back. Coffee was given overtime.

"Okay Book, talk to me." Coffee pulled up a chair and studied her work partner. "I know you. When you have a lot of things you can't control, you look like you're stuck."

"I do have a lot in the air. Sometimes I just have to think it out. I told you about the phone call I got, and I can't stop thinking about her."

Up by the assignment desk, Lacie Grandhouse was getting her story for the day. She was doing a follow-up to the firefighters rescuing the truck driver. A ten a.m. news conference was planned, where the driver wanted to thank the firefighters.

Booker finally seemed to pull out of his funk. "Those firefighters are heroes."

"For them, it's just another day." Coffee took a sip from a cup of tea. "Let me know if we're on today."

Booker stayed out of the morning meeting and, within four minutes, Claire Stanley came to him. "Okay Booker, Serenity Hart has you on her S list. I spoke to her yesterday. Long talk."

"I'm not surprised."

"I think if she could, she'd tie you up and drag some information out of you. She doesn't know it, but she's right about you having information."

"I was hoping she would tell me something about the witnesses, but it didn't happen."

"Book, here's the deal. I've got you going to a news conference. Maybe we pull a short sound clip for the five p.m., or maybe it's your story for the day. The producers would like to see your face on TV today."

"I get it."

"I'll email you the information on the newser." She was gone, headed back to the assignment desk. Booker's cell phone rang. Unknown caller.

"Booker."

"If I give you an address, are you ready to move?" He knew the voice on the phone.

"I can meet you. Where am I going?"

"Take Steeper Avenue north to Palm Street, all the way out to U.S. 27 and wait for my call."

"I'm on the way." Booker called out to Coffee, and she immediately went toward the door. He waved to Stanley and yelled, "Gotta go. Trust me."

She waved back a goodbye. Before he had a chance to reach the SUV, he got another phone call. "Booker. I can't talk long."

"This is Fila's friend, B.B."

"Can it wait? I'm heading out on a story."

"Booker, I think I found something, and it could be really important. I just thought you should take a look at it."

"I can't right now. Will it wait until tonight?"

"Ok. I'll make some changes on my end. I was supposed to fly out later."

"Thanks, B.B." Booker tucked the phone away and jumped into the passenger seat. He gave Coffee the directions and they were off. Headed north, Booker could not stop thinking about the other balls in the air. Just who was in the SUV following Demetrious? What information did B.B. find? He pleaded with Demetrious to change up his driving habits and look for anyone following him. He even spoke with Misha about what happened.

Now west on Palm Street, the destination was another fifteen minutes away. In some areas of South Florida, the distance between the ocean and the Everglades was just fifteen miles. Booker knew every inch. For others, travel was a mundane part of driving. For a reporter like Booker, certain locations carried horrific memories of past news stories. They were like news landmarks. They passed the house where a victim was discovered in the front patio, dismembered. In that story, the culprit was a disgruntled neighbor. There was the canal just off Palm Street where they found a suitcase filled with body parts. A suspect was never caught. Twice during the year, police diving teams and crews with special equipment found cars in the green-black canals near the road. Most of the cars were empty. A few held human remains and closure for families looking for loved ones who had disappeared. In some cases, missing person reports were from decades earlier. Almost all of them were drivers who went off the roadway. Two miles west on Steeper, a man walking his dog had smelled something coming from a house. When police checked, they found three human heads in a refrigerator. A rival gang member was caught in that case.

And far to the south, in Miami, before Booker arrived, he was told about the numerous murders during the time of the cocaine cowboys. Victims shot many times. All part of the history and lure of the cities by the ocean.

Three blocks from the U.S. 27 connection, Booker looked for anything —a car, a person on the road, a clue. They found a parking lot. The lot was a spot for fishermen to leave their boats and push off into the waters of the Florida Everglades. They pulled in and stopped. And waited.

Booker got out. He liked it here. The air was empty of traffic noise. If he stood by long enough, there would be splashes from fish tapping the surface. They kept waiting.

His phone came to life. "Booker...I'm here."

"You weren't followed?"

"Far as I can see, it's just me. My photographer is with me. Her name is Coffee."

"Okay. Take U.S. 27 north into the next county. When you get to Prairie View, go East two miles until you reach a farmhouse. You can't miss it, there's a huge horse statue out front. Turn in and I'll meet you there."

Coffee overheard everything and was now going north. On the left they saw the vast spread of the Glades, where alligators and pythons were rival neighbors. On the right, in the distance were neighborhoods. Every city and county along the divide made promises to not build homes in the Glades and preserved drinking water.

When they turned onto Prairie View, Coffee slowed down and both of them looked for the horse. They also kept checking to make sure there was no one behind them. Out here, traffic was scarce.

Coffee pointed. "There it is." She pulled in and parked near what looked like a three-bedroom house, stopping near a large sun-bleached gray horse statue. Strange to see such a small house, since there was plenty of land to build a larger residence. Coffee got out her camera. Booker carried the sticks, or tripod. The front door opened before they got there.

A woman stood in the doorway. She had short black hair, shorts and running shoes. Her blouse was sleeveless, and her arms were fully muscled. Booker thought her biceps were as large as most men who worked out.

"Come on in. I'm Mercedes Campana. You can set up in here."

Here meant a small living room. She already had two chairs lined up in interview-style. Her eyes kept flicking back and forth from Booker to the front windows. She was clearly watching out. Her eyes were dark like her locks. "There are no cell phone towers out here so calling will be spotty. But I like it that way."

"No problem. Coffee will fit you with a microphone and we'll talk."

While Coffee fitted the microphone, Booker checked out the small house. There was a quaint kitchen with all green cabinets and a nice wide window to the back yard. He could see trees in no certain pattern or formation, just a wild assortment of bushes needing a trim and uncut grass.

When he turned back to Campana, her eyes connected with his. "I see you checking out my yard. It's a mess. A friend lets me stay here." She pointed toward the window. "What you don't see is I have a car and a motorcycle out there and two different paths in case I need to get away." She sat down in the chair facing the front door. Coffee gave the signal she was recording.

Booker said, "I hope you are okay. From our conversation on the phone, it sounded horrific."

"I was out on my run. Just before sunset. Just as I got to my car, after my cooldown period, someone tried to stab me. I was terrified."

"You see the person?"

"Not really. He had a mask. Looked like a man. I managed to dodge the stabs and hid under the car and when there was a free moment, I got out and took off. He chased me. I ran off into the woods, turned around and got back to my car. He was hanging on the hood of my car. I'll never forget it."

"What happened next?"

"I got him off my car and I drove away and didn't stop until I was a long way from there. I haven't been by my house."

"Any idea why you were attacked.?"

Her arm muscles tightened, and she flexed her fists like she wanted to hit someone. "I know exactly why. At least I think so. I was about to speak with detectives about the murder of Shanice Rocker. I was going to make a statement. I kept telling people one thing, and now I wanted to change it."

"What did you want to change?"

For a moment Campana looked like she was about to stand up, but she didn't. Her eyes kept moving from Booker and the camera to the front windows. She stared at them like an intruder was about to appear any second. "Back then I was going to tell detectives I overheard William Rocker arguing with his wife. A loud argument and that he threatened her. I was very clear about that. At least that was what I was prepared to say."

"And now?"

She licked her lips like her mouth was dry. Campana used her head to flick back a line of curls about to slide across her face. The eye movement was back. "William Rocker never had an argument with Shanice. Never. I just said that to a couple of people."

Booker leaned toward her just a little. "Clearly, the question is why would you do that, and did you say those things on your own or did someone direct you?"

"You're getting into an area that I'm going to hold for police."

"Still, why would you say there were arguments when there weren't any?"

"There was a reason. I just can't say right now. And I was not the one who told William to leave the country. Others did that. I just know I want to change what I said and now because of that, I'm a target."

"Just one little area if I can. Tell me about Shanice? And why do you think anyone would hurt her?"

"I've been thinking about her and the judge every day since it happened. Every day. I just know we were close friends. Ate at our favorite restaurants, shopped together. She had this really great laugh. Her laugh made me laugh. Her death leaves a hole in my heart."

"You say you first told some people Judge Rocker had argued with his wife. Who did you tell you were going to police?"

"Ken. Ken Capilon. He knew I was going to the authorities. Clear this up once and for all. When he was murdered, I should have left then. I thought I was safe. Now I know I'm not."

"You think Ken told anyone?"

"I just know Ken did actually tell detectives William argued with Shanice. A false statement. Now, today, we were ready to settle up and tell it right. Ken would change what he said before. I would be seeing detectives for the first time."

She pulled off the microphone, handing it to Coffee. Booker wanted to press her about what happened four years earlier then gave in to her wishes to stop.

"Mercedes, what do you plan to do now?"

"Now that I said something on camera, I'm headed to the police. I'll just wait in the lobby and speak to whoever will hear me."

"Okay if we follow you?"

"I like that. Let me get my things." She went into a side bedroom and came back with a small duffle. "I'll drive around to the front and I'll meet you at P.D."

"No problem. Thank you."

Booker loaded the tripod into the SUV and got inside. He sent a text to Claire Stanley saying he had a story for the five p.m. Details to follow. When Coffee got into the car, she turned to Booker. "Okay, maybe I'm wrong about the judge."

Campana drove around to the front, got out of her SUV and walked to Booker's car window. She handed him a piece of paper. "Look, I'm not using my cell phone, only burners. This number will be good for the next day or so then I'm gonna change it."

Booker took the paper. "This address, is this your place?"

"Yes. I know my mail is stacking up. Once I check in with police, maybe I'll go there next. See you there." She got into her SUV and drove off. Coffee followed.

They traveled the same route back, south on U.S. 27, then to Steeper Avenue. Once they reached Steeper, they joined afternoon traffic. One, then two more cars got behind Campana.

"Stay with her." Booker examined the cars in front of them. Campana's car was now ahead with four cars between them. Coffee stepped on the gas, moving around slower cars. When they got to the turn for the police station, Campana's car was nowhere to be seen.

"Sorry Book. Too many cars in the way."

"Maybe we'll beat her to the P.D."

In the next few minutes, they witnessed a South Florida phenomenon. Under a bright blue sunny day, raindrops pelted the windshield. "Only in Florida," Coffee muttered.

Booker examined the sky, dotted with a few clouds. "That's why they call it liquid sunshine." For the next mile, rain hit hard, then suddenly stopped. They looked for Campana's car and she was no longer in their vision.

The police station was six more minutes away. They pulled into the lot and Coffee got out the laptop to check out the video. Booker got on the phone with Stanley, letting him know they had an exclusive interview with Mercedes Campana.

"Book, how did she sound. Believable?"

"To me, she did. Very believable. I know she looked scared. I don't see her car here and I'm thinking about letting Detective Jensen know what's coming."

"Okay. Later."

Booker was told he was the top story at five p.m. He called Campana's burner phone.

Coffee yelled from the back of the SUV. "She answering?"

"No." He tried two more times. Got nothing. Now, concern filled his thoughts. He went over the images of her car in front of them, the added traffic, the rain, and then she was no longer there.

For the next forty minutes Booker and Coffee put together a video package. Once uploaded to the station, Coffee put out her tripod. Even if another station showed up now, they didn't have the interview.

Booker called for Detective Jensen and left a voicemail. The newscast was twenty minutes away. He checked three times with others in the Public Information Office. No Campana. The directive from Channel 27 was to go ahead with the story, maybe she would still show up. Booker again called Stanley. "If you have a free crew, can you send them by Campana's home. I sent you the address earlier."

"No problem, Book. I'll send someone now."

"Maybe police sent a unit to do a wellness check."

Two minutes before news time, Stanley called Booker back and told him two police units were at the Campana residence and Brielle Jensen was there. Booker said he would go there as soon as his live story ended.

One minute past five p.m., Booker Johnson looked into Coffee's camera and told South Florida viewers the story of Mercedes Campana. He let her explain what happened in her own words, let Coffee's video show the sheer concern in her face. And then tried to explain the unexplainable. "When we last saw Campana, she was supposed to show up here at the police department with a mission to speak to detectives. She is not here, and authorities, at this point, do not know her whereabouts. Please know we will stay on this story. For now, we are live at police headquarters, Booker Johnson, Channel 27 news."

23

Coffee's worried look matched the one on Booker's face. He tried calling Campana two more times and got no answer. They were about to head to her home address when Claire Stanley called them. "Booker, head to Federal Highway and Croaker Street. I'm hearing it on the police scanner. I think they found her car. Abandoned."

"We're going."

"I hate to keep you on the clock."

"No problem, Claire. We're on it."

Booker and Coffee said nothing as they rode. Hours earlier, they had talked with her, even followed her. Now, could she be missing?

When they arrived, two other news crews from other stations were already there. Booker was actually the last to the scene. The near black SUV was down a slight embankment, the nose of the car almost in a canal. The car had a sizeable dent on the front driver's side. A fire rescue truck was there, along with three police units. And Brielle Jensen. She searched out Booker. "Book, what time did you last see her?"

"About 3:45 p.m."

"Thanks. Your assignment editor, Claire, she gave us some other details."

With some hesitation, Booker asked, "Is she here?"

"No. The car is open. Her purse is in the car, in a duffle bag. The car key is on the front seat. Everything is in the car but she's not here and we are searching."

She walked off and Booker knew that would not be the end of it. He might have to make a statement. He was prepared to do so, even if it meant he would then become part of the story. Coffee was busy photographing everything. She panned and videotaped the car, detectives walking around, a crime tech team ready to process the car once they got an okay, traffic slowing down to rubberneck. She got it all.

One detective stood near the water, looking into the shallow depths of the canal.

Booker was going through a wide range of emotions. He had never lost an interviewee before. All of his planned excursions always worked out, somehow. The painful thought of something bad happening to Campana set him back a bit. When Coffee finally turned her attention to Booker, she made him sit in the car.

"Book, this is not your fault. Or our fault. We got separated. The police are here. They'll track the cameras. We'll find her."

Booker wiped down his face and tried to settle himself. From deep inside, a renewed energy bubbled to the surface. The intense need to question moved to the forefront and in a few more seconds, Booker again resembled Booker. He called Stanley. "If the producers want, I can do some live TV. Let's get video of her car out there. We can be ready to go in about two minutes."

"You're on Booker. Get ready and we'll come to you."

5:46 p.m. There was another forty-four minutes of Channel 27 news before the station turned it all over to the Network. Exactly three minutes later, Booker was again on the air, pointing to the now-damaged car, telling his audience this was the same SUV and license plate he saw earlier in the day when he interviewed Mercedes Campana.

He let Coffee turn and show live pictures of the search scene and the yellow crime tape going up. When he was done, Booker made an appeal. "Police are asking, if you were driving by and saw this car, if you saw her or if she was with anyone. If you saw anything, you are being urged to call police."

He pulled out his earpiece and let Coffee get more video. Off to one side, Jensen was on the phone. By the edge of the water, there were now three detectives and two uniformed officers. All of them looking at the water. There was about one more good hour of daylight. If they weren't already there, nighttime was the active search time for alligators. For now, Booker did not see the familiar gator tail swirls in the dark water.

Two members of the crime tech team, in white outfits, searched the car. They first took several photographs of the inside before they moved or touched anything. Wearing gloves, they carefully removed the duffle and placed it on a white sheet on the ground. And then more photographs. Booker was always amazed watching TV crime shows depicting actors just picking up evidence without being photographed or not using evidence markers. Probably in lieu of time, they just skipped a few steps.

On the street, another officer was waving traffic to keep on moving. The flashing police car lights lit up the roadway. An all-white Audi pulled alongside the arrangement of news vehicles. A woman got out and started walking toward the crime tape. Four steps across the uneven grass and assorted weeds, the four-inch heels dug so deep into the soil she had a hard time keeping her balance. The woman turned around and went back to her car and pulled off the heels, changing them out for a nice pair of runners. Now, her steps were fast-paced and she didn't stop until she was right behind Booker Johnson.

Her eyes must have burned into the back of his head, and he turned around to face Serenity Hart.

"Mr. Johnson, I see I have to pay a lot more attention to you and your news stories."

"Please, just Booker."

"I saw your story. Anything that corroborates what my client said or did, I'm interested in that. Is that why you came to my office, asking that really vague question?" Her eyes were searching Booker's face.

"I was just looking for an update."

Hart looked over the collection of police and news crews. "I had a feeling you would be here. I just stopped to see you for a South Florida moment." Hart pivoted and turned toward the Audi, then looked back. "I hope she's okay."

A few more steps and Hart drove off. A dive team arrived and a flat boat was moved into place near the water's edge. Booker joined Coffee and followed her gaze across the top of the slow-moving water. Coffee said, "What did she want?"

"She's just concerned."

Booker took seriously one tool all reporters needed. The practice of simple observation. A year earlier Booker had been sent to an apartment fire. He'd been less than two minutes from standing in front of a camera and telling what he saw. He'd looked left to right, taking in everything, turned and was on the air. He told an audience the number of floors for the building, the number of fire trucks, what type of fire equipment, where the smoke was coming from, the number of people on the ground getting assistance, and—from hearing the radio transmissions from a nearby ladder truck—he'd been able to report that the blaze was now a three-alarm fire. He took in all of the information in less than one minute. Observation.

Now Booker was observing all things in front of him. Everything moved so fast there wasn't time to write anything down, just seal it to memory.

They watched the dive team carefully surveying the water. Booker scanned the green-black water, checking the surface for any bubbles. Many bodies of water in South Florida were controlled by the water management district and, if a hurricane approached, the water level would be lowered, allowing for the pending inches of rainwater to come. This, however, was not a controlled waterway. The lake eventually circled back until it reached a number of homes. The exact spot where Booker and Coffee were standing was a run-off location so rainwater from Federal Highway was directed into the lake.

Booker trained his eyes on the other side of the lake, staring into the edge of the bank some eighty feet away. This section was still far from homes and was lined with South Florida foliage of sawgrass and a few cattails.

Booker's visual search of the area also included watching Detective Jensen. Her focus seemed to be one area on the other bank. Booker followed her gaze. There was a strand of rugged looking Saw Palmetto palms and a clean area where someone could stand and fish. When he looked at Jensen again, she was waving her arms and pointing. Booker froze. "Coff, look straight ahead at those two palms. Directly across from you on the other side. Jensen sees something. Zoom in and tell me what's there."

Coffee zoomed all the way in with her camera. Rather than say anything and mess up the ambient audio, Coffee started waving her free hand, like she had just won a bingo game. She stepped away and let Booker study the small eyepiece. He saw exactly what Jensen was transfixed on. The detective started yelling to the man and woman divers in the flat boat, frantically waving and pointing them to the spot on the other side. She yelled, "There's movement! Get somebody over there now!"

24

While the dive team moved across the water to the other side, the fire rescue truck backed them up on ground, lights flashing, toward the bank and parked, ready. Booker called into the station and Stanley made arrangements to break into programming. Forty-seconds later, Booker Johnson was again speaking to a live TV audience.

"Police have not confirmed this is the missing woman, but you can see movement across the water on the other side. A police dive team is there and the person they are attending is getting help. They are now moving her to a backboard where they will carry her to a waiting boat."

Booker described the operation. He recognized the hair, the fully developed arms and shoes of the person he'd interviewed. Without some conformation, though, he could not say it was her. Clearly, she was alive. Her eyes remained closed, her arms were tucked in, and Booker could see her chest rising and falling from heavy breathing. Coffee and other TV crews remained on the rim of police crime tape and relied on the camera's zoom feature to get in close. Before she was placed into the rescue truck, paramedics checked her. She opened her eyes.

Booker had no idea what happened to her. Jensen got into her car and as the rescue truck moved forward, so did the detective. Police officers got traffic to stop, and the rescue unit pulled out into the roadway, along with two unmarked SUV detective cars. All three vehicles moved away from the bank. Above Booker, a Channel 27 helicopter followed the vehicles. Once the vehicles were out of sight, Booker ended his live portion. The station went back to regular programming.

Coffee took a ten-second break. "Who do they have at the hospital?"

"I think Yang is there."

"We headed that way?"

Booker checked his watch. 7:20 p.m. "I think our day is over. Yang and a night reporter will cover it. I'll pick it up in the morning. Thanks for your hard work, Coff."

"No problem. At least we know she's okay."

"Yes."

Twenty minutes later, Yang was waiting, set up with a photographer, when Police P.I.O. Brielle Jensen came out the hospital doors and approached the spread of three camera crews.

"I'm going to make a statement and, for now at least, I will not be taking any questions. This afternoon, a driver was rammed by another car. Both vehicles were traveling northbound on Federal Highway. The victim in the car was forced off the road and came to a stop by the canal. Fearing for her life, she jumped into the water and swam away from a possible attacker. At this time, we are not naming any victim and, for the moment, there will be no more information released at this time." Jensen turned back toward the doors, reporters respecting her wish for no questions.

In the Channel 27 parking lot, Booker was on the phone with Misha. "You've had a busy day." Her voice was like a refreshing respite.

"You watched?"

"Every second. How is she?"

"Don't know yet. I'll try to find out more in the morning."

"You up for a late dinner?"

"That's why I'm calling."

"Let me guess. You've got to make a stop and won't be coming home right away."

"You know me. I always like to let you in on everything. I'm going to see a person who might have some info on a death some five years ago. This is separate."

Misha's voice continued to sound teasing. "And you're going to see a woman, at her apartment, and you're concerned about what I think about that."

"Her name is B.B. She's a flight attendant."

Booker could hear Misha take in a deep breath. "Booker, you have to know by now. I trust you. I think we're good together. And I know wherever you go, you have me in your heart. So, go see this C.C."

"B.B."

"Yes, B.B. Go see her. I'll be right here when you get back. Is that clear, Mr. Johnson?"

"Clear."

Booker sent a text to B.B. to let her know he was coming. A quick look at the Crummick app showed four people had opened up discussions about Booker's story on the rescue of Campana. Best he could tell, one post reached a half-million hits. Booker's story had gone viral on the app. There was a lot of interest in what happened to William Rocker.

B.B. opened the door before Booker had a chance to finish knocking. "C'mon in, Booker."

B.B. was dressed in what looked like free-flowing pants and a short-sleeved blouse, barefoot with toe and fingernails in a matching shade of probably coral. Booker had no idea. He sat down in the big chair opposite the couch.

"Want anything to drink?"

"Just water." Booker was tired. The traveling up to another county and back, an afternoon in the sun, concern about Campana, all of it became his worry pile. And now, in a soft chair, with no dinner, he pushed himself to stay alert. She handed him a cold bottled water. "Thanks. So, you say you found something?" He took a sip.

"I got to thinking about what we found in the suitcase, the large envelopes, and until now I didn't touch them."

"Okay..."

She reached behind her and pulled out the two big envelopes, placing them on the table. "I didn't find much. I wanted to let you look through them." She got up and went into the bedroom, returning with a stunning black dress. "But this is why I called you."

"A dress?"

"Yep, Booker. A dress. The more I talk about Fila, the more I start to remember things. All of a sudden she was very happy about something."

B.B. stretched the dress over the top of the couch. "This dress is special to me. It was Fila's dress." A matching tiny black purse rested on the back of the couch. "Please know, Book, she searched and searched until she found this dress. We were planning to go to my yearly company party. We talked about it for months. This dress fit her to a T. The party was two days away. She said she wanted to tell me something very important. And that's why she was happy. She would not kill herself with drugs just before that party. Never."

"She say why she was so happy?"

"She never got to tell me. And then the overdose."

"Maybe she tried to experiment."

"Not Fila. I would know!" B.B. bellowed. Her cheeks puffed out, fists balled up tight like she wanted to hit something. Booker could see the anger pulsating through her. B.B. picked up the purse and threw the bag against the wall. The bag popped open, and a few papers spilled out onto the floor. Calm returned to her face and B.B. picked up the purse and papers.

Booker was interested in the contents of the purse. "Can I see them?"

There were three very worn pieces of paper from the small-sized legal pad. On one Booker read: REMEMBER HOUSE. He put the paper to the side. "Any idea what house means?"

B.B. shook her head.

The next piece of paper had four dates. All of the dates were days prior to her overdose. Again B.B. had no idea what the dates meant. When Booker examined them, he handed each page to B.B. for more inspection. The third page was just a phone number, underlined four times. Booker took out his cell phone and photographed each page. "Any ideas on this phone number?"

A puzzled look stayed fixed on B.B.'s face. "I have no idea."

Booker gave all the pages back to B.B., and then he went back to the table and chugged on the water. He put down the bottle and reached for the envelopes. He pulled out papers and found Fila Mackee's copy of the apartment rental agreement, more paperwork about moving to Florida, and additional photographs with B.B. somewhere on a boat.

"Nothing about where she was from?"

"She never talked about it. Always changed the subject when I brought it up. All I know is she wanted to be here. Florida."

Booker placed the materials to the side, then finally stuffed the pages back into the two envelopes. "You said she came here to find something."

B.B. pulled out a glass of white wine. "There were times I heard her talking to someone on the phone but she wouldn't say who."

Booker picked up the yellow piece of paper with the phone number. "Have you called this number?"

"Me? No." She took a long hard chug of the wine. "Never saw it before tonight. I need another glass. You want any wine?"

"No. Water is fine."

She got up, went to the fridge and reached for a bottle. "There was one other thing I thought was strange. When the police finally let me in after she..." B.B. stopped. Her voice had cracked, and she stood there as if she was being held by the pain of losing someone. "When she died. When I got back in here, everything was off."

"Off?"

"Yeah. It was strange. Everything was in its place, just not quite in its place like somebody picked up a cup and put it back but an inch off from where it used to be."

"Just one place?"

"Here in the living room, it just looked like everything had been moved. Especially in her bedroom. Mattress moved around and put back. The end table was an inch off. I could tell cause there was always a mark on the floor where it's supposed to be. It was off the mark."

"You mean like someone searched the place?"

"Exactly. A careful search of everything here and then put back but just a tiny bit off. Weird."

"You tell police about this?"

"Heck no! They'd think I'd lost it. No, you're the first person I've told."

Booker kept staring at the phone number, turning the scrap of paper over a few times. There was nothing on the back. He grabbed his phone and punched the phone number into a Google search. The phone actually worked this time in the apartment. When he found something, he did a bit more searching. Three minutes later, he was still reading information. He found two more bits of information and continued to read.

"Well, I actually got my phone to work."

"Okay, Mr. Booker, you've got me in suspense. What's up with the number?"

"Well, first, if someone was in here looking for something, the last place they would look is in that tiny black purse. All of those pages mean something." He was done with scrolling up and down on the phone, reading information. He looked into B.B.'s anxious eyes. "Well, everyone said Fila came here to find something. I don't think it was a thing. I think the real reason Fila came to Florida was to find a person."

"A person? Who?"

"This number you found. Underlined. It's to a state agency helping people find a biological parent. I think Fila was adopted."

25

The driver of the blue car turned off the lights and eased into the comfort of the after-midnight calm of the Florida Everglades. He got out and took in the eerie peace of the Glades. Just yards away out on the water, the red steady eyes of alligators watched as if someone even dared enter their domain. The location was U.S. 27 where there were no homes, no street-lights and possible death for anyone venturing too far in these exotic reaches. The man couldn't see them, yet the crawling monsters, the Burmese python would be just over in the sawgrass. He got out and stood, watching and listening for any approaching cars or trucks on the highway. There was no hurry, no time clock on what he had to do. There was move-ment in the water. The red eyes were silently encroaching on their visitor, moving and creating S curves behind their tails in the water. The trunk was opened and the man pulled out three large cans, placing them on the ground near the car. The figure opened the glovebox, pulled out a knife and began ripping up the seats. Nothing could be left for discovery later. The car windows were left in the up position.

One by one, the man emptied the contents of the cans over and inside the car, trying not to splash any of the gasoline on himself. He pored over the top of the car, letting the liquid drip down all sides. When all the cans were empty, he placed them far from the car, back toward the entrance to the boat ramp. In the morning, fishermen would be here, launching boats. For now, this was the place where evidence would be destroyed. He walked around the car, making sure gasoline covered the hood and doors. When there was full satisfaction, he took out a gas-soaked rag and held it near the lighter.

For a second, everything in the Glades stopped. The alligators held in place and the chirping of the bugs ceased. The rag was in flames and the man approached the open door and tossed it in the car. A second lit rag was placed on top of the car. He stood back and waited.

In twenty-seconds, yellow flames moved across the seat covers and licked up the armrest and windows. The top of the car was a roaring dome of heat. The car of fire looked like a pyre in the middle of a natural habitat. The man took six steps backward, all the time watching the end results of his work. There was a crackling noise coming from inside the car and tall red arms of fire reached up into the blackness of the night. He grabbed the cans and walked with ease to the road, waiting for another car to pick him up before there was an explosion.

26

On Sunday morning, Lacie Grandhouse was just one of two reporters working the weekend shift. She sat at her desk, going over newspaper articles and incoming news releases and was about to head to court to check on overnight arrests. Grandhouse had watched the style of Booker, and she remembered when he always came to work ninety minutes early to peruse for news stories.

"Hey, Grandhouse." The quiet of the newsroom was shaken by the shouting voice of Randall Culmer, weekend assignment editor. "Come up here and tell me what you think. I'm listening to something on the police scanner."

Grandhouse grabbed a notepad and went up to the assignment desk. Thanks to the construction of the Channel 27 newsroom, the editors worked on a riser, built two feet higher than the desks for reporters and producers. The police scanners consisted of two machines on the desk and also a computer website, dedicated to scanner traffic. Grandhouse stepped up on the desk and listened.

"Unit 39 can handle. 41 can do a washdown. PD contacted. Car fire now out. Waiting for PD. Possible connection to hit and run."

Grandhouse was scribbling notes. "Where is this?"

"U.S. 27, north of Alligator Alley on the west side by the boat ramp. What do you think?"

"We go get the video, then figure out if it's connected to running Mercedes Campana off the road." She was down off the riser and running for the side door to inform her photographer Rolando.

Grandhouse ran to the parking lot and found Rolando Acosta closing up his trunk.

"I'm ready, Lacie. Where are we going?" he asked.

They drove westbound, with little traffic to slow them down on a Sunday morning. Acosta was the oldest on the staff of photographers. He had the most experience and, in his nineteen years in broadcast news, he had amassed seven Emmy Awards.

Acosta reached for his sunglasses. "Glad I ate something. We got a car fire? They're really interested in that?"

"If it's what I think it is, this could be a break in the story Booker's been covering."

"Okay. We got about fifteen minutes there, max."

When they reached the scene there were no other news units. Two fire trucks were there, one had firefighters rolling up hoses. Acosta parked the car, ran around to the back and pulled out his camera. Grandhouse headed for the fire chief. Acosta was videotaping.

Grandhouse studied the name on the bunker gear. "Chief Buckner, what do you have here?"

"Car fire reported by two fishermen who arrived this morning. The car mostly out but still smoldering when they got here. We arrived, made sure the car was out and no flames spread to the grass."

"Thank you. Police coming?"

"Yes, and when they get here, everything will have to come from their P.I.O."

"Understood. The car was unoccupied?"

"Yes. There was no one inside. From what we can tell, an accelerant was used. The car was probably set on fire early this morning."

"You find any gas cans? Anything to help in your investigation?"

"As you can see, this whole area is asphalt. No tire tracks to speak of. And no, we didn't find any cans. We'll keep looking but nothing so far."

"Thank you."

Grandhouse moved behind her photographer. Acosta went through the standard set of movements. He videotaped a wide establisher shot, then went in on various angles. There were long push-in zooms of the inside, all charred. Grandhouse looked with surprise toward the passenger-side front fender. There was a huge section of the fender untouched by the flames.

"Rolando, you see this?"

"Yep. On it. I'll get some more video."

The fender was damaged. The long thin dents looked like the paint of another car was embedded into the smashed folds of the fender. Acosta took several minutes getting every angle he could. When he was mostly finished, Grandhouse looked in the direction of the two fishermen who were still there, standing next to their bass boat.

Acosta needed no explanation. His camera was up and recording when Grandhouse extended her microphone toward the men. "I'm Lacie Grandhouse from Channel 27. If it's okay, can I ask you what you saw when you arrived this morning?"

Both of them started talking at the same time. The one on the left, the taller one wearing a Marlins baseball cap, continued. "We saw the car soon as we pulled in. Thing still had some flames coming from the back seat. We called the fire department."

"You see anyone here? Anyone connected to the car?"

The shorter one, wearing long-sleeved protective gear from the sun, pulled on his weather-worn Florida Panthers hat. "We didn't see anyone, but we checked the car to make sure there was no one in there. But no one would survive that."

"What do you two make of this?"

Marlins hat pointed to the burned-out wreck. "I don't understand people. I know we're way out here in the Everglades, but this is not a dumping ground. It's not perfect but the Glades is a great place. We don't need no dumpers here. That's why we're staying. Waiting to speak with police."

"Thanks for your time."

A police unit rolled up next to the fire trucks, along with a tow truck. Acosta got video of the officer talking with the two fishermen and the inspection of the burned car. When he got the okay, the tow truck driver hooked up the blackened car and moved it onto the bed of the car mover. The fire trucks left and moved on down U.S. 27. Grandhouse and Acosta waited until they got video of the car being hauled away. Police gone, the calm of the Glades started to return.

Later that afternoon, police put out a news release stating they had recovered a car suspected in the hit-and-run of the car driven by Mercedes Campana. Grandhouse had her story for the day, and she prepared to send a message to Booker.

27

On Sunday morning Booker woke up early, dressed in sweatpants and his best basketball shoes, and was ready to head for the gym. He was also on standby in case Campana was being released from the hospital or there was any new development in the Rocker murder. More than anything, Booker wanted to be outside the hospital where Campana was recovering. He kissed a sleeping Misha and headed out the door.

The gym was a five-minute drive. The workout club had seventeen treadmills, every muscle stretching piece of equipment imaginable, two swimming pools, pickleball, and even a bowling alley. What interested Book most was the basketball court. He used the b-ball court to work out his thoughts. He did a short bit of stretching, signed out a basketball, and started with short jumpers. Ten minutes later, he was hitting fifteen-footers. All net. For Booker, this was therapy. He could work out all the demons of the week, and let the down moments come out through the sweat. When he was in college and got a cold, he'd used a remedy he would not try today. When sick, he would down a half-glass of whiskey and play two hours of basketball. The sickness came through the pores and went away. That's what he'd told himself at the time. Today, he just wanted to work up a good sweat.

Thirty minutes into his workout, he turned down two offers to join a three-on-three basketball game. A game could turn into two or three more. Booker just wanted to shoot some hoops and go home. He kept his cell phone slanted up and tucked into his gym bag, so if the phone rang, he would see an incoming call.

The phone was silent, and Booker kept shooting. The bag contained clothes, so if he was needed, he could go immediately, stinky body and all.

He tried to let the stories of the week float to the bottom of his thoughts. Now, there was concentration on a hard dribble, a smooth layup or a rebound. He moved from free-throw line to corner shots and beyond the arc. Everything was about the shot.

Booker had a strict rule about shooting baskets. Before he left the gym for good, he had to make three baskets in a row, all perfect shots, no rim, just the sound of strings poppin' and nothing else. He made three shots, then missed the third, several times. Three in a row finally came and Booker turned in the ball.

Freshly showered and wearing a cleaners-pressed fishing shirt over khaki shorts, Booker picked a table nearest the water. He gave Misha the best seat, looking out at the Atlantic Ocean, and he sat across from her. Boater's Landing was built close enough to the water so sand from the beach covered the concrete floor of the restaurant. Booker could never understand the name of the place since there was no place to anchor a boat. The area had no boat slips, just one of the best viewing spots in the county. Misha ordered an iced tea while they both checked the menu. She took a sip. "Coffee would love this tea."

"She likes hot tea, thank you very much."

"Oh, sorry. Hot tea it is."

Since they'd had a very small breakfast, Booker was more than ready for lunch. He settled on a Mahi-Mahi sandwich and fries. Misha kept running her finger up and down the menu. "I like everything," she grinned. "I'd like the shrimp, but the salmon is calling my name."

Booker liked bringing her to Boater's Landing. The sun caught her face just so, lighting up her cheeks, clouds reflecting in her eyes. Her smile was warmer than the growing heat of the day. Booker liked to keep staring at her until she made him stop.

He looked down at his cell phone and let the news stories creep back into his daytime. No messages from the assignment desk on Campana.

"I can tell when you're deep into it." Misha put the menu down.

"Sorry. A lot going on this week."

"I know. You're the star of the week on TV and the Internet."

"Didn't mean to drift off." He turned his phone face-down. "I promised you no news talk at the table. I'll just enjoy the ocean view."

She grabbed his hand and held his fingers in hers. "There was a time when I thought all these news stories were coming between us. Now, I'm in. I'm interested in everything you're working on."

Booker started to speak, to tell her he had to make concessions as well. He never got the chance to say anything. Misha seemed determined to make her point.

"Book, I know now, your stories are not just important to you but to this community. You're documenting history. That's one of the reasons I came back to you, moved in with you." She leaned in and pressed her lips to his with the intensity of the first time they shared a kiss.

When they looked up the waitress was standing there, looking a bit embarrassed. "You two take all the time you want."

"I think we're ready. Misha?"

"I'll have the grilled salmon with steamed vegetables and a bowl of chicken tortilla soup."

"And for you, sir?"

"Mahi-Mahi sandwich, fries, and can I get your smoked fish dip to start?"

"For sure." She headed back with the menus.

Booker pushed his phone away and gazed out. Somewhere off to the right, he thought he spotted frigate birds, the friend of fishermen. From his many times out on the water fishing, Booker knew frigate birds spotted fish and would hover over them. Boat captains moved in and fished just beneath the birds, catching fish in great numbers. The water was a dark blue in the deeper water, turning turquoise closest to the shore. Off somewhere, they heard the shouts of people on the beach, sunbathing.

Booker turned to her. "We need to settle on a vacation spot."

"Last time we talked, we had it down to three places."

"I like the cruise idea. Alaska is always beautiful. And there was Napa Valley."

She leaned back in the chair. "I don't mind staying local. We can jump on down to Key West."

"No one jumps down to the Keys. Travel time, everything down there is slower."

"But I love it."

The soup and the smoked fish with crackers arrived as Booker's phone started to ring. The incoming call was from Channel 27. No matter the subject, he was not going to let the call interfere with the lunch.

"Booker, sorry to bother you." The voice was Culmer, the Sunday assignment editor.

"No problem. What's up?"

"I just wanted to give you a couple of updates. We've had a crew at the hospital, waiting and checking on Campana."

"Okay. And?"

"Well, an hour ago, when I checked, they made her a no-information patient."

"Understood." Booker knew no-information meant what the term implied. No further information or updates would be given to Channel 27 or anyone. "Anything else?"

"Yes. And there was one other thing. The hospital did say she is no longer a patient."

"So, she's gone."

"Yes. Thanks Caesar." Booker's mind raced for only a moment or so. If she was gone, Campana was now probably in the safety of police. No more interviews and no contact whatsoever.

"And, Book, one last thing Lacie wants to tell you." Booker waited.

"Book," Lacie said. "I didn't mean to mess with your Sunday, but I thought you would want to hear this before the newscast tonight or you see it on our web. Police think they found the car that ran Mercedes Campana off the road."

"Really? Where?"

"Out in the Glades by a boat ramp. Burned to a crisp. However, someone screwed up. One small section of the car did not burn. The part where, I think, police will be able to get some color scrapings and match them with Campana's car."

"Thanks. Great work. I'll watch tonight."

"Later, Book."

Booker pressed his phone down on the table, leaned over and kissed Misha. "No more news talk. Let's eat."

28

Demetrious Moreland watched two more people walk into the Core Zone Cyber Café and sit in front of two free computers. Some rented by the month and had full access twenty-four-seven. Anyone looking for work was given a freebie. Any veteran was also given free access. He had watch over the tables of computers and the small gaming room. On the other side, there was a café with food choices and an entire vending wall of juices behind compact boxes with clear fronts. Demetrious was responsible for the computer side, and two co-workers operated the food area.

Core Zone was part of a block-long strip mall, sandwiched between a greeting card store and an empty location. Sunday afternoon business was good, and Demetrious had drawn up plans to knock down a wall and extend into the next-door vacant space. He just needed more time to finish the mock-up before presenting it to the corporate office.

Outside, in the parking lot, a car was positioned so the driver could look into the Core Zone and watch Demetrious. From where the car was located, far away from the front door, no one would suspect anyone was outside casing the place. The figure in the car pulled up a pair of powerful binoculars, focusing on areas deep inside the café. In the passenger seat, a writing pad detailed information on comings and goings, time at the motel, and the trips to the apartment of Booker Johnson. The figure had new information, rested the binocs on the console and pulled up the pad to write. There were notations on start times and when Demetrious left for the day. The page was full of notes and even had a big circle around the words BEST TIME TO HIT.

Inside, Demetrious went about his work, stepping in to help someone on a computer, informing another of how the café worked, and even spending a short time taking food orders so someone behind the counter could take a bathroom break. He did not see the car that had been outside for hours now, or when the vehicle slow-rolled away into the sprawling outline of five dozen parking spaces.

Monday morning, Booker Johnson answered a message from Claire Stanley to meet her before the meeting. She only had five minutes since she was responsible for putting together the list of story ideas. A collection of producers and reporters would discuss the options and anyone around the table could pitch a story. Stanley spent few minutes in her office, probably best since she spent so much time on the assignment desk. Her office was near the center of the arrangement of desks.

"So, Booker. Where do we stand on the Rocker story?"

"We have a few sound clips from Mercedes Campana we have not used yet. We could try to get an update on where she is or at least how she is doing and do an update. Rocker is still in shutdown mode and not saying anything. If I could just get an update from police on people who were supposed to come forward, that would be a way to advance the story."

Stanley barely blinked during the exchange, as if she wanted to take in everything he said and not miss anything. Booker said, "At this point, I don't think police will let us get anywhere close to Campana. P.D. is going to work this hard and that means no contact with media."

Claire reached for the first stick of gum for the day.

Sitting on her desk was a reddish potato. Booker had to take notice. "So, who got the hot potato?"

"Dolan." She snapped up the potato replica and squeezed the thing in her right hand. Dolan was the executive producer. Martin Dolan. He had a habit of being demanding, in need of information in mere seconds, and rarely, if ever, giving a compliment. Whenever anyone became a distraction to gathering the news, Stanley threw the so-called hot potato right at them. The foam toy was a favorite of Stanley's.

"Hope you never throw that thing at me."

"Booker, just don't give me any gray hair."

"I'll make it a point." While staring at the potato, he hesitated to make his next point. "Before you take off for the meeting, there is one thing I have to share."

"Oh..." The potato got the squeeze.

"There is another story I've been working, separate from the Rocker story."

"Something for today?"

"No. It needs some work."

Stanley's jaw started working on the gum, moving like a tiny machine. "A hunch?"

"I'll continue working the main story, but in my spare time I've been checking on something else. A girl who died five years ago. A suspected drug overdose."

"Okay, I remember Grandhouse telling me something about this. There's no story there, right?"

"Well, maybe there is something. I'm still checking. Again, this is on my spare time, I promise. Some things just aren't right."

"Your hunches have almost always turned out to be good stories, but Booker, this is a cold case. Did police reopen the investigation?"

"No."

"Any family come forward?"

"No family."

"Okay. You got me. I don't see a story right now. But if you think something is there, go ahead. Just don't forget the other story."

"I won't. Trust me."

Booker's few moments with her were over. She tossed the potato on the table and put her head down to her computer, followed by a flurry of fast typing. She had fewer than eight minutes to get ready for the meeting.

Booker eased out of her office and sat down at his desk and started making phone calls.

When he didn't get anywhere with the phone checks on his list, Booker again looked up the adoption information he had on Fila Mackee. One call and he found out what he'd imagined: not much information from the agency. However, they did direct him to a website with a registry where adoptees could look for biological parents. There was a phone number.

"Hello, this is Booker Johnson with Channel 27."

"You have to contact our public relations firm. They're in Atlanta."

"I just want some general information. I'm trying to find out if a certain person posted her profile on your site."

"We don't give out information like that. Again, I can give you our contact in Atlanta."

"Okay. Thank you."

Booker wrote down the information and made another call. Again, there was resistance to giving him any information. He did, however, get an idea from them. He could post his own message to see if anyone remembered Fila. Booker spent the next twenty minutes writing a detailed post about his efforts to find out about Fila Mackee, and who she might be trying to find. He might make more calls later.

His cell phone received a text, a message from Mercedes Campana. Her message said, *I have just a few minutes to speak with you. I can call in ten minutes.*

Booker answered yes immediately. He turned and called out to Claire Stanley, letting her know he would be recording an incoming call. He got Coffee involved and she set up a camera inside a video edit booth. The booth would offer a much quieter place than the bustle of the newsroom. Booker's phone was put on speaker, with Coffee's microphone resting next to it. Four minutes later, there was a call. Coffee zoomed in with her camera on Booker and the phone on the small desk.

"It's Booker. Mercedes?"

"I'm here."

"Let me say first, is it okay with you if we record this conversation?"

"Yes."

"Mercedes, are you okay?"

"I'm fine, now. I'm sore in a few places and I'm going to get therapy soon. For now, I'm resting and healing."

"We're glad to hear you're okay. After we did the interview and we were following you, can you tell us what happened? We got separated."

"I know. Well, I'm in a safe place and some of this I can't talk about yet. And other parts are a blur. I just know there was something on my right and I had to get away. Then, I was out of my car, running. I kept running, then I was in the water, swimming. I don't know. I got to the other side, and everything went blank."

"You say something was on your right. Was it a car?"

"I really can't say much more. I'm pretty tired and they're still checking me out. Just know I'm somewhere safe and I have to go."

"Please get better."

Conversation was over. Coffee indicated she needed more video of him sitting by his phone. When they were finished, Booker informed Stanley he had a story for the newscasts. He had a recorded phone call, but he wanted to add to the story.

29

Booker and Coffee were on Federal Highway, retracing the driving path taken by Mercedes Campana. Booker drove while Coffee leaned out the window videotaping everything on the route. They ended up in the same location where Campana went into the water. Coffee got out and used her camera to try and show the path Campana would have taken to the water. Once they had most of the elements needed for the story, they backtracked once more, this time looking for any possible home or business surveillance video.

Coffee pulled a giant blue scarf from the back seat and wiped down her face. September in South Florida was almost as hot as August. "Two crews already checked for surveillance and didn't find any." She tossed the scarf backward to the rear seat.

"I know. Just rechecking."

The problem with surveillance video in this area was the road was a long way from a camera. Federal Highway was a busy area and wide. The cameras with the best angles there belonged to county traffic and Booker had no access to them. Just police.

Booker pointed down the road. "Let's eat."

He had just about everything needed for the story. He had the audio-taped phone interview, video of the scene and the roadway with water.

While Coffee was inside eating, Booker took out a large legal pad and started making phone calls on the side story, the one about Fila Mackee.

Booker got an email from a person familiar with the adoption process and finding a biological parent. The email in question told him to contact a Conrad Vermika. There was a phone number. After three rings, a voice.

"Hello."

"Hello. This is Booker Johnson with Channel 27. If you have just a few minutes, can I talk to you about adoptees finding a loved one."

"Who is this again?"

"I'm Booker Johnson, a reporter for Channel 27 news. I'm tracking down some information, if you can help me, regarding a Fila Mackee. I understand she was looking for someone?"

"Oh, Fila. Yes. We talked a bit."

"How did it go for her?"

"We spoke a bit. I met up with her through True-Find."

"What's True-Find?" Booker was writing notes as fast as he could.

"It's call Florida True-Find. It's both a message board and a site for posting information."

"What kind of information?"

"Say you were adopted, now you're over eighteen and you want to find your bio. You can post your information. At least the very little info that you have. And you can read what others have posted."

"Why would Fila start her search here in Florida?"

"Well, I don't know where, but she got something that told her to look south. In Florida."

"So, you heard what happened to her?"

"The overdose? Yes. It really took me by surprise. I really liked her. She was fun."

"Hang out much?"

"Some. Went to the beach. One time we did that airboat ride in the Everglades. That was great."

"One thing I'm interested in Conrad is whether—"

"She found a bio? Well, I know she looked hard. Sometimes it's a two-way street. The biological parent can keep an agency up-to-date when they move, change phone numbers, that kind of thing. If they don't, it makes it harder."

"And in Fila's case?"

"I know she was getting close, but I'm not the person who would know what happened."

"Do you know who would be that person?"

"I think so. Hang on a minute. It's been a long time."

There was a pause. Booker heard a shuffling of papers. Then another long pause. Conrad came back to the phone. "I think I got it. His name is Percy Mayweather. Lives down there. She was close to him. Give him a ring."

"Thanks." Booker took down the information and said his goodbyes. Coffee returned from lunch. "Book, you on a hunger strike? You need to eat something."

Booker went inside and ordered something to go. They returned to the body of water, edited the story, and prepared to be the third story in the five p.m. newscast. He kept checking and found no updates from police or anywhere else. Even the Crummick app was quiet.

When it was Booker's turn to report, he delivered smooth lines, showed a decent videotaped story to a South Florida TV audience, wrapped up his comments, then watched Coffee break down the tripod. She kept a good stare on him. "This Fila thing has really got to you. I can tell."

"I'm close to something but I'm not there yet."

When they pulled into the TV station parking lot, Booker's phone rang. "Booker."

"This is Percy. You called about Fila?"

"Yes. You have some time?"

"Sure. I live just outside Apton County. I can be there in forty minutes."

Booker set up a meeting at a park. Neutral grounds. He chose Palmetto Palm Park, two miles from the Atlantic Ocean. Here, the closing hours were late. Booker parked his car and sat at a wooden bench near an empty pavilion. Mayweather was more than forty minutes late and Booker knew one accident somewhere would slow down the arrival time for anyone. Close to one hour late, a car pulled into the lot. The driver stared hard in Booker's direction, then got out.

Mayweather was much shorter than Booker imagined from the phone conversation. He had a receding hairline, green polo shirt and brown shorts. The conversation started before he reached Booker and never gave an indication a handshake was needed.

"So, it's Booker Johnson, is it?" He stood and did not sit.

"Booker is fine."

"I don't know what you're doing or what you're up to, but we are very apprehensive about people asking about Fila Mackee."

"I understand you don't know anything about me. I report for Channel 27 news. I know what was in the report about her death, but I don't think that's the full truth and I'm looking into what happened."

"Where were you five years ago?"

"I admit, I was doing other things then. Let's be honest, most overdoes cases don't get any attention. I want to change that in Fila's case. I talked with her roommate."

"B.B. is a good person but she doesn't know all the details."

"So, what are the details? Percy, what can you tell me?"

The next ten seconds seemed like a year. Percy Mayweather had the look of someone who was not going to say another word, let alone factors shedding light on Fila's death. Mayweather turned and started for his car. Booker stood up. "Where are you going? Don't you want to find out what went down?"

"I just don't trust you, Mr. Johnson. Not you, the police, anyone. There is a circle around Fila where we are protecting her memory. You just don't understand."

"Help me understand." Booker moved within three feet of Mayweather. "I told you I'm working on finding out facts. You should be receptive to what I'm doing."

Mayweather looked like he was considering Booker's words. "I'm part of a support group for people who were adopted. Please know, adoption is the best thing in the world. But some of us just need to talk things out. For some, it's in the separation from your bio. Fila was too young to feel any of that, but she had feelings."

"Again, what can you tell me about why she moved to South Florida?"

"I'll do this. Meet the group tomorrow morning. Right here in the park.

Ten a.m. No camera, just you. You convince the group and maybe we'll tell you some things."

"I'll be here."

With that, Mayweather got into his car and did not look back. Booker stood for a moment and took in the natural silence of the park. He heard the birds sifting through the oak trees before heading to his apartment.

30

"So, you want to continue gathering facts on something the police haven't even deemed a cold case?" Claire Stanley was chewing her morning gum so hard, Booker thought she would break her jaw.

"You've trusted my hunches before. And, for the most part, they have worked out."

"This is a lot of trust though, Booker. You are spending so much time on this overdose and you're leaving the Rocker story uncovered."

"Just let me meet with this group. Give my pitch, see what they have to say, if anything. And I'll be back in the fold, working on the Rocker situation."

"And you're working without a camera?"

"No camera."

"Okay. I trust you on this." The gum chewing stopped. She picked up a stack of notes and headed off into the morning meeting. Booker waved bye to Coffee and he left the newsroom.

Heavy a.m. traffic was starting to wane, and he made it to the park in under thirty minutes. They were there waiting for him when Booker parked. He was all smiles, they looked grim.

"Thank you for coming. I'm Booker Johnson."

There were just three of them. Mayweather and two others. "Mr. Johnson, this is not the whole group. The others did not want to meet just yet. I'm gonna set a few rules. You know my name, but they won't be giving you name information. We did some research on you and from what we can see, you were due some respect. We'll let you know if you're moving out-of-bounds."

Sitting next to Percy was a tallish looking man Booker estimated to be in his late thirties, heavy-set with big hands. Next to him was a Black woman, late twenties, with very long perfectly made braids lining her head, stretching down her back. She kept putting them back in place only to have the strands fall over her cheeks, blocking her left eye. When Booker could see her eyes themselves, they were gray in color.

Booker stood before them. "Just let me be blunt. I didn't know Fila at all. I only know her through her friends. But from what I know about her, she did not overdose on purpose. Something happened that night. She had a history of not using drugs. But she also had a real burning desire to know more about herself. That's why I believe she moved here. But I need some information from you all to unlock some doors. I understand you don't know me. If someone wanted to do her some harm, I need to find out what or who she bothered to push someone to do this."

Every time the woman moved and flashed silver nails, she looked like the front cover of a magazine. Her gray eyes bored into Booker. "We all have different stories. I loved my adoptive parents. But I wanted to know the whole truth about where I came from. So did Fila. We bonded with her. She found us and we talked things out. We agree with you, but I'm not sure how you can do anything. It's been too long."

The other man spoke up. "I have no idea how or where I would have ended up if it weren't for the people who adopted me. They gave me a good life. When Fila joined the group, she had this obsession to find her bio parents. There were some factors suggesting she might find out more here in South Florida.

Booker moved a few feet, so he stayed in the shade. "Did you ever hear her talk about using drugs?"

All three responded with Mayweather being the loudest. "No. Never."

"Did anyone threaten her at the time?"

Mayweather and the woman in dreadlocks looked at each other and shook their heads. The second man said, "I got the feeling she was scared of someone."

"Who?" Booker pushed for answers.

"I'm not sure," he continued. "You see we didn't ask or talk about our jobs, work situations, things like that. We just shared stories about being adopted. One person had biological parental separation problems, but we all benefited from being adopted."

The woman in braids took both of her hands and smoothed over her hair, then addressed Booker. "You're asking things about us and Fila, what about you?"

"Okay. I like to be called Booker, or Book. Originally, I'm from California. My mother still lives there. I found out I have a half-brother named Demetrious. I don't mind telling you his father is a drug dealer who has an outstanding warrant for his arrest. We share our mother's eyes and she didn't know his dirty past until much later. Then she left him. My brother lives here and we're pretty tight."

Gray eyes smiled. "Well, I don't know much about my birth, but my adoptive parents got me when I was a baby. I owe them the world. They put me through college and today I'm a microbiologist research assistant with a doctorate from the University of Miami and a master's in information technology."

"Wow. Impressive. I just have my bachelor's in TV." He looked at the big man who said, "I have a master's in marketing. The people who raised me were always there for me."

Booker checked his watch. Any moment Stanley would be calling for him to return. "So, you don't know where Fila was working? Or what she was doing to find a bio?"

Mayweather spoke. "She talked about her roommate. Nothing about a job. But now that you mention it, she did say she was afraid of someone."

"Did any of this change? Did she experience a happy moment?"

The lips of all three closed shut. The woman knotted her arms. Mayweather looked down at the ground. Booker broke the quiet. "Let me guess. She made you all promise not to say anything. I know she was extremely happy about something. She bought a black dress and was excited. Now, what do you know?"

Mayweather looked at the others before he faced Booker. "They don't know about why she was happy, but I do."

"And?"

"She was happy because she said she found her birth mother."

"Birth mother? She say who?"

Mayweather looked like he didn't know how to proceed. "The only one who knew was me. After she told me, I moved away for three years when I got a job in New York. I left and I heard about her death when someone called me. Fila gave me the name and I put it away until this very moment. And now, I'm just shaking for what I'm about to tell you."

"This would really help me. Who was it?"

Mayweather got up and walked over to Booker. He leaned in and spoke softly. When Booker heard the name of the birth mother, he was shaken as much as Mayweather.

31

Before Booker had a chance to speak with Stanley, another person on the assignment desk called him. "Booker, we need to send you somewhere right away."

"I need to speak with Claire. Is she there? It's important."

"She's out but I need you to meet Coffee. We're not sure if it's a murder or suicide."

"Okay. Give me the address."

The location was in the exact middle of the county, a neighborhood landlocked, far from the ocean, with no canals or bodies of water nearby. The apartment complex was open, no fencing around the parking lot. Anyone could walk or drive in and out of the place with little notice. Booker drove up, parked, and looked for Coffee. She was busy getting video of the scene. Police tape blocked the entrance to the first-floor apartments. Coffee's face was clouded in frustration.

"This ain't pretty, Book. The other stations were here two hours ago. We got a lot of catch-up to do."

"You see any P.I.O?"

"Not yet. I'm pissed we missed this."

Booker's phone rang. He got it on the third ring. "Booker, I'm sorry."

"Claire, what do we know?"

"Well, we missed hearing this on the police scanners, we didn't get a phone call tip and there was no news blurb from police letting us know about it. We just missed this and the other stations are kicking our ass."

"They have much?"

"Well, one just posted a couple of sound clips. We are way behind on this story. See what you can scramble for the noon."

"I'll call you in one hour." Booker scanned left to right. While he studied the scene before him, the new secret from the adoption group was burning a hole in him. A burn he couldn't pass on until he could confirm what he was told. He had to hold onto it for now. He decided not to tell Stanley.

"Coff. We're gonna split up. You move around, get all the video you can. I'm headed for another angle and an interview. I'll zap your phone if I get something."

"No problem." She was off, camera on her shoulder, recording all movement before her. Booker stepped back and walked away, heading for the apartment building next to the original scene. He walked up the stairs, noticing there were no surveillance cameras anywhere. He got to the third floor of the adjacent building and looked down. From there, he saw Coffee joining the other photographers getting video of detectives moving in and out of the building, crime techs loading a bag of evidence into a van. Booker got a text, the Channel 27 helicopter agreed to stay out of the area for a while so police could continue to investigate and do a grid walk of the parking lot. Helicopter blades stirring things up might not be good, even if the chopper was five-hundred-feet in the air.

A woman moved in next to Booker. She was in a full-length robe, hair layered in uncombed gray, sipping on a Yeti cup of coffee. "We get a lot of police out here. Car break-ins are very big around here."

"Morning. I'm Booker..."

"I know who you are. Seen ya on TV."

"You know anything about that apartment? They tell me it's one-twenty-seven."

"I try to keep my nose out of everything. Safer that way. But I hear things."

"Oh? Like?"

"Well, if you don't put me on that camera of yours, I heard something right around one-thirty a.m. Sounded like two pops. I came outside, didn't see anything and I went back in."

"You say one-thirty a.m. You're sure about that?"

"Very sure. I have more clocks and watches than anybody." She drew a long pull on the coffee and wiped her mouth with the sleeve of the robe. "Something happened down there. Not surprised. Too much stuff goes on here."

"Thank you."

"I'm going back inside. See you on TV." She smiled on the way to the door.

Booker looked down. A police officer walked around the left side of the building, clearly out of view of the news crews. He kept going and stopped at a bush. For the next two minutes he poked around the bush without disturbing anything in the dirt. He called out to someone. Booker used his phone and called Coffee. "Without letting others know, casually look up to your left, up on the third floor."

"Yeah, I see you."

"Quietly, discreetly, leave and join me up here."

"I'm on my way." Coffee put away her phone, pointed the camera to the ground, and in a slow pace walked back to her SUV, made a turn around the back of the vehicle and walked to the next-door apartment building, headed up to Booker. Once there, without saying a word, she looked over his shoulder and began putting up her sticks, finally snapping the camera into the holder. She aimed her lens toward the officer. He was joined by a detective and a crime tech. The tech put down a crime scene marker and started taking photographs. Lots of photographs of the hedge. Next came the equipment used to measure distance, placed on the ground. More photographs. With the supervision of the detective, the tech reached a gloved hand behind the hedge and pulled out a gun. The weapon was photographed more than a dozen times by another tech and placed into a brown evidence bag to be marked later. Coffee had video of everything. Booker noticed the other crews were not aware of the weapon pickup. The tech walked around to the front and made the short trip to the crime scene van. The officer was now left there to guard the find location.

Coffee finally looked up from her camera. "Nice view up here."

"We've got about ninety-minutes until news time. I want to make a short trip across the street."

Booker and Coffee made their way downstairs, again moving about like they were just as unaware as the other crews. They walked across the parking lot and stood in front of the third apartment building in the complex. This unit was six stories tall like the others. There was one difference.

Booker tilted his head toward the building. "You see the apartment on the second floor?"

Coffee looked up. "A door cam. Think they got anything?"

"It's the only one around I can spot."

Coffee followed Booker until they reached the second-floor apartment. He knocked. They waited a full minute before there was an answer.

A young man answered the door. He wore a faded near-brown sweat-shirt with the sleeves cut high to reveal muscled arms, his skin tone close to the color of his shirt. "Before you ask, I didn't see anything."

Booker introduced himself. "I was just asking if your camera has a view of the apartment across the street?"

"You mean where all that stuff is going on? I might. I have it cause someone broke into my car twice two months ago. I bought the best camera I could find." He pointed to the camera mounted outside his door. "This baby will record your nose hairs seventy feet away."

"Okay, can I ask you for your feed for around one-thirty a.m. Some-where in that range."

"Stay outside. I'll check." Booker guessed he was a former football player, probably six-five and up to two-hundred-sixty pounds. Booker felt sorry for any would-be car thief caught by the man in front of him.

While he checked the video, Coffee kept an eye on the crime scene. If the P.I.O. stepped in front of the cameras, they were screwed. Two minutes later, he came back. "The lights are poor. Can't see much really. But I think right around that time you can see a flash coming from that apartment."

"A flash?"

"Yeah. Wanna take a look?"

Booker and Coffee entered the apartment. They kept their vision away from the disarray of clothes and the dirty plates in the sink and went straight to his laptop. He pointed to the monitor. "See. You can spot that apartment and right around that time you mentioned, there is a flash."

Booker stared down at the video. "No, it's not just a flash. There's two flashes. Very clear."

The muscled man re-examined the video. "You're right. Well, damn, there are two flashes."

"Is it okay if we shoot some video off your screen?"

"Sure. Your station give out rewards for video?"

"No, but once we're done, the police would be very interested in the video you have."

"The police? Sure."

Coffee put up her sticks, loaded her camera, and started videotaping the surveillance video. The flashes were visible. However, Booker could not see a person leaving or entering the apartment building. "Thank you. You want to say anything on camera about your video?"

"No, I'll leave that up to you. But I will contact police."

Booker had to look up at him. "Again, thanks."

Booker carried the tripod for Coffee. They made it back to the SUV. He needed to check in with Claire Stanley. He called and after two minutes on the phone, she reacted. "You got the possible murder weapon? And maybe the shooting caught on video? And no one else has this?"

Booker made another visual check for the P.I.O. "We think so. Just us."

"Booker, sometimes I think you work better under pressure. Good work. Feed in the video of the surveillance, then edit your package. We want to look at this vid."

"No problem."

While Coffee fed in the surveillance video to the station, Booker wrote a script. He closed the door to the SUV and recorded his voice. Once finished, he left the editing to Coffee and went back to the crime tape for any new developments. A police officer told the assembled reporters a P.I.O. would talk in a few minutes.

Booker turned around and Detective Brielle Jensen was facing him. "I understand you have some video that might interest us?"

"We just got it."

Jensen gave a short smile. "Don't worry, I'm just here asking if I can see it. We have a detective on the way to the apartment. The guy called us right after you left."

Booker opened the door to the SUV and Jensen said a hello to Coffee. She quickly cued up the video and hit play. Jensen watched the video and said little. "Thanks for showing me." She was off, walking and ducking under the crime tape.

Four minutes later, Jensen stood in front of reporters and photographers. She waited until all of them were recording. "At approximately nine-twenty a.m., workers were concerned when a fellow employee did not show up for work. We were called to make a wellness check. Inside apartment one-oh-seven, we found a deceased male, shot twice. A weapon was found nearby behind some hedges. We will determine if the gun found is the murder weapon. The apartment has been disturbed and it will take more time to process the scene. We are working on the possibility this happened around one-thirty a.m. If anyone saw or heard anything around that time, we would ask you to please call us or the TIPS hotline."

Booker jumped in. "Do you have a working motive for the shooting? And are you ready to release the name of the victim?"

"We are in the process of contacting next of kin, so no, we do not have a name just yet. Also, anything about a motive is part of the investigation."

Booker could tell by her body movements, Jensen was ready to leave the line of microphones. Another reporter asked, "Was there anyone else in the apartment? And can you say if police have been to this apartment before for any reason?"

"From what we can determine, the victim was alone in the apartment at the time. The second part of your question is part of the investigation. Thank you. If I have more, we will release it." She walked toward the crime tape. A uniformed officer lifted the crime tape up so she could walk underneath.

Everything Jensen said was fed live to the Channel 27 website. Far as he could tell, Booker was the only crew. No second unit. Coffee set up for the noon newscast.

Booker told the noon audience about the shooting at the apartment, how neighbors heard something at one-thirty a.m. Booker's edited news story was just over ninety seconds long. He included the gun recovery video and the surveillance video showing the two flashes of light in the window, possibly representing the actual gun shots. Booker wrapped up his live portion and waited until he heard 'all clear' before he started talking to Coffee.

"If you don't mind, I'll call Claire to arrange for another crew in here so you can take a break."

"Book, I'm good. I can keep going."

"Okay."

Before he could turn and check out the next move, Booker got a call on his cell.

"Booker." It was Demetrious, and he was out-of-sorts upset.

"Demetrious? What's wrong?"

"I know that apartment. I saw you on TV."

"You know this complex? How?"

"I've been there, Book. I know that place. I have to talk to you right away."

Booker heard desperation and fear in his voice. "Talk to me, what's wrong."

"We need to talk. That's the apartment of Eddie Beck."

"And he is?"

"Book, he's the guy who supplied me the information about Fila Mackee. And now he's dead."

32

For the rest of the afternoon, there were no new developments. Booker and Coffee watched a line of reporters knocking on the door of the man with the surveillance video. Everything looked like he let all of them get the same video Booker released on the noon newscast. They would not be able to backtrack and get video of the gun being recovered. For now, the video was the sole exclusive of Channel 27.

Booker worked throughout the day, going through all the motions, yet stayed continuously worried about his brother. They made plans to meet in the evening. Right after the call from Demetrious, Booker called Claire Stanley. "I need a favor. Can you give me all the information you can on Eddie Beck. The same address as the murder location."

"You have the victim's name?"

"I think so. We just can't use it yet. But I would like to know as much about him as I can."

"No problem. We're on it." She was gone.

Coffee pulled a now-warm bottle of water from the back seat and took a long draw. "Okay, Book. You can't leave your partner in the dark forever. And there's a big hole you're not telling me."

"Coff, the guy who was murdered here might be linked to Fila Mackee, the woman who overdosed."

"Man, that's a big leap. She died what, five years ago?"

"I have to talk to someone tonight and then I'll know more. For now, I just can't say much."

"No problem." Coffee chugged the water. Both of them kept watching the parking lot and the apartments for anyone new who could be interviewed. The police update gave the age of the victim but no name. By four p.m. Booker got a call from Stanley.

"You ready to write?"

"Go ahead, Claire."

"Everything I'm telling you will be in an email soon. Edward Beck, age thirty-three. Far as we can tell, he was arrested once for loitering. Another time for theft but the case was dropped by the state. After the nolle pros drop, he comes up in the system again for passing bad checks but again that case was also dropped. By the way, the charges go back ten years ago. He would have been in his twenties. Since then, a clean record."

"Social media?"

"Yes, he's everywhere. All the platforms. Nothing special. He's apparently been living at this current address for two years. I don't see a girlfriend on any of his posts."

"Thanks, Claire. You sending a night crew?"

"I have to since they could be confirming his name any second now. We'll do this tonight and reassess in the morning."

"Thanks." Booker did not reveal what Demetrious told him. He needed a bit more time to check on a few more things. He thanked Coffee for the hard work and told her to enjoy a well-earned meal.

On his way home, Booker got another call from Stanley. "Book, this just came in."

By the sound of her voice, he knew something was not right. "What's up, Claire?"

"Your witness who came forward, Mercedes Campana, well police just put out a short news release. Something happened medically. She's in a coma."

"Coma?"

"For now, yes. We're going to run something on the website and later in a newscast, but she was going to be important to the Rocker case."

"And she might have information on who hit her car."

"Sorry, Book."

"Thanks for the update."

33

Demetrious Moreland kept pacing in the apartment and checking his phone.

Booker pointed to a chair. "Dude, sit down. I've never seen you so nervous."

Moreland ignored the chair. "They shot Eddie and I'm next."

"You can stay here tonight. Don't go back to that motel room."

He finally sat down. "Eddie's dead and I know they've been watching me."

"You mean the other day?"

"First, I spot a car downstairs here, then I'm almost positive the same car was parked outside my café, just sitting there all day."

"You see the car?"

"No, but someone who works with me saw something. Told me a car's been out there most of the day. Stays in one spot for an hour, then moves to another location."

Booker was adding up all the incidents. He'd seen the car himself, the one with no license plate. Now, with the murder of Eddie Beck, there could be some truth to Moreland's concerns. "Have you thought about going to the police?"

"And tell them what? I think somebody is following me? That won't exactly make my case a priority."

"And all this started after you asked him about Fila?"

"Yes."

"If you want to contact police, see if you can contact Brielle Jensen. She's working Eddie's case."

"Jensen. Okay. Just so you know, I signed the papers, and I will be moving in tomorrow. The apartment upstairs is mine."

"Great."

Moreland got up again and went to the window in Booker's kitchen, pulling apart the curtain and peering into the street below. He spoke over his shoulder. "I don't want to disturb Misha with my problems." He came back to the chair. "No one down there."

"Misha is in the other room with her headphones on, working. She's okay. But I will tell her later. We have a rule. No secrets between us." Without saying so, Booker, so far, had the same relationship with his half-brother. He wasn't raised with Demetrious. For Booker, early life was with his mother. His father divorced and moved on to another wife. Booker wrote him out of his life at that point. He knew his mother was pregnant but didn't question what happened. Booker would learn years later that his mother rejected the lifestyle of Moreland's father. A life built on drug money. Demetrious spent his life away from Booker. That was the agreement. A drug thug stayed out of her life, but he convinced her to let him raise Demetrious, who spent his time in boarding schools. Now, together in the same city, Booker wasn't about to lose touch with him again.

"When you last spoke with Eddie, did he sound concerned? What did he say, exactly?"

"Just that Fila was upset about something on the job. And that she was looking into it." He thought for a moment. "I think he said he was going to look into something else."

"Those words?"

"Yes."

"Okay Demetrious, explain to me again. How did this car thing work?"

"First, I pumped this up a bit too much. These weren't really that many classic cars. Just mostly old cars. The one I showed you that day, well, that was the best of the bunch that I drove. Company called Green Wave Drivers. We would get a text to find the location of the car. The text would have a code to open a lockbox, get the key, and drive the car to a certain location. Once I got there, another car would be waiting for me. I would drive that car back to another location, get out, and leave it."

"Didn't that seem strange to you?"

"At first, yes. Then, I just got used to the money. The money was great. My problem was I thought it would be a good news story." Demetrious used his hands and wiped down his face. He kept looking down and talked through his fingers. "I started all this Book. I got Eddie killed."

"Look at me." Booker waited until he had his brother's full attention. "You didn't get anyone killed. These are killers and I've got to learn all I can about them."

For the next twenty minutes, Booker wrote down information about the car transfer plan. When he was finished, he set up Demetrious in the second bedroom, then went in to explain what he could to Misha. When he was done, Booker reached for his wallet and keys.

Now, worry moved into every pore of her face. "Where are you going? It's getting late."

"Don't worry. I'll be back. There's something I have to do."

When Booker pushed open the front door of the complex and walked out into the street, he didn't see the car tucked neatly behind a Ford Bronco, some six to seven car lengths away. Inside the car, the man let the Sig, mounted with suppressor, rest on his right leg. He always kept his eyes on the front of the place. No matter what, there was no way he was going to move.

34

Well past eleven p.m., a hard night wind kicked at the front of Booker's car, making him keep a firm grip on the wheel. All afternoon and evening he'd been holding onto a secret. A secret that overwhelmed his heart, and he knew there was only one way to possibly confirm what the adoption group leader told him earlier in the day. This had to be done, he told himself, before he could package up his entirety of information and present all the facts to Claire Stanley.

Gray clouds gave a strong hint rain was about to follow. Booker was the lone car moving down the side road. Federal Highway was a mile behind him, and when he passed the stores on Wepner Street, they were all closed. Huge blank store windows made the drive almost claustrophobic. A half-mile later, Booker pulled over, deciding to park under a large banyan tree, hidden as much as possible from the street. There were no other cars, just Booker.

He stared out the front windshield at the cemetery across the street. Booker felt like an assassin, waiting in the shadows. A rough breeze actually moved the front of his motionless car. In the cemetery, trees bent at the will of the wind, leaves kicked from boughs, and the street was littered with a rolling collection of broken branches. Booker guessed the wind speeds were kicking well past thirty miles per hour, enough to tip over a bus.

Maybe this idea was a bust. For the next few minutes he thought about going home, just leaving, then he gave up on the change-of-mind, opting to stay put.

Booker stayed in the car, rather than getting out and risking being seen. He beat himself up for not bringing a cup of something hot. For as long as he waited, Booker tried not to look at the headstones. The combination of the wind howling, leaves smacking against the granite markers, and the wicked sky made this venture only for the strong-willed.

He thought about what he would do if this idea turned out to be a nothing. Going to Stanley with half-confirmed information was not on the table. And what if the information he got on what was about to happen at the cemetery was incorrect?

The info he got foretold a specific day of the week and a specific time. Right now, the allotted time was past, and Booker remained in place. He gave himself another twenty minutes. If nothing happened by then, he would turn around and go home. He worried about Demetrious. Someone was tying up all loose ends connected to Fila and now maybe Demetrious was a loose end. Booker even thought about contacting B.B. Maybe she was also in the cone of danger, just for being Fila's roommate. He put B.B. on the top of his next-day things to do. She should, at least, be warned.

Five minutes left and Booker would leave.

The wait reminded him of hours spent in the station surveillance van, with the inside windows covered in black drapes, a tripod bolted into the floor. The van itself was a beat-down excuse of a car, with a myriad of faded colors and ugly wheels. The van was made for fitting into the background, while inside, Booker kept notes and Coffee would focus in on the person in question. One photographer kept a piss bottle nearby and never needed to leave his watch-post. Most news stations, like Channel 27, cut back on extended investigations. The van remained in the parking lot, getting older and better adapted to blending in. Now, Booker was in his own car.

The wind calmed and, for the moment at least, the weather seemed to settle. The cemetery still looked foreboding. Bad B-movies, with creatures stirring out the mist, pushing up out of graves, crept into Booker's mindset. He waved off the thoughts and focused on the task in front of him. Booker even stopped the constant glancing toward his cell phone for the time.

His peripheral vision caught sight of a car approaching from his right. Booker ducked down in his car, leaving just his eyes exposed over the top of the wheel. The car moved slowly until it was in front of the cemetery. A figure got out, looked around and started the short walk to the front gate. The man went inside.

Booker got out of his car and followed.

35

This would be uncharted, new territory for Booker. Following someone into a cemetery wasn't on his agenda when he started the day. The figure walked the path until he moved off to the right when the cemetery roadway split. Booker kept moving, not sure if his steps would echo loud enough for a response. The man kept going.

After another forty feet the man stopped and walked into the vast arrangements of headstones. In another five steps, he stopped. Booker walked onto the grass, not looking down and keeping his eyes on the back of the man in front of him. The figure was now in front of a gravesite, head bowed. He had flowers in his right hand. Booker was almost near his left side. The time to speak was now.

"Judge Rocker, it's Booker."

William Rocker snapped his head backward toward Booker. "What are you doing here?"

"I know I am imposing, but I had to be here. To ask you something."

Rocker kept the questions going. "How did you know I was here?"

Booker felt he had to come clean. "The day of the truck accident, I saw you drive this way. I didn't know about the cemetery. I found out later. They told me when you came and that they always left the gate unlocked so you could have access. Don't be angry with them."

"I won't. I just like to spend some time here. Alone."

"Okay if I ask you...?

"No problem, Booker."

"You were here the night Ken Capilon was murdered, weren't you?"

"Yes. I stopped by his place to hear for myself that he was going to the police and change his testimony. When I got there, I didn't see his car, then I thought what I was about to do was wrong. So I left."

"And came here?"

"Correct."

Even though Rocker had stepped away from his judgeship four years earlier, Booker still gave him the respect of the bench and always called him judge. "Judge, did you know about the witness Mercedes Campana?"

"I had no idea who she was until I saw her in your report. So, she was about to come forward for the first time. My attorney didn't even know about her. I have to thank you for that."

Booker contemplated what he was about to ask, then waited for the tall man to do what he came to do. "Book, okay if I place these flowers?"

"Go ahead judge."

Former judge William Rocker placed flowers in the metal water cup near the headstone of Shanice Rocker. Booker and the judge stood silently for the next two minutes or so. Booker let the moment stay solemn. It was the judge who spoke next.

"Booker, you're probably wondering why I come at this time."

"It crossed my mind."

"Well sir, it's because the police and the medical examiner's office tell me this is about the exact time of night she was murdered. I wanted to remember her when her life was taken."

"I understand, judge." Booker backed up. "I have something else to ask you but I'm moving back for a while to give you some time."

"Thank you."

Booker sidestepped other gravesites, a task made harder with the darkness. He moved back a good fifteen yards and gave the judge privacy. From where he was standing, Rocker appeared to be talking and holding a conversation, telling Shanice something Booker would never hear. The only sounds were the remaining bits of wind piercing the night air and rustling the branches of the few Live Oak trees in the cemetery. Death had not come to Booker's family, with half-brother and mother still around. He had no intention of contacting his natural father. Booker had come to know the pain of loss through others. Relatives of those murdered, and horrendous car crashes brought tears to the microphone. Booker's words of comfort came from personal habits to treat people a certain way. Even his grandparents were gone when Booker was young, and he was spared the childhood experiences of a funeral. He just wanted to make sure Rocker had time alone since Booker had invaded that treasured territory.

Booker waited several minutes, until the judge seemed to be at peace. He walked toward the grave. A whisper of wind pressed the tops of the grass. When he got within a few feet, he noticed the judge was holding more flowers in his right hand. Booker looked down and to the left and was shocked to see his discovery.

36

Booker stood and stared down at the gravesite of Fila Mackee. "Judge, Fila Mackee. I didn't know...I was here to ask about her."

"Fila? You know about her?"

"Judge. Was Fila..."

"Fila Mackee was the daughter of Shanice." Rocker moved within inches of Booker's face. His voice grew louder. "Why are you asking me about Fila? What do you know?"

"That really is the key question I was going to ask you about. I don't know where you live these days. I know your attorney won't let me anywhere near you, but Fila Mackee is a person whose name came to me, and I wanted to ask you about her."

Rocker looked over Booker's shoulder. "Judge, I come here alone. There are no cameras. My cell phone is off. It's just me. But I am asking you on the record about Fila. So, are you willing to confirm Fila Mackee was the daughter of your late wife?"

"Yes." Rocker seemed to settle into a state of willingness, a resignation to Booker's questions. "It was Shanice who made all the arrangements. Had Fila buried here."

"That's why you had us meet you in Chicago."

"Correct. Fila's adoptive parents live there. I had no information other than she overdosed. I promised them I would find out more. But so far, I let them down. I haven't found out anything."

"I have been looking into Fila's death."

Before Booker could say another word, Rocker tossed questions like he was throwing darts. "How did you find out about Fila? What exactly do you know?"

Booker stood there for a moment, absorbed in the surroundings of death all around him, and thought about what was happening. Booker Johnson, the one bent on asking all the right questions was now being questioned himself. "Judge did you know where Fila was working part-time?"

"No idea. Shanice shared very little with me. You know way more than I do, that's why you need to tell me everything."

"I will, but I have to ask, how did Shanice find out about Fila?"

"Fila apparently did all the work, posting on a message board, finding out what she could from the state of Florida. Her parents in Chicago had no information. They just wanted Fila. Got her right after birth. Then, one day, Shanice said, Fila just showed up at the door. Shanice knew right away it was her daughter."

"Did Shanice tell you what happened?"

"With Fila? Well, I wasn't supposed to know. Ever. Shanice got pregnant in college. Some guy who was married. Shanice didn't know what to do but she wanted to have the child. She gave up Fila right after birth and moved on. It was Fila, when grown, who didn't give up on Shanice. She kept going until she found her."

"And then?"

"First, she kept all this from me. She was afraid it might hurt my political career or even the judgeship. Didn't want me to know anything, but one day she told me bits and pieces. And then, Fila was found dead."

"Overdose."

Rocker heaved a sigh. "That's what the medical examiner said. Shanice went on a mission to find out what happened to her daughter. She didn't get very far. She went out one night, and someone attacked her. The whole world said I killed her. My own friends convinced me to leave the country. I'm still looking for answers."

Booker started to form in his mind what he could or could not say. His own TV station didn't know all the facts. The threat of rain had passed, and the clouds now covered the entire sky. Rocker stood waiting, still holding the remaining flowers.

"There is a lot to be confirmed, judge, before I tell you a great deal. You're going to have to trust me. Fila had a roommate here, seemed to have a good life. She had friends, others who were adopted. Now, as to what happened to her, I'm still working on that."

"How do you even know about her?"

"That's what I can't say much about just yet. Some things have to be confirmed."

"I told her people in Chicago I would get facts. Please share anything you find with me. Is that okay?"

"I will. I just need some more time."

William Rocker turned and carefully placed the flowers on Fila's gravesite. "I wanted Shanice buried next to Fila."

Booker again gave him time to reflect. Rocker appeared ready to leave. "If Shanice was looking into Fila's death, she didn't say much. I just know she was devastated. Knowing Shanice, she probably started investigating how Fila died."

They both walked the roadway back toward the gate, Rocker doing most of the talking. "I can tell there's a lot you can't tell me yet. I'm not in a position to do a lot of investigating. I'll leave that to you."

They reached the gate. Booker tried to reassure him. "Until I can confirm certain things, I can't say too much."

"I understand."

Rocker put his hand on the car door. "You know, beside killing my wife, they also say I killed Ken Capilon."

"Why? He was about to speak in your defense."

"I hear things. I read stuff. People claimed I killed him for revenge. For not telling the truth four years ago. But I was right here. With Fila and Shanice."

They both departed, Booker leaving first, heading back home. When he reached the apartment, he looked around and did not see any strange cars on the street. He opened the door to find Moreland was asleep on the couch with the television still on. He turned everything off.

37

There were several chairs added to the office of the news director at Tuesday morning's meeting called at the request of Booker. After some discussion, Stanley looked up from the notes she had taken.

"So, the Shanice Rocker case is now directly tied to the death of her daughter, Fila Mackee. And you believe, but can't prove, there's more to her overdose death. And Eddie Beck was a friend who knew Fila, and now he's dead too."

"That's correct." Booker stared out at the assembled. Coffee sat off to the side. Inside the meeting were reporter Lacie Grandhouse, who always wore her Nikes on news stories. There was reporter Merilee Yang, who asked for a lot of background information since she was not aware of the facts. Stanley wanted all of them to be there when Booker gave his update. Stanley had more questions. "How much of this can go on television? And when? Or are we still in the investigation-mode where we're researching before we put something on the air?"

News director Acevedo clarified, "We wait for now. Let Booker do some more investigating. We need a bit more. The mother-daughter angle is a good start. Thanks, Booker, for getting us to this point."

"The judge coming forward was huge, but a lot of the initial effort came from Lacie. When her story about the car drivers was cancelled, she started looking into this and found out about Fila's overdose."

Acevedo added, "Good point. But again it points out we need more information. What do we know about this car-driving thing? Who runs it? How did it start? There's way too much we need to gather before we put something out there. Booker, keep going. Pull in Lacie to help if you need someone. Everyone report to Claire and she will update me. My door is always open."

Meeting over, Grandhouse filed out and Yang went to a story she had lined up for the noon newscast. Booker had another small meeting planned with Stanley. When they reached her office, she tossed him the potato. "It's hot, Book. Don't drop it. Now, tell me where are you going next?"

Booker put the potato on the floor. "There is an element to this I haven't told anyone. For now, I will share this with you and no one else."

"Sure, Book."

"We know about the death of Eddie Beck. We have not formally connected him to the car-driving company. Beck was supplying information about Fila to my half-brother. Excuse me, brother, Demetrious. We think someone has been following him."

Stanley grabbed her familiar gum. "Is your brother safe? You need some help with that?"

"For now, I think he's okay. We can't prove it yet, but Fila's death might not be an overdose of her own doing. And Beck was shot and killed. Two people connected with this company have been murdered."

"I understand. You want to bring police into this?"

"Trust me, I think they are doing a lot without me. We just have to keep going and draw lines of connection. If we can do that, truth will come out."

"And you don't want Acevedo in on this?"

"Please, I'm trusting you to just keep this between us until I know more and prove more."

"Okay, but please keep me in the loop."

"I will."

Booker picked up the potato and placed the plastic toy on his desk. Coffee walked up behind him. "Are you going somewhere just now or checking things out?"

"I'll be on the computer, but I want to go somewhere in about thirty minutes."

"No problem." She was off.

He caught Grandhouse just before she left the building. "I want to thank you for bringing all this to my attention."

Grandhouse, hands out, tried to wave off the compliment. "You did all the work. Amazing turn. So Fila was the daughter of Shanice."

"Rocker knew but didn't think it mattered. Kept it to himself. But thanks Lacie."

"No problem."

Booker sat down, pulled out a yellow legal pad and started writing things down. On the top of the page, he wrote Car company—Green Wave Drivers, Inc. Next, he went over some information and looked for new angles. He again checked Sunbiz.com the state website for business listings. From the information from Demetrious, the company worked by text messages, left cash for the drivers, all tucked tightly into the lockbox. Even with the name, Booker could not find a location, not even a PO box. He started with the online ad for new drivers—an ad taken down right after Grandhouse wanted to do the news story. Booker had a screen capture and was studying the online pitch for hiring drivers. The ad was short. There was a mention of driving older and classic cars, that they needed to be driven to keep them running efficiently. There was a listing of an email and no phone number. A demand for drivers and no formal address. He tried putting the email info into the state business search website and got nothing. The whole thing was hush-hush, and Booker wondered why anyone would sign on. It was just too mysterious.

He tried the email and later saw it bounced back. Whatever existed before was now a memory. From conversations with Demetrious, Booker knew drivers did not take down VIN numbers or any plate numbers. Next, Booker tried every social media platform he could reach. Finding nothing, he needed to get outside and time to think. He called out to Coffee and they took a ride.

He called first to make sure B.B. was in. She had just an hour before heading to the airport. Coffee stayed in the SUV while Booker went to the apartment. B.B. wore business attire, with a white blouse and navy skirt.

She put her key in the lock, and they talked as she locked up. "So, you said on the phone Fila found a parent but you can't say much about it now?" The large black eyelashes flashed at Booker.

"Until I do one or two things, I just need to keep it quiet for now. But it seems that big surprise she was going to announce had to be about a parent she found."

"Thanks for that." Her eyes probed him. "There's something else wrong, isn't there?"

"You're leaving. For how long?"

"A couple of days, maybe. Why?"

Booker took a second to spit it out. "Just be careful. One person connected to this was murdered. Just watch out."

"When I get back into town, I'll stay with a friend. I'll text you then."

"Thanks." They reached the elevator, B.B. rolling a travel bag. She pushed G on the panel. "You're probably wondering why I only go by B.B."

"I wondered but I just thought you wanted to keep it personal."

"My mother liked a TV show character and so she named me Beatrice. I'm Beatrice Boxworthyton. And since I don't want anyone in life to call me Bea, and my last name is longer than a football field, I just go by B.B."

"Fine with me."

"I promise. I'll be careful. Let me know when you can explain all this."

"No problem."

He walked her to her car, then reconnected with Coffee. He gave her the next place on his list. Twenty-minutes later, they were parked in front of the vacant home of Judge William Rocker. Coffee rolled down the SUV windows, turned off the engine, and they were surrounded with the sounds of nature. "Okay, Book. Why exactly are we here?"

Booker got out, and, like his first visit to the house, he stood outside and stared at the place. Coffee strolled up next to him sipping water. "You still have the keys, don't you?"

"I'm not going in. I'm thinking."

"Bring me up to speed."

"The night they found Fila dead, things had been moved around. We know Ken Capilon's place looked like it was searched. And we know people broke into Rocker's place here twice. Coff, what are they looking for?"

She poured out the remaining splash of water from the bottle. "We couldn't see into Eddie Beck's apartment. But I get your point. If they've been looking for something since Fila's death, maybe it started with her."

"That's what I was thinking. And maybe somebody thought Shanice had access to whatever it is they want." Booker walked all the way up toward the front door, looking into the windows, then turned around and headed to the SUV.

Coffee started the car. "Back to the station?"

"Yes. I have to nail down the car company."

38

When he entered the newsroom, Claire Stanley was waiting for him. A man was with her. "Booker, please meet Ronny Oliveson. Ronny is here to help you."

Booker sized up the guy holding a notepad, wearing large glasses, a white shirt and green tie, and with a briefcase on the floor. Stanley was all smiles. "Ronny has a degree in business administration and a master's in computer engineering. We borrowed him from IT. He's going to help with your search of the car company." While waiting for Booker's reaction, Stanley picked up the potato.

Booker was apprehensive. "I really don't need any help."

"Just let him try. See if he gets any results." Stanley turned to her many other duties. "You two play nice together. If you need me, you know where to reach me."

Booker was left with the computer expert. The man with the degrees adjusted his glasses. "You need help with the shell companies, correct? I can assist you with that."

They both sat down at Booker's desk. Oliveson pulled out a laptop and a sheet of paper. Booker spilled all the available information he had on Green Wave Drivers, Inc. He told him how they operated, the pickup patterns for drivers, the key drops and the short life of the Green Wave website. Oliveson took Booker's comments, closed up his laptop, and left.

Booker and Coffee had an off-the-record invite waiting for them.

———

Twenty minutes later, they were standing in front of a row of antique cars. Coffee looked uncomfortable, standing there without wielding a camera. Before them was a 1957 Chevy. A large placard, mounted on a metal stand, contained information about the car. Booker leaned down to read the engine was a V-8, 238 cubic inch.

A voice called out to him. "Welcome. And thanks for coming." She was tall, slender arms in a sleeveless white blouse, dark green pants. Her hair looked locked in place and her eyes were clear blue. She extended a hand, first to Coffee, then Booker. "I wasn't sure if you were coming."

"I always want to learn."

She smiled the way a parent would showing off the accomplishment of a son or daughter. "This is one of my beauties. 57 Chevy." She walked around the car like a model would show a vehicle at a car show. "All original parts, even kept the colors original. Matador Red for the body, Imperial Ivory for the top. Drive it twice a year. I'm Salanna Stock. Booker, I know you. And this is?"

Coffee said, "Junice Coffee. Photographer."

"Thank you both for coming. I have five other cars in my garage." The concern moved into her eyes. "The reason I called you is because I'm hearing you're investigating a company with a few antique cars?"

Booker was now a couple of yards from her. "Don't know how you heard, but yes, we're looking into them."

"I belong to a car club. All of us from South Florida, three from here in Apton County. The reason we heard about this group, and I use the term loosely, is because some people thought we were behind this group. I want to be clear, we are not. This is a pop-up company, not sanctioned by us or recognized by anyone, and they appear and disappear like a ghost company."

"And I understand you don't want to say anything on camera?"

"Heavens no. At least not yet. We have tried to track them down and gotten nowhere. We are really hoping you can find out about them and shut them down. They are not associated with us. We take great pride in our cars."

"You ever hire anyone to drive them?"

Her head kicked back with the question, nostrils flared. "I drive my cars myself. Would never just hand them over to a stranger like that. And yes, I heard about what they do."

Booker smelled the fresh-cut grass, looked over the layout of five acres of property, surrounded by landscape islands and new plantings of Southern Magnolia trees. Salanna Stock saw how Booker was eyeing her property. "My husband and I owned a few restaurants. Sold them all. Bought and built up this place. He's gone now, but we bought cars together. Please know, a lot of car owners are not well-off. If it's your life's dream to buy one of these beauties, then do it."

Coffee walked around the Chevy. "I once owned a red Volkswagen in college. Still miss that car."

"What about you, Booker? Is there a car you wish you could own?"

"Well, it was before my time, but I loved that Chevy Nova muscle car."

Stock nodded. "See. There's always a car you always wanted. Some owners in the club are store clerks. One is a bank employee. Another is a handyman. We all share a love for our cars. We meet bi-monthly. And we also hate what this ghost company is doing. If we find out anything, Booker, we will pass it on to you."

"How did you hear about them?"

"Like I said, people mistake our club for them. Call us for jobs driving our cars. We don't hire anyone. Ever. That's nonsense. Please find them and expose them."

Booker was ready to leave. She made one last plea. "If you want, I can give you a drive."

"No. That's okay. We have to go."

"Okay. In the garage, I've got a 1927 Bugatti worth two million. There's a 1964 Jaguar E-type in British Racing Green. Anytime you want, you can take a look."

"Thank you." Booker was on the way back to his SUV. "I will contact you if I learn anything about them."

"Please do."

Coffee got behind the wheel. "Man, I really miss that Volkswagen. You never had an old car?"

"Naw. There was actually a long time we just used public transportation." Booker pulled up his laptop. "But I understand now why this Green Wave Drivers would not want to be anywhere in front of a camera."

Booker kept checking for an update on the health of Mercedes Campana. He sent two emails to Detective Brielle Jensen and so far, he heard nothing. No updates.

Coffee parked last in a long line of cars next to a park pavilion. She pulled out her camera and Booker moved in, finding a position near the back of the small crowd. Standing in front of a podium was Branson Landale. "I want to thank everyone for coming. Ken Capilon wasn't just a great employee at our company, he was a great person. Everyone at Find-A-Way knows and remembers how he liked to help people. This is a celebration of his life. A celebration of what he meant to his co-workers and to the charity he loved. And that's why we are here. At this park, at this pavilion. He spent a lot of time here helping kids."

Booker scanned the gathering. On the far side of the wooden shelter, he saw Ray Aldon, the charity's director. Not too far from him, Booker was surprised to see William Rocker. The front row seats were filled with notables. Munis Grant, the Mayor of Everpalm, the second largest city in Apton County, sat next to the county administrator. There were two former city commissioners and one prominent business owner. All of them came to champion the life of Ken Capilon.

A movie was played on a large screen showing Capilon interacting with high school students. Then a series of quick pieces of video, all of Capilon helping people with their move to Florida. Capilon, while in his forties, had the face of a much younger man, almost teen-like. He looked like a former athlete, with short blond hair and the muscles of a weekend warrior. The video showed him playing basketball with youngsters in the charity program, Gold Breakthrough.

Grant, the mayor, was in his second term. He had amassed a large portfolio of land in key sections of the city and county. In doing so, he vastly increased his wealth. A few of his properties were part of major building projects. During his second run for mayor, he personally paid for the entire campaign. Grant was about five-five, partly balding and always wore a sport coat even in the oven-like conditions of South Florida.

Coffee walked in and around the pavilion, picking up short video clips of Landale talking, people listening, and single video shots of the mayor, Rocker and others.

What surprised Booker most was the moment Rocker himself got up to speak. Coffee used the top of a chair as a makeshift tripod, balancing her camera for an even video frame of Rocker. There were soft whispers and a few fingers pointed at him while he came forward.

"I've known Ken for a very long time. He was generous with his time and was a believer in hard work. His company will miss him and so will the charity, which my late wife also put so much time into." Rocker sat back down.

Landale was back at the podium. "I thank you all for coming."

Coffee moved back to the outside of the pavilion and kept getting video. Booker didn't approach anyone and took a few notes.

They left, with Booker calling Stanley to give her an update. He had one more stop to make before Coffee's lunch break.

39

Given the joint stories of Fila Mackee and Shanice Rocker, Booker was permitted free rein to go wherever he deemed necessary. He had to check in, text, call or email. Coffee parked more than a hundred feet from the entrance to the Internet Café where Demetrious Moreland worked.

Coffee had her camera resting on the floorboard behind her seat. "So, we're not going inside to check on him?"

"No. I'm just checking to see if anyone is parked out here waiting for him."

Both Coffee and Booker went into surveillance mode. They watched all cars entering the area in front of them, paying attention to people getting out of cars. They were also looking for cars parked for a long time with no special purpose. Twenty-minutes into their stay Booker finally gave notice it was time to move on.

Coffee drove off.

Demetrious Moreland emptied two waste baskets, wiped down two desktops and answered more than twenty phone calls in the span of one hour. The wipe downs and basket cleanups were not part of his duties, yet he took them on since one person was out sick. The Café was a steady movement of people searching the web. A corner of the place was dedicated to just gaming. With one person down, he stayed well past his time to go home. In the next two hours he interviewed four prospective employees, asking questions and taking down information. The hiring was done through a panel of two people, Demetrious and one other. The main office in Boynton Beach, Florida, just wanted to be kept in the loop.

Traffic into the place began to slow after eight p.m. By nine, Demetrious made sure everyone was headed for the exit. The kitchen area had been closed and cleaned an hour earlier. The staff left for the day. Now, it was just Demetrious to close up the café.

He had developed a new way of leaving. First, he checked the very limited surveillance cameras. They only captured views immediately in front of the place and not the lot. Since the death of Beck, Demetrious added even more steps before going to his car. He turned out the lights and now waited a full five minutes before opening the door. In that time, he surveyed the lot. In a darkened Café, he took time looking for a stray car. When he was absolutely sure there wasn't a problem, he walked to his vehicle.

He headed to his motel room to pick up the remaining four boxes, then he would head to the apartment in Booker's complex.

The drive out to the edge of the county had Demetrious circling the motel three times to make sure he was not followed. He also checked the cars in the motel lot and they seemed to be the regulars. He realized the task was almost fruitless with so many people checking in and out daily. New cars and new faces all the time.

Demetrious got out of his car and did not hear the footsteps coming toward him. He worked the fob to lock his car door and still did not see anyone in the lot. A person stepped out from behind a parked car.

Demetrious felt the gun at his back. "Hands on the hood." When Demetrious started to turn toward the stranger, the barrel of the gun dug deeper into his back. "I said hands on the hood and don't look up. Don't you understand, dumbass?"

Demetrious did what he was told, placing both hands on the hood of his car, staring down. "What do you want? I don't have much."

The stranger kicked his legs apart and kept him leaning against the hood and fender. The move left Demetrious in a weaker position, one where he had almost no leverage to do anything.

The gun moved up from between his shoulders to the back of his head.

"Okay Demetrious Moreland, we're gonna take this nice and slow. And yes, I know your name. You made contact with Eddie Beck, didn't you?"

When Demetrious didn't answer, the gunman's voice was calm and even. "I'm not going to yell 'cause I don't want to wake up these fine folks. But I will pull the trigger and wake up everyone here, but you'll be dead."

"Yes, I spoke to him, but he couldn't help me. He told me nothing."

Ten, fifteen seconds went by. The gun stayed pressed to the head of Demetrious, like the man was weighing what he heard. Demetrious was getting tired, bent over, legs wide. If he nudged his glance just a bit to the right, he might be able to check the windshield and see his gunman.

"You two had words. What exactly did you ask him and what information did he give you?"

"Nothing. Just stuff about the job, driving the cars."

The hard kick against his inside right knee sent Demetrious sprawling to the ground. He was facedown, lips rubbing up against the pitted, dirty gravel, tongue out, tasting a small pool of green-black engine oil. Demetrious spat out the liquid, fighting back the hard urge to wipe his mouth but he stopped any movement when the gun was repositioned against the nape of his neck.

"You must really think I'm some sort of dumbshit. Now, one more bad answer and a bullet will enter right here and probably exit through your right eye. Now, let's try this one last time. What information did Beck give you about Fila Mackee?"

Demetrious remained prone taking in the question. "Let me up and I'll tell you everything. I can't talk like this."

"You know what? Let's get you up. But this time, we're gonna take this conversation over there, into a dark place." Demetrious looked over from his place on the ground toward a large outdoor table. And behind the table was a path leading to a grouping of overgrown weeds and plants.

"Get up! Don't look at me. Start walking."

40

Slow to his feet, Demetrious felt the gun move away for the first time in minutes. He moved like a person convinced a weapon was still aimed directly at his back. He walked past the parked cars, past the row of dented garbage cans. Demetrious paced in an unhurried cadence like a man concerned about what was about to happen. Even if the man got the information he wanted, would that be enough? Others connected to Green Wave were murdered or died mysteriously. The short walk, in measured steps, could be a way for Demetrious to come up with a plan, a fast plan to escape or avoid a bullet in the back.

There was another, second table two or three yards away. The gunman didn't want that. "Stop here. That's far enough." Now they were away from prying eyes.

Demetrious stopped. "Who is Fila? I forget the last name you mentioned. Fila? I don't know her."

They were a good twenty yards from the nearest motel door and the stranger's voice boomed with anger. "You're testing my patience. You have a few seconds to tell me what I want to know, or you'll join Eddie."

Demetrious was now eyes down toward the wooden patio table. He reached up and wiped parking lot dirt from his cheek. "You remember I just got here a few months ago. When was this Fila here?"

The man ran up to Demetrious, grabbing and placing his right hand on the bench, then jamming the barrel into the skin. "I'll blow a hole right through your hand. Before he died, Eddie told me he talked to you. Told you about Fila. Why are you asking questions about her? Who wants to know all this information? You? Or someone else?"

The barrel pressed hard into the top of his hand. If Demetrious moved an inch, a bullet would tear through bone and tendon. He would survive, if that would be the one and only bullet. There was a lot of risk in his next answer. Demetrious moved like a man running out of options.

"What if I told you what you want to know, would you let me go?"

The barrel stayed jammed down into his skin. "Here's the thing, Demetrious Moreland. You keep answering my question with a question. That has to stop. Right now. You just have to know if you don't answer my question, I'll end it right here."

Twenty feet from them, the figure stood behind his car, a Sig Sauer 9mm P226 in his right hand, topped with a suppressor. The figure just barely heard the two men by the patio table, so he moved in closer, stepping ever so quietly so he wouldn't be noticed. The more the figure heard, the more urgently he raised his weapon. When he was within fifteen feet, he heard each word and each question. The man holding a gun to Demetrious was wearing a balaclava. Demetrious had his right hand on the table with the gun barrel directly on the dorsal side. The stranger was still in the midst of asking a question.

The figure with the Sig aimed and pulled the trigger. The suppressor coughed.

The bullet smashed into the top of the table, kicking up splinters. There was hardly a sound from the gun. The Sig stayed in the weaver position, aimed directly toward the gunman.

Now it was the figure's turn to talk. "That was a warning. Get the fuck away from him or the next shot takes off your head."

When the stranger did not move, the Sig coughed again. The bullet just missed the leg of the stranger, landing somewhere in the leaves in back of them with a hard thud.

The Sig man stayed partially hidden behind a car. "You don't seem to understand. You will be very dead if you don't move away from him."

The stranger pulled his gun away and ran, pushing Demetrious toward the figure. The push put Demetrious directly in the shooting path and gave the stranger a block. The masked man ran into the small grouping of trees and did not turn back to offer a shot of his own. Demetrious heard the stranger running off with large steps, taking advantage of the black sticks of trees and the lack of proper street lighting. Within seconds, the stranger was gone. Demetrious was alone with the figure holding the Sig. He looked up and into the eyes of his father, Roland Caston.

41

"What are you doing here?" Demetrious rubbed his right hand until he could no longer feel the pain caused by the gun barrel. Caston looked around like he was looking for witnesses to what happened.

Before Caston could answer, Demetrious had another, more pressing question. "I don't think he's coming back. Could you please put that away?"

Caston looked down at the Sig, retreated to his car, then came back, empty-handed. "Look, I've been following you for days. You need my help, son."

"Son? You have never earned the right to call me that. But following me?"

"Days ago, I was gonna stop by your café. I found a car casing the place. I know bad when I see it. This guy, I couldn't see his face, he was watching you come and go. So, I started watching him."

"Outside my café? I thought someone was there."

"Not just the café, outside Booker's apartment, and here at the motel. I don't know anything about what you're doing, but somebody has it out to get you and I'm not gonna let that happen."

Demetrious leaned up against his car, still rubbing his hand. "I started all this. Booker's been trying to help me. People around me have been killed. All because I asked for just a bit of information on a girl. Her name is, rather was, Fila Mackee."

"And so, these people don't want anything to get out about her, is that it? And you're in the way?"

"I think so."

Caston was just as tall as Demetrious. He wore a black and gray fishing shirt and black cargo pants. Missing was his usual business attire and ultra-polished shoes. Demetrious took notice. "You're not wearing the business shirts and tie."

"That stuff is gone. New me, new clothes."

Someone slid a curtain aside for only a few moments, then put it back in place. "Thank you for what you did." Demetrious dug into his pocket for his keys. "Glad you came along when you did."

"I want to be clear. I'm not here to kill anyone. I just wanted to protect you."

The words from his father didn't quite ring true for Demetrious. He was used to the ways of the *before*, when his father's drug ring took over an apartment building, intimidated occupants, ran drugs all over the county, threatened anyone who might testify against the group, and was rumored to be the one who ordered a murder. In the compromise worked out with the mother of Demetrious, Caston could raise him, but only if he kept him out of the drug life. The promise meant Demetrious would spend those years in boarding schools. When he turned eighteen, Demetrious took off. The Caston before him now looked different somehow.

"You said, 'new clothes, new me.' What do you mean? You still have an outstanding warrant for your arrest. Before there's a conversation that resembles father and son, you have to deal with that first."

"Maybe I have." Caston moved back to his car.

"Meaning?"

"The old me would have someone kill that guy. On the spot. Protect the blood. The new me says let him live and let the authorities deal with it." Caston stood still like he was conjuring up what he was about to say. "Please don't say anything to your half-brother. Booker would blow this all up, and I can't have that right now or get my name linked to this mess of yours. I've got the authorities to think about."

Demetrious looked shocked. "The authorities? You've never said one thing good about the authorities. And he's my brother."

Caston walked around and picked up his brass. "Things change, son." He opened the door to his car. "I placed my cell number on the windshield of your car. If you need me, just call. But please know, I'm watching over you."

"Okay, what are you up to?" Demetrious came close to him.

"When I say I've changed, I mean it. I'm no longer into the drugs, at least not illegal. I made my peace with the law. And please keep this just between us. My life depends on it. I'm now working with them. Undercover." He soft-slapped Demetrious against his unbelieving cheek, fired up the car, and slowly backed out.

42

When Demetrious reached the apartment, by prior commitment, Booker had agreed to help him bring up the boxes to the new apartment. Demetrious had a hand truck, and they were able to pack all four boxes onto the truck. The elevator had just enough room for them.

Booker posed his question to the back of the boxes while pinned against the fake woodgrain wall of the elevator. "It's late. Everything go okay with the move from the motel?"

From his position on the other side of the boxes, Demetrious stood next to the panel of floor numbers. He couldn't see Booker and maybe that was a good thing. Booker would not be able to see his eyes. The half-bruh wouldn't be able to see the deception on the face of Demetrious when he spilled the forthcoming lies. "It was good. No problems. Just had to drive slow. My car isn't the biggest."

The entire body-language for Demetrious was of a man who was not going to tell what happened, the gunshots, the threat on his life or the possibility of being killed. The elevator doors opened, and Demetrious kept the boxes in between him and the probing reporter eyes of one Booker Johnson.

Inside the apartment, the place was strewn with empty boxes from fast food restaurants. The two-bedroom-two-bath top floor apartment had a slight reek from the older boxes and some uneaten food.

"Man, Demetrious, you've got to air this place out. I can help you with that."

Demetrious kept his facial expressions away from Booker, concentrating on unloading the boxes. "Don't worry about moving them into any rooms. I'll get to that tomorrow."

"It is tomorrow. It's like one a.m." Booker pushed a box into a corner. He then searched until he found a plastic garbage bag and started stuffing it with paper plates and containers of all sizes.

Demetrious moved about and decided the best weapon he had to avoid Booker pulling the truth out of him was simple: change the narrative. "You talk to mom lately?"

Booker snapped his attention, full-bore, toward Demetrious. He weighed what a question like that meant in the past, not that they had that many experiences together. Their interactions mainly came from the short period of time when Demetrious lived with Booker. The question, out-of-the-blue, meant something, though for Booker, he didn't know what. "You reminded me. I really should call her. We could do it together. Get her on the phone, yak it up. Get her laughing. You tell me a time and date soon and we can do it."

Demetrious had his back to Booker. "Sounds great. I'll text you. We'll set it up."

"Demetrious. Look at me."

The person who grew up without family gatherings for the holidays with a father who spent all his time selling drugs, the teen who enrolled himself into college and refused to accept any financial help from Roland Caston, now turned to the closest thing he had to a family: Booker Johnson.

"What's up half-bruh?"

"Demetrious, is everything okay? You seem a bit off."

Demetrious Moreland knew his eyes were telling and they looked weak, like he had been through something. Booker noticed.

Demetrious gave a soft laugh. "I'm fine. Been a long day. One person called in sick and I had to do the work of five people. I'm good."

"Well, you know if something is wrong. If you need my help in any way, I got your back."

"I know. I appreciate it, Book. Naw, I'm fine."

The two spent the next hour cleaning, finished stuffing the garbage bag, spraying Lysol, wiping down the kitchen counter and setting up a television, all connected to the WiFi. Just past two a.m., Booker headed for the door.

"Later, Book. Thanks for everything." They had spent all that time apart and now they were spending more time just being brothers.

"Remember. You need anything. Call me."

43

Booker was tired and worn out on Wednesday morning before he even sat down at his desk. He brought Coffee a cup of spearmint tea with her required adjustments of three packets of honey. The unloading of boxes with Demetrious merely hours earlier would have been easy for the much younger Booker Johnson, not the mid-thirties version. He rubbed his eyes and was about to make a trip to the restroom for another dash of water on his face when Lacie Grandhouse approached him.

"Book, check this out. Maybe I'm seeing things but take a look at this photograph." Grandhouse had printed out photos from a fund-raising event from years before where Shanice Rocker was a participant.

Booker stared for a few seconds. "You got me, Lacie. I don't see anything."

She pointed down. "Take a look in the far right. I know it's blurry, but do you see a figure? Someone on the outside of the house, looking through the window?"

Booker was again examining. Outside the large floor-to-ceiling glass window was a slender-looking male, eyes dark as raccoons, staring in on the gathering. "I didn't see him before, but you're right, there's someone there."

"Now that I have your attention, think back to the Eddie Beck's mugshot. Could that be our murder victim Eddie Beck?"

"Wow. If that's him, that would be a sure connection to someone at the charity, but who?"

Booker took the photograph into his hands and continued studying it. "Now I'm trying to figure out who he was looking at? And why would he even be at the party? Even though this is four years ago, he would still be too old for any of the programs funded by the charity."

"You guys need this." Junice Coffee handed Booker a magnifying glass and snatched up the tea in one move. She walked away drawing a sip.

Booker held the magnifier over the photo. "I wouldn't swear on it, but I think you're right. That's Eddie Beck, Green Wave driver and now dead."

Booker and Grandhouse shared the magnifying glass, and for the next ten minutes, both of them pored over the photographs of the event and only found Beck in the one photo.

"Again, good catch Lacie."

"Just trying to help."

"Unfortunately, we can't go on the air and say it's Beck, but it gives us something to confirm."

Grandhouse smiled and withdrew back into the tiny maelstrom of office chatter, shared overnight experiences, and the daily splitting of news stories matching a reporter to an assignment. Booker stayed fixed on the Rocker and Mackee cases. Now, his worn-down eyes were accompanied by a sore back, thanks to all the moving of boxes. If he could, Booker reasoned he needed another three hours of sleep.

He got up to wash away the sleepiness, and was just about to leave for the bathroom, when he got a phone call. "Booker," he said, answering.

"Morning, it's Ronny Oliveson from IT. Did you get my email?"

"Email? No. Haven't even turned on my computer yet. Long night. You sent an email?"

"Yes. I can't come down to explain it all. Involved in a project for the boss. Plus you don't want to hear all the steps I had to do, but the bottom line is the shell company Green Wave, well, I was able to find an address to a location. I know it's not much, but I wanted to pass it on."

"And is there a name connected to this location?"

"No. Not yet. Need more time. Just that Green Wave Drivers was somehow connected to this house address. Hope that helps."

"Thanks. I'll check it out."

"One more thing. If you check the county website on the property, it won't say Green Wave Drivers. If you check the name that's listed, you could go down the rabbit hole. I'm saving you a lot of time. Trust me, I found some corporate records with the address."

"Thanks."

"And Booker, I don't have time to check what's there. I'll leave that up to you."

Booker got off the phone and pulled up the email and the property address: 197743 Willdrift Lane. Apton County. He added the address information to his phone, then typed in the address on his computer.

Coffee was done with her tea and looked like she was ready to head out the door, if needed. "Whatcha got? Anything?"

"Coff, why does Willdrift Lane stand out? I should know that address." Booker started snapping his fingers. "Willdrift Lane, Willdrift Lane."

Then, he got it. The information on the computer confirmed what he was thinking. "Coff, let's take a ride. I got an address from our guy in IT. Maybe connected to the driver's company." Booker tapped the computer monitor screen hard.

"This house is the same location where Shanice Rocker was found murdered."

44

Neither Booker nor Coffee had been there before. They'd both only seen file video of the scene, police tape across the front walk. There was video of William Rocker being held back by officers when Rocker demanded to get into the house and see his wife. They refused to let him inside a crime scene. He'd stood outside, pacing and wringing his hands.

Now, the place looked abandoned. The house on Willdrift Lane was the last spot on the block, ending with a cul-de-sac of trees. Coffee got out, put her camera on sticks and started getting video. A few minutes later, she opened the SUV doors and sat down. Booker had gathered a few notes during the drive. The taxes on the house were paid each year. The owner's name was still hidden in the shell company maze. A hedge was recently cut and the mailbox looked like no human had touched it in years. Booker started walking toward the front door.

"Book, you need me?"

"Stay there, I'll be right back. We just need some video of the place."

He had to be careful since this was still private property. Booker knocked on the front door and heard nothing from inside. He stepped to the right and, without touching anything, he tried to look inside. He saw a heavy rug on the floor and a clean living room. An L-shaped beat-up leather couch rested in the middle of the room. The kitchen was nearby, and Booker was sure the house was small, inside and out. Booker tried to imagine Shanice, cut and near death, trying to get away from an attacker. Booker kept peering and couldn't make out anything by looking through the windows. All he had was imagining why Shanice would come to such a dismal looking place. He ruled out going to the back yard and walked the distance to Coffee and noticed the layers of gravel. A few weeds popped up through the tiny rocks.

Coffee sniffed at the surroundings, the darkened windows on the second floor. "Looks like a haunted house. Can't understand why she would come here in the first place."

"I know. It's far from her place. My guess is she was lured here. By who, I don't know. But this is not where she would want to be at night unless there was a good reason."

On the right, a man came walking, almost running to them. He was wiping down his face with a towel, looked to be in his seventies, and the watch face on his wrist had moisture inside of it. He waved the towel. "Hi. Glad you're here. You come to buy the place?"

"No. I'm Booker Johnson, with Channel 27. We're just here for a few minutes."

His face and forehead twisted into lines of disgust. "Dammit, I wish they would sell this place. Worst house on the block."

"Live here long?"

"Almost eighteen years. A nice couple lived here. Sold the place and we never once saw the new neighbors. No mail ever comes here. Some weeds grew up like beanstalks so we complained to everyone we could, but we couldn't find the owner. Someone removed the weeds and put down rocks. What a mess."

Booker asked, "How did you resolve it?"

"We didn't. This is the only house here with gravel, probably so they wouldn't have to deal with cutting the grass. Things changed right after the murder."

"You were here for that?"

"Oh yeah. What a scene. Police and reporters all over the place."

"So, you never saw the owners of this place?"

"Not once. This whole area is nice cause no one comes down this block.

We're off by ourselves. The only problem is we could use some new street lighting. That's a problem we've had for decades."

Booker pointed to the back yard. "What's back there? I mean beyond the yard?"

He wiped the towel against the back of his neck. "There used to be a farm back there. Guy grew all kinds of plants. He stopped growing one day and the place has been vacant." The man's gaze moved off Booker and rested on the house. "I was sorry to see that woman killed like that. I heard she was cut up pretty bad. We didn't hear a thing. Police questioned us."

"Yeah, I know it was bad. I didn't cover the story. Only read about it later."

The man looked like he wanted to pick up some gravel from the yard and throw the tiny rocks at the house. Instead, he started walking to his own property, where the grass looked trimmed to perfection and there was a small feeder for the birds.

Coffee packed up the gear. They sat in the SUV. Coffee flipped the visor down to block out the sunlight. "Okay Book, what do you think?"

"Shanice came here for a reason. I strongly feel she was told to come here. Maybe it has something to do with her daughter."

Coffee scoffed at the idea. "You have no proof of that. You told me Rocker himself didn't know anything about Green Wave Drivers until you told him. For now, you're just assuming she knew."

"Right, right, right. I'll stick with just what we know. She came here and we have to find out why."

Booker got a phone call.

"What's up Claire?"

"You know where Judge Rocker's home is located, right? Well, head that way. We're hearing the place was broken into again."

Booker and Coffee were not the first news team there. His rival, reporter Clendon Davis, was out front of the Rocker home, photographer set up and taping. Davis was beaming like a lotto winner watching Booker arrive after he did. A police unit was parked by the gate and a team of crime techs was already inside.

"Bit late, aren't you Booker?" A huge smile ripped across the lips of Davis like a shift in tectonic plates creating a break in his sun-burned chin.

"Hello, Clendon. Gloating is never a good idea in this business."

Coffee set up and got the normal series of video: establish wide-shot, zero in on any action, and then get what photographers called a cut-away. Booker walked around to the side of the house, looking for any other activity. During his walk, Booker noticed a white Honda parked down the road. Without saying anything, making sure he didn't give anything away, Booker kept looking for the owner of the Honda somewhere within the confines of the home. A good twelve minutes later, Booker found what he was looking for. William Rocker was inside his home, standing off to one side, probably where the crime techs told him to be and not in the way of the investigation. Booker rejoined Coffee and whispered into her ear.

For just a home burglary, even for a possible murder suspect, there would be no police Public Information Officer. Another twenty minutes went by, and Davis was getting antsy to leave the scene. He kept pacing and checking his watch. Booker stood by and said nothing.

"All yours, Booker." Davis and crew were about to leave.

"Seeya Clendon." Booker kept his watch on the front door of the house. Both crews had already recorded video of the techs bringing out bags of evidence. Davis appeared to have all he needed. They got into their car and left the neighborhood.

Coffee looked up from her camera and nodded in the direction of the door. Former Judge William Rocker walked outside. He had anger in his eyes. Rocker stood a few feet from his door and just stood there shaking his head. He rubbed something off on his pants. There was no crime scene tape, not for a burglary call. Booker could have approached but instead gave him some space. He uttered some unintelligible words that sounded like cursing and slapped his hand, hard, against his right leg. Coffee recorded all of the movements. Rocker marched toward Booker.

He pointed to the house. "They tore up the floors. Can't believe it."

"Hello, Judge. Okay if I can get a word on camera?"

"Sure." He sounded agitated and upset. Coffee was up and recording.

"What can you tell us about what happened here?"

He calmed down a bit. "I got a call. Police said a neighbor saw the front door was open. Police think it happened overnight. They were obviously looking for something. Ripped up my wood flooring. I think they thought I had a floor safe, which I don't. Problem is they looked in a few places, each time tearing up floors and carpet. The bedroom, my old office, it's a mess."

"Any cameras here?"

"Here? No. As you know, I've been staying elsewhere." Rocker turned away from Booker and stared directly into the camera. "Whatever you're looking for, it's not here. You already took my knife set, now leave me alone."

"Any prints? Maybe there's some evidence."

"I think they were wearing gloves. That's all I got to say. I'm just fed up."

Coffee put the camera down. Rocker called Booker over toward him. "I need to ask you something away from the camera." They walked a few yards away from Coffee. "Booker, what can you tell me about Fila's death? Anything new?"

Booker wasn't prepared to tell him about the discovery of the black dress, the possible search of her apartment of any of the other facts. Now was not the time to say much. "Sorry, I just don't have enough confirmed to tell you anything. What I can say is I'm looking into some things."

"You promise to let me know when you can?"

"Of course."

Rocker got into his Honda and eased down the street. Booker called Stanley and gave her an update. He would be a story at the end of the first block of news, meaning he would be live in front of the house around five minutes into the noon newscast. There was still work to do. With Coffee standing nearby, Booker knocked on doors looking for a witness or ear witness if someone heard something. And he was looking for surveillance video. There was nothing on all accounts, no witness or video. He gave his report in the noon and wondered what Davis must be thinking, watching the interview with Rocker—an interview Davis would have had if he had stayed.

Stanley called him after his live shot. "Do you think they found anything?"

"The burglars? No. They've hit this place at least twice before. There's simply nothing here."

"Book, you're getting close to something. Someone out there is getting desperate."

"Maybe. But they're getting desperate in the wrong place."

Stanley said, "I used to work with an assignment editor who used to always say 'Keep shakin' the tree, something's gonna fall.' Booker, you're shaking things up. Keep going, but just be careful."

45

On the ride back to the station, Coffee kept fidgeting in her seat. "Okay. Coff, what's up?"

"You didn't ask Rocker about Shanice going to the house that night? I mean maybe he had something new to say."

"I've already talked to him about that night. And I have nothing concrete. I have to keep working at it."

"Understood."

The afternoon was quiet with no new updates from police or Rocker's attorney. A check with Detective Jensen's office revealed Mercedes Campana was still in a coma and soon she would again be a no-information patient, meaning all updates about her would end once more. By the five p.m. newscasts, Rocker appeared on two other stations answering questions only about the break-in. His information was the same he had given Booker.

Booker's story on Rocker was reduced to a vo/sot, a bit of video from the scene and a short sound clip with Rocker.

Still exhausted from the night before, Booker was glad to head home. On the drive home, Booker got a phone call from Misha.

"You need me to bring something home?"

She sounded worried. "No. Come right away. Somebody left something stuck in our mailbox."

"I'll be right there." Booker stepped hard on the gas pedal, and when he reached the apartment, parked at an angle. He didn't care, he just wanted to get inside quickly. Booker almost ran out of the elevator, got inside the apartment and found Misha staring at a piece of paper on the kitchen table. "I didn't want to touch it anymore until you got home."

It was a short note:

WE TRIED TO GET D.M. ONCE. NEXT TIME WE WILL SUCCEED UNLESS YOU GIVE US WHAT WE'RE LOOKING FOR.

Misha looked upset, then she was fuming. "It's a threat, I guess aimed at your brother? Cowards always hide behind their threats."

"Yeah, looks like something directed at Demetrious. It says they tried once. He never said anything to me." Booker texted Demetrious and didn't get a response right away.

Misha put her finger close but did not touch the paper. "You want to call police?"

"Let me check with Demetrious first. Anything on the surveillance?"

"It's been down for two days."

Booker went downstairs to the mailboxes and checked around. He went outside and surveyed the street, checking for any cars, and found nothing out of the ordinary. He walked a half-block, turned the corner and continued his search of the neighborhood. Nothing. By the time he reached the front door of the complex, Demetrious had texted him back indicating he would be there in the next ten minutes.

Booker opened the door of his apartment before the second knock. "Take a look at this and tell me what you think?"

Demetrious stood over the paper, as if reading the short message a few times. Misha had her hands on her hips.

Booker said, "You okay?"

"I had a run-in yesterday."

"Yesterday?" Booker pulled out his cell phone and took a photo of the paper.

Misha pointed again to the table. "What kind of run-in?"

Demetrious stood back from the two of them. "I don't want to talk about it."

Booker tried to keep his voice from sounding like a demand. "Please, what can you tell me. This is a threat. And indirectly, a threat against me. And since it was left at our mailbox, the threat also includes Misha. Please. What happened yesterday?"

"Some guy. Couldn't see his face. Had a mask. It had something to do with Fila."

Booker tossed more questions. "What did this man say? Was he armed? How did you get away? You never said anything."

"No I didn't. All I can tell you is I'm fine."

"Does this have something to do with rubbing your right hand all night?"

"Just know I wasn't hurt."

Booker started to dial. Demetrious pulled on Booker's hand. "What are you doing?"

"I'm calling the station first, then police. You were attacked."

"Don't do that. Booker, this was handled. I don't want to involve the police. Besides, look at it. The whole thing is vague. It could be another D.M."

Misha leaned back against the kitchen sink, shaking her head. "If you don't want to contact police, then what is it they are looking for? They think Booker has this, whatever they want."

"I don't have anything to give anyone," Booker said. "I feel I'm close to something but not yet. There's something you're not telling us. Demetrious, this is us. Misha's involved. What are you leaving out?"

Demetrious looked toward the floor, then the ceiling rather than face the two of them. His expression looked like a swirl of inner thought and conflicted memories he did not want to share.

Booker didn't have much to guide him on the next move by Demetrious since they didn't grow up together. Tendencies and habits, born out of years of closeness did not exist between them. Booker had little idea what Demetrious would say. There was another question he wanted to pose, and instead waited to see if he would say anything.

"I'm sorry Misha for getting you so close to this. Just know I'm asking you again, Book, don't bring the police into this."

There was one thing Booker did know. He could rely on the woman standing just feet from him. By now, after a break-up, getting back together and mending a relationship, he could just about predict what she was about to say. "Well, I trust you two gentlemen. I know I'll be safe with you guys around and when you're not, I can be ready for anybody coming through that door. I'm going back to my computer and phone, I've got more work to do. Booker, dinner is in the fridge. Just heat it up. Demetrious, please stay if you want. Love you both." Misha Falone went back into the third bedroom, now an office, and closed the door.

"I wish I could say more, Book. I do."

"You can't answer this, but I think I know what you're doing. This has something to do with your father, doesn't it?"

While lack of a life around each other was one thing, Booker was still able to decipher tells in the eyes and face of Demetrious. A tell or sign of what he might do was so slight that if Booker didn't make a point to watch closely, he would miss the tell altogether. Demetrious blinked twice and remained quiet for a few seconds.

"I just can't talk about it. And please, no police." Demetrious turned toward the door. "I promise, I'll be careful. You do the same."

"I'll honor your request for now. Take care."

46

At four minutes past seven a.m. Thursday, Booker got out of his car, leaned against the front passenger side fender, and looked out over the house and property of William Rocker. In the cup holder was a fresh mix of banana, pineapple and pomegranate juices. The juice would have to wait. Right now, Booker again concentrated on the house where he'd been just twenty-four hours earlier.

Coffee drove up in her SUV and walked over to Booker. "So, why are we back here again?"

"I got your tea in the car. Just don't touch my juice."

She opened the door, took out the tea and let the cup warm her hand. "Left the camera in the car until you explain why we're here."

"I just wanted to think."

"Think? Okay." She took a long sip from the cup and joined his gaze toward the door of the place.

"Just rolling things around in my head, Coff. All the break-ins, the stolen knives. Just trying to put the pieces together."

"Let the police do that." Another sip, this time louder than the first. "Know what they're saying on the Crummick app? That Rocker tore up his own floorboards. Made it look like someone was trashing the place. There's still people out there who think he's behind all this."

Booker walked the front sidewalk twice, moving to his right, checking the side of the house, then walking to the other side. The entire time, Coffee just watched him walk. Booker retrieved his juice and swallowed half the cup. There was only another thirty minutes left and he would be on the clock, with the mandatory check-in with Claire Stanley. "The app say anything else?"

"Just that more than half the comments go in the judge's favor, that they believe him. Seems like every time he's on TV, he gets support. Comments in his favor go up."

Booker was just about ready to get in his car and leave. He downed the rest of the juice. He tried to separate the events, circling Demetrious out of his thoughts for now. Misha told him she was going to the home office to work there for the next few days. He was planning to swing by the café later in the day sometime after lunch and check on Demetrious.

All his movements in front of the house were being watched by Coffee. She stayed quiet during his thinking time and left him alone.

There were moments in Booker's career when subtle pieces of information turned into a major turn of events. In those times, wherever he was, he would snap his fingers, a signal all the unpressured moments in thought led to a big conclusion. Right now, he was definitely under some pressure. The kind that could slow and cloud a person's reasoning. Not the thing one needed for making the right move.

Booker checked his watch, realizing his time was just about over. He spent the next few minutes anticipating most of his morning movements. There was the daily check with police on any new movement on the two cases. He already had updates on Campana. His only card to play was returning to the office.

"Hey Book, I'm headed to the shop. Claire might have something for me, but if you need me, I'm ready."

"Thanks."

She crushed the cup and carried it with her to the SUV. Booker considered himself lucky to be able to work with her. She was patient as the first rays of sunshine, but he'd seen her swat away anyone who got in the way of her camera shot. Stanley told him other reporters were lined up to work with her, but management didn't want to break up the team. He watched her drive off, leaving him with just the house and his thoughts.

He spoke out loud to himself. "House, house, what is it about the house that they're looking for?" Booker turned around to see if anyone was around to catch a man speaking to no one. It was time to go. Booker got into his car, sat behind the wheel and checked the residence one last time.

He snapped his fingers.

Booker sent a text to Stanley indicating he would be checking in soon. Then, he called B.B. "Morning. You home?"

"I was planning to go out soon. Why?"

"There's something I want to check out. Stay there and don't move. I'll be right there."

47

During the drive to B.B.'s complex, Booker kept a steady watch to make sure he was not followed. The letter about Demetrious had him taking extra precautions. He had no idea what information Demetrious was holding back. The threat level toward his brother had increased and he wasn't sure how to address what did or did not happen. When he reached the apartment, Booker circled around four times and made sure no one was behind him when he parked.

B.B. opened the door just when he was about to knock. Her hair was pulled back and her nails were red. Even in bare feet, she was just as tall as Booker. The moment she said, "Come in," Booker moved quickly to the center of the apartment.

"That case that belonged to Fila, can I see it again?"

"Sure."

He waited for her at the kitchen table. When she came back into the room, Booker took the case from her since it looked heavy, and he eased the case onto the countertop. B.B. opened the case. "And what are you looking for?"

"Not sure. I just remember something, and I want to see it again. Remember, there was a sock in her running shoe."

"Yes. We only saw a piece of what was inside. The keyring."

B.B. raked her hand through the belongings and the photographs until she found a shoe. Booker was about to grab the shoe, but opted instead to let B.B. handle it. She pulled the sock out slowly and placed it on the table, then removed the keyring.

Booker saw the same thing he saw before, a small window. Finally, the entire keyring spilled out onto the countertop. B.B.'s eyes widened.

Booker leaned in. "The keyring is a house. Largest keyring I've ever seen." He had looked over William Rocker's home and the ransacking that had taken place. In Booker's view, the person or persons involved in Fila's death, Ken Capilon and Eddie Beck, were all looking for something that Booker thought was in an actual home.

"B.B., when Fila wrote the word HOME, she must have been talking about this, the keychain. This is the house she was referring to. See if you can open it." Booker held up his hand. "Wait, you have some gloves?"

"No problem. Way ahead of you. If this is something, you want to preserve her prints if she handled this." B.B. opened a kitchen drawer and pulled out a pair of purple hospital-styled plastic gloves.

"Okay, let's open this." B.B. grabbed it, holding the keychain in the air, which was big and detailed upon more inspection. She twisted the keychain with anticipation and after three tries, the entire front of the tiny house popped open. A thumb drive fell onto the counter.

"She hid it." B.B. leaned down, taking a closer look.

Booker's thought process was moving a hundred miles an hour. "The next few things we do are extremely important, so hear me out. It's vital we keep things in order. I, myself, am not going to touch this thumb-drive. You have a laptop?"

"Yes."

"Where is it?"

"Right there on the coffee table."

"Okay." Booker retrieved the laptop, opened it up and let B.B. turn it on. "Now, insert the drive and we'll see what she was saving."

Four files appeared on the computer screen. All of them were labeled Green Wave Drivers. There were dates. "These dates might correspond to the dates she wrote down on paper. Okay, open the first file."

Once open, they were watching a video. For almost two minutes, nothing happened. From what he could tell, Booker and B.B. were watching an angle that looked like it was from a hidden camera. The camera must have been mounted somewhere in the back seat of a car and pointed toward the driver's seat. Then three men approached and one man reached into the car behind the driver's seat and popped open a compartment. Then he took out a large packet and handed it over to a second man. There was recorded audio. "Here you go. Consider this delivered. The driver, she doesn't know what's in it. There's forty thou there. Enough for this one-third of the kick. Another fifty K coming soon. They want this project to move forward. Once the driver makes the stop, I want confirmation."

The man who got the money spoke up. "The deciding vote is secure. Tell them I'll make sure it happens."

Again, the first man. "The same deal as the others, there will be a note put in the usual place. The note will just have the letter D on it. D for done."

The money receiver said, "Got it. Done." All three of them started laughing. The video ended.

B.B. opened up the second file. The same scenario like the first instance. A lump sum of money was handed off to two other men. Using a different car this time, one of the other men took what looked like a money packet from a compartment built into the back of the driver's seat. Like before, a lid was opened, the packet pulled out and the lid closed again. And there was more conversation. "This is working out great."

Over the next twenty minutes Booker and B.B. watched videos of money being taken out of a car in the same manner and, in other cases, money put inside. When they got to the fourth and last video, B.B. gasped. "That's Fila. She recorded herself."

"You want to stop? We can stop now if you want."

A single tear formed at her left eye, rolling down her cheek and hanging there, leaving behind a wet streak. She dabbed at her hazel eyes. "She wanted me to see this. I have to continue." She started the video. Fila was speaking, holding up a small device. "This is Fila Mackee. If you look at all the videos, you will see I was able to record twenty-three transactions. I used a pin camera with audio. I recorded this so someone, one day, can do something about this. These are payoffs. Please know, I attached a tracker on the bottom of one car and I located the garage where all the cars were being hidden. Also, and this is important, on my last trip with Green Wave Drivers, I stole their payment. The money is in the spare tire compartment in my car. I think they might have discovered one of my cameras. If for some reason, something happens to me, please do something with the videos." The screen went blank.

A separate file was marked "P's taken by Eddie."

"You think P's means photographs? And Eddie has to be Eddie Beck." Booker waited for B.B. to respond on whether she should open the file.

"Let's see."

The file contained sixteen photographs, all from various locations. Three pictures Booker recognized immediately. "I know this event. This was the charity fund-raiser. This is a picture of everyone there, along with, if you look close, that's Fila in the background."

B.B. was locked in on the photos. "That's my girl. You know these people?"

Booker said, "Some of them." And there was a photograph of Shanice Rocker. "This is Fila's mother. Her real mother. This shows the two of them were in the same room together. Maybe that's where she confirmed the information that Shanice was her mother and later showed up at her door.

Booker was taking notes on his phone. "The car she mentioned, that was five years ago, did she sell it?"

"I have the car."

"You have the car? You have Fila's car?"

"Well, to make a long story short, I was helping her out so we both signed for the car together. We shared the car since I was out of town so much."

"So, you haven't looked inside the spare tire boot?"

"The car runs great. No problems and no flat tires. I've never looked inside there."

"Okay. Keep the drive with you and let's look at your car."

B.B. put the thumb-drive into a plastic baggie, pushed it down in her pocket, and the two of them went downstairs. Booker looked around and found nothing unusual outside. The car was parked under a shade tree.

Once the rear of the SUV was opened, B.B. lifted the carpeted top. Inside the compartment, there was a clear plastic bag. Booker counted three long rows of stacked bills, neat and ready for spending.

B.B. started to touch the package, then stopped. "Damn. Just like she said. It's been here all this time."

Booker took out his phone and snapped off eight to ten photographs of the money. "This is what they've been looking for. She didn't say anything before her death?"

B.B. closed up the compartment. "No. But I recognize one person on the video. I've seen him before."

Booker started to dial, then saw he only had one bar. "I have to move to another location to call out. I've got to make a few calls then come back."

"Understood."

Booker got ready to leave. "Listen to me. After I leave, I want you to do the following things. Lock up the car, go back upstairs and don't let anyone inside."

"Okay. No problem."

"And that person you recognize. His face should be familiar. The guy taking all that money, that's the mayor of Everpalm."

48

Booker had a lot to share with Stanley. He drove out of the grouping of buildings, headed to a main roadway. His plan was to make the call and return to B.B.'s place, and have Coffee meet him there. A half mile into his drive, Booker pulled over. He was about to make the call to the station and first started writing a text message. He was almost finished when his car was bumped from behind.

His airbags did not deploy, and Booker checked his mirror. The mirror itself was filled with the image of a gun barrel pointed directly at him. Booker typed in one more sentence and sent off the text. The voice behind the gun sounded forced. "Get your foot away from the gas pedal."

Booker looked up and into the face of someone with a balaclava. "Lower the window, Mr. Johnson."

A hundred thoughts raced through Booker's mind. He could ignore the directive and stomp on the gas anyway. He could comply or he could get out of the car and confront him.

"Listen, Mr. Dipshit, your brother's life depends on what you do. By the time you touch that gas pedal, you'll get four in the head. Is that clear? Now lower the fucking window."

Booker was trying to determine whether he had heard the voice before. The man tapped the window twice. Booker let down the glass.

"Good," the man said. "Make sure the doors are open. We're going to take a ride." The man quickly moved around the car, the gun trained on Booker the entire time. The figure kept his head down as if avoiding the small number of cars moving down the street. The man got into the car, moving to the back seat directly behind Booker. He aimed the gun so the barrel was about two inches from Booker's right temple. "Give me your phone."

"What did you mean about my brother?"

"Demetrious? We've been following his ass for a long time. We almost got him before, but you had someone step in to prevent it. It won't happen again. If you don't comply, he will die. The phone!"

Booker held onto it, thumb pressed into the front of the phone, attempting to press buttons. "Where are we going?"

"I have a place in mind. You just drive."

Booker's concerns about Demetrious were confirmed. Someone must have tried to kill him the other night and Demetrious stayed quiet. And the person who stepped in to help must have been Demetrious' father. Booker took in every detail he could about the intruder. He figured he must have been following him at some point coming out of the complex. Booker tried to guess the man's height, decipher the fake voice, and recognize he was right-handed. Booker tried to push the narrative in his direction. "What do you want?"

"I know you must know what I'm looking for. The information you have on Green Wave Drivers. All of it. Now for the last time, hand me the phone."

"The only way I'll speak to you is we go to a public place. We go to Limestone Park and I'll tell you everything I know."

"We're not going to any park. Just drive and I'll tell you where to turn."

"You can shoot me right now if you want. Go ahead! And you won't hear what I have to say about the video."

Even through the mask, Booker could tell he made an impact. The gun was moved even closer now, pressed right up against his head. "What about a video?"

"Nothing else. We go to Limestone Park and I'll tell you everything. And you leave my brother out of it."

Booker gambled his life on what the armed man would do in the next few seconds. And possibly the life of Demetrious. The wait grew longer. Any attempt to drive off now would end in Booker's death. The man pulled out what looked like a burner phone, dialed and whispered a short message, then returned full attention to Booker. "The phone!"

Booker handed him his cell phone. He took Booker's phone in his left hand, then dropped it in his lap and lowered the window. "Pull over."

"What, here?" Booker kept driving.

"Pull over." The barrel was pointed in the direction he wanted to stop the car. "Now drive toward that canal."

Booker saw a thin body of water next to the road. In the next twenty seconds Booker could change the direction of what was happening. He could hit the gas and drive full-speed into the canal. In another scenario, Booker quickly thought, he could drive into a car, causing a huge wreck. The ensuing crash might give him a chance to escape. He even thought about jamming into reverse and driving fast, causing confusion. There were all kinds of escapes running through his thoughts. He decided to use none of them. Let things play out. Booker stopped, pulled to the side, and in the mirror, he watched the gunman move the weapon to his left hand. He used his right to promptly throw the phone like it was a disc, far enough to reach the narrow canal.

He yelled. "We're going to Limestone Park, or it will be your last drive."

From their current location, Booker knew the travel route would take them twenty minutes. Booker's car windows were tinted, letting the gunman travel without much concern about being seen. Booker gave up trying to question him. The gun stayed fixed on Booker, and did not move. Four times during the journey, the man made it clear the trip to the park better be beneficial or Booker would know the power of the gun held near his head.

Booker drove past strip malls and neighborhoods. There were several times when he considered stopping and jumping out of the car. He dismissed all those ideas and kept the safety of Demetrious as his main priority. Even if he could get word to police, would that stop someone from getting to his brother before help got there? And during the drive, he knew at any given moment, the figure could simply have him pull over somewhere else and pull the trigger. The information they were seeking must be critical if they quickly agreed to meet in a public area.

While he drove, Booker's thoughts were on the identity of the man behind him. He weighed all the factors he had amassed in the past several days and was moving toward a name. The first hint of a brief end to humid days had arrived in the morning. The temperatures were much cooler, and Floridians enjoyed a morsel of what the pending months would bring. Yet, even with the car's AC running and the lower temp, the man with the gun reached up and tried to wipe away a line of sweat moving inside his balaclava toward his eyes. Booker recognized the movement because he had seen the move before. If he said anything, he wasn't sure what action the man might take, but he decided to go for it anyway.

"You can take off that mask and stop the garbled voice. Ray Aldon, charity director, I know it's you."

49

Limestone Park got its name from the makeup of the soil and rock covering virtually the entire state of Florida. Booker drove past the tall green and gray welcome sign near the entrance. He parked near a hiking trail and a small pond.

"This good enough?" Booker put the car in park and waited for an answer.

"Get out!" Aldon got out of the car, keeping the gun pointed at Booker's head.

Out in front of him, Booker saw people arriving, parking cars and pulling out blankets and containers of water. Aldon did a quick look around like he was looking for a spot away from most other people. Booker walked toward an empty bench. He made a decision to sit down, not knowing if Aldon would agree to the location. Booker sat. Aldon kept the gun under his shirt, barrel in Booker's direction.

Around them, park goers were enjoying the sun, some throwing frisbees. Others were taking selfies and checking to see if everyone was in the photograph. Booker saw a woman off by herself with a book. Four more couples sat with their backs to Booker. The park was alive with a lot of visitors, and all of them looked to be young, college-aged.

"Okay, Mr. Booker. You got your wish. We're in the public. Now talk."

"What do you want to know?"

He held the gun aimed at Booker. "We know Fila had cameras. Did you find any recordings?"

"Maybe. What if I did?"

"Look. This isn't the time to be coy. If I make one call or if someone does not hear from me soon, your brother is dead."

"I need to know if my brother is okay. If you can assure me of that, I will continue." Booker tried to look resolute, something not easily done with a gun just two feet away. Other couples were now entering the park, and small bits of chatter echoed across the grass. Booker knew the park well and had already outlined escape routes in his head if he got the chance to run. The routes would offer little help if a bullet found him first.

"Stop dictating how this is gonna go down. We need some answers right now."

"We?"

Aldon's eyebrows crashed together and his jaw clinched. "Talk now."

"I'll give you a piece of what I know. There's video of transactions going down. And it won't look good if those videos get into the right hands."

"You saw these videos?" Aldon picked up the cell phone and made a call. All he said were two words. "Here. Now." He put the phone down and lifted the gun just a bit higher, now pointed at Booker's face.

"There's people on the videos. And you can hear all of the conversations. Deals going down. Very clear video."

"Where's the video now?"

"Ah, if you want them, I want to know Demetrious is okay. Make that happen and we'll go from there."

A man appeared at the back of Booker. He heard him walking on the sandy soil, stopping near Booker's left shoulder. Booker took a guess. "I'm thinking this is Branson Landale." Before Booker's suspicions were confirmed, a large-bladed knife moved in close to Booker's neck. Branson Landale stepped around until he was facing Booker. The knife was held downward, the day's sun glinting off the metal. Landale took his free hand and slammed his fist into Booker's shoulder.

Booker stiffened and looked up and into his face. "You worked with Ken

Capilon. Worked with him on the charity. And you had a hand in his death. I'm guessing that knife was stolen from William Rocker."

Landale shook back his blond locks. "What has he told you?"

"He knows about the videos." Aldon, the gunman, looked determined to shoot.

Landale slid the knife into a holder, hidden now from view. "And how do you know about the two of us?"

"Well, even though neither of you are seen, there is a lot of talk about you both. Conversations with the mayor of Everpalm. But answer this. Why did you have to kill Fila Mackee?"

Landale said, "Because she wouldn't give up the tapes. We found her camera hidden in one of our cars."

"So you conned your way into her apartment and fed her fentanyl and watched her die."

Landale moved in closer, almost striking distance with the knife. "We have to kill him."

Aldon looked upset. He wiped sweat from his forehead. "Stop talking. Let this moron Booker talk. We're gonna ease on out of here and get back to the car."

Booker played another card. "And you don't want to know where the money is?"

Both men looked surprised. Booker kept up the curiosity. "That's correct. You should be missing a big clear bag of money. You wondered where it's been all these years. Well, I know where it is, and it has to be just laced with fingerprints."

The gunman started to yell, then lowered his voice. "He's bluffing. He doesn't have any money."

Booker looked first at Landale, then to Aldon. "You know what this is all about? One word. Greed. You had it all set up. Kickback payments going to shell companies. But that wasn't enough. You both had the bribe pipeline going then you got into this let's-have-fun mode. You got bored and started stuffing cars with cash. You used Fila and Eddie Beck as money mules. Unknowingly, they drove bribe money back and forth. Until one day, Fila found out about it and installed a hidden camera. Who is the one who killed her? I'm guessing you were both there that night. And guess what? A so-called close friend of yours, she woke up this morning from her coma. And she's probably talking with police."

Ray Aldon stood up for the first time. He started looking around like he wanted to make a run. Booker kept going. "Mercedes Campana called you after she did an interview with me. Said that she was going to police. That's how you knew to send a guy to force her off the road. Isn't that right?"

The knife came back out in plain sight. "Mercedes knew too much. She had to go." He stopped speaking.

Booker pointed to him. "You can tell me. I don't have a camera. No cell phone. No nothing." Now Booker was raising his voice. "After Fila died, Shanice contacted you both about her daughter. She was looking too hard. Might stir things up. You lured her to that house. You cut her up."

The blond yelled back. "It wasn't just me. He was there. We had to get the videotapes."

Booker's shoulders squared up. He fought within himself to remain in control and not get himself killed. "And you both killed her. You must have demanded the video, but she didn't know anything about the videos."

The two men were standing, hovering around Booker like they were both ready to silence him. "One last thing. As we speak, the videos, the money and the thumb-drive are in the hands of police. I instructed the person who had them to give them over. And yes, I have a copy as well."

Aldon yelled. "Cut him, it's neater. A quiet death. A bullet will draw too much attention."

Booker could no longer contain himself. "Have either of you heard of the social media platform called Crummick? Well, Crummick has literally thousands of followers to this story and some of them are here today."

Aldon and Landale pivoted, casting looks at the people who were once casually enjoying the day and were now all aiming cell phones in their direction.

"You can kill me if you want but let me tell you first. One person over there has two million followers. The one there on the right, well, she has four hundred thousand. From the moment we all entered the park, we have been live on Crummick, video going to all those millions of followers. And they are just waiting to see what you will do next. You both have now gone viral."

Landale raised the knife in Booker's direction, then lowered the blade and took off running. Aldon, at first, just stood there, looking perplexed, then he ran after Landale. Both got into Landale's car and drove fast toward the entrance. Once they turned onto the roadway, Booker heard the wail of police sirens.

Booker sat there. Off to his right, the woman who was once reading a book, had a cell phone of her own. Junice Coffee ran toward Booker. She stopped, almost out of breath, looking him over like she was checking for any injuries. "You okay, Book?"

"I'm fine. Glad you got my second text."

"I got it. The first one told us about B.B. That text was clear to understand. We sent two crews over there. Got there just a bit ahead of the police. There's a lot to process. And I understand you had the presence not to touch anything?"

"B.B. handled everything. And I saw your text about Mercedes. Glad to see she's okay."

"She sent word through the hospital. When she's better, she wants to speak with you."

"Obviously, we have crews on the arrest?"

"Yep. We have Grandhouse down the street. I heard police caught them two blocks from here. Stanley sent Merilee Yang to the police department. They'll go there first for questioning. And we have another crew at the apartment where your friend B.B. has been waiting for us and police to pick up everything."

"And the mayor?"

"Booker, they just now got their hands on the evidence. It's gonna take a while. You know that."

"You're right."

Coffee sat down next to him. "You had me scared Book. When I saw the gun and a knife appear, I almost ran over here when that jerk pushed you. But I left you alone."

"I thought they might turn around and see any of you."

"They were so caught up talking to you, they didn't pay any attention to us. I was close enough to hear everything. A few of us out here had high-sensitive microphones attached to our phones using XLR cables and adapters. These guys have expensive stuff."

"Thanks for figuring out my text. I could only say it out loud, then hit send."

"At first I didn't quite understand Limestone Park. Then I got my butt over here. Stanley took care of the rest. She put out word on Crummick and our own website that a major break was coming. Then, she texted where you were going."

"Wow. Everyone could have seen that, including some bad folks."

"She thought the more people saw it, the better."

Booker searched for his car keys. "We've got to get a report ready."

50

The general manager of Channel 27, the senior producer of the newscasts, the news director and someone from H.R. all wanted to know if Booker wanted to go home and rest or stay on the story. Booker learned later it was Stanley who firmly told them he would be just fine. There was also the question of police who insisted on talking to Booker about what happened and the weapons involved. Booker knew charges could be pending of kidnapping, assault, and possible attempted murder. The only thing Booker wanted was to get in front of a camera and tell his story.

Grandhouse had her own story to tell. She was on scene where the car crashed with Landale and Aldon inside. She would stand in front of the car, all surrounded with crime scene tape and do her report. Booker's own car was now in the custody of police. Booker was right where all reporters do not want to be: part of the story. He had no choice.

The two other TV stations were also there reporting since they had to see the social media feeds. Crummick made the whole thing available to the world with just a tap on the phone or clicks on a computer. Booker looked around. The people in the park who fed to Crummick could also be potential witnesses. Booker had never experienced anything like this before. Coffee used her cell phone to feed a live signal to the Channel 27 website. She and many others had used a snap-on high-grade microphone and, in Coffee's case, the microphone was covered in a windsock, resembling a furry animal. The sock blocked out noise. Like she told Booker, the two assailants were so caught up with him, they didn't notice the equipment being used. Booker called Stanley. "How are you all blocking this out for the newscasts? Umbrella lead with me and Grandhouse?"

"For sure. We will use two in the box with you and Grandhouse in the picture for just a tease. Then we will come to you. Booker, you okay doing this?"

"You're the fifth person to ask me that. Yes, I'm fine. Anything else I should know?"

"We have two crews at the hospital since these guys got banged up in the crash. We have another crew at police HQ. We're not sure if they're talking to them at HQ or the hospital."

"Gotcha. We're all ready."

Booker stood ready in front of Coffee's main camera and tripod. In his earpiece Booker heard the anchor in the studio: "We're breaking into our regular programming for something that played out live on social media and our own website. Channel 27's Booker Johnson taken at gunpoint to a park by a man wearing a mask and making demands. I can say Booker is just fine. He joins us now from Limestone Park. Booker, how did this whole ordeal start?"

"What happened today started as an investigation going back days ago when former judge William Rocker returned to the United States. Rocker was questioned in the murder of his wife Shanice four years ago. Since his return a lot has come to light. Channel 27 has learned Shanice was reunited with a daughter she had given up at birth. Fila Mackee was raised by a family in Chicago and, five years ago, found her mother. Mackee worked part-time for a company that used drivers to move cars around the city, especially older models. Mackee discovered a scheme to transport bribe money and made recordings. Fila Mackee died of an overdose and what you will hear and see are videos of the men who cornered me, demanding to get those videos back. The videos are now in the hands of police. Based on the videos we have seen and the comments made live, the men talked openly about murder and bribery. Channel 27 contacted the mayor of Everpalm about his appearance in the videos and, through his office, the mayor put out a statement saying 'they were going over the video and they are not prepared to make a comment right now, other than the mayor has always worked in the best interests of the citizens.' As for the men here at the park, they are under arrest for what happened to me with police looking at them for a connection to the murder of Shanice Rocker."

Channel 27 showed the home viewing audience three videotaped recordings made by Fila Mackee, followed by several video clips of Landale and Aldon in the park, confronting Booker. The segment ran almost six minutes. Much longer than a regular news feed. Booker kept his portion short for his wrap-up. "There are several more videos to share with you. Please know, Channel 27 has sent copies of all of the videos to the mayor. There will be more to come on what happened today and the hope that police will reopen the investigation into the overdose of Fila Mackee. Booker Johnson, Channel 27 news."

Booker heard an 'all clear' in his ear. Then he heard the lead-in to Grandhouse who was in front of the smashed car. Booker didn't get to hear a lot since police Detective Brielle Jensen was standing, waiting for him.

"Detective."

"One of our detectives is ready to take your statement. We'll keep just to what went on today. But are you okay?"

"Yeah, I'm fine."

"Sorry about your car but it's part of the investigation now. You'll get it back as soon as possible."

"Trust me, I understand."

In her capacity in the P.I.O. position, Booker and Jensen had shared conversations at various events. One time they both spoke with students in an elementary school for career day. He admired her tenacity to cut to the truth on any crime scene. She ran her hands over her sun-worn locks, making sure they were all tied in back.

"Booker, I know you've been working hard on this. But while I can't say much right now, please know we've been working hard as well. There will be a news conference later. Take care of yourself."

Booker used a smile as a way of saying thank you. He was surrounded by tiny beehives of conversations.

The last thing Booker or any reporter wanted to do was involve himself in an investigation, large or small. He listened through his earpiece as Grandhouse deftly explained how the car with Landale and Aldon left the park at a great speed, avoided two other cars, missed a police unit, then crashed. She had video of one man being taken by fire rescue. The other, Aldon, was put into a police vehicle for transport. Together, the two reports spanned more than eighteen minutes. The anchor then returned everything back to regular programming.

The statement with police was brief with the detective telling him they would be making a follow-up visit soon.

Booker thought about the task ahead of him. He was locked down to the park area and would remain here for all other live reports throughout the day. Channel 27 texted him to say they would be bringing food and water over, Booker was to stay in place and not move. Grandhouse was in the same position. She got video of the car being processed by crime scene techs, then an hour later, the car was towed to the crime lab. Both of them had to stay in place.

Booker also had to interview people who witnessed and fed video to Crummick. That task alone would take the next fifty minutes.

Elsewhere, other crews would have to follow the story. An hour later, a car pulled up and William Rocker pushed open the passenger door. The driver was Serenity Hart. They walked toward Booker.

51

Booker didn't expect to see them. Within ten minutes, reporters from the other stations, newspaper reporters, and some of the Crummick content creators all assembled in a spot near Booker's location. Coffee got her sticks in place and snapped the camera into the mount.

Hart, as usual, controlled the moment. "Thank you for coming. I called this news conference to make a few statements about what transpired here this morning." The arc of cameras were all pointed at Hart. "We are thankful to police and to Mr. Booker Johnson for bringing facts to the public which clearly prove my client, Judge William Rocker, did not have anything to do with the death of his wife, Shanice. We hope that police will move forward with the investigation and make the appropriate charges. Mr. Rocker has been waiting for this moment. He will make a statement, but he will not be taking questions. When he is finished, I will answer some of the questions you have."

Rocker, looking straight ahead, stepped up before the cameras. "My wife Shanice was looking for answers when she died. Answers on what happened to her daughter, Fila Mackee. We do not believe Fila overdosed and, indeed, she was a victim just like her mother. For now, I want to thank the detectives working on this case and I, too, want to thank Mr. Johnson for uncovering so much and for putting his life on the line. Some would say on the line for a news story. But it's much more than just a story. We're talking about the murders of four people. Thank you."

There was a whisper of questions which was quickly drowned out by the voice of Hart. "Any questions for me?"

A woman off to the side of the group asked, "Can you explain why his wife was at the house that night?"

Hart looked right to left. "She was lured there because she wanted to find out what really happened to her daughter. Fila had just met her biological mother. They were just starting to know each other. Shanice did not know about the transporting of money. None of it. Then Fila was taken from her. She started her own investigation and when she got too close, she was killed."

Booker asked the next question, "Can you speak to why people would change or lie about the judge during this investigation?"

There was a quick spark in her eyes, like a fresh-lit flare, then her expression calmed down to one of a court-ready attorney. "There is an answer to that, but I can't say anything just yet. I'll let police handle that. Thank you for being here." Hart turned and directed Rocker to leave with her. During the walk back to the car, Rocker turned and nodded an approval to Booker.

Forty minutes later, Detective Jensen made comments. She spoke about the crash and the arrests of two men, without naming them. Beyond the brief statement, there was little else. Even though a Channel 27 camera recorded video of crime techs taking away evidence from B.B.'s car, the money and thumb-drive, Jensen would not comment. For Booker, it was clear police didn't want to reveal a lot of what their investigation contained and how much work needed to be done.

52

Eight Days Later

Booker got out of his car and started looking for her. It was 7:30 a.m., and Booker found himself in the park, just where he was instructed to be and told to wait. A Lincoln Navigator pulled up next to Booker's car. Mercedes Campana got out, walked to the rear of the Lincoln and opened the rear hatch. She sat down and pulled over a pair of running shoes. "You just gonna stare at me?"

Booker joined her at the rear of the SUV. "Going running?"

"This is the spot where I was attacked and managed to get away. I'm taking my spot back. Make some new memories. Replace the old." She pulled up the laces and tied both shoes. "I usually run in the evening but I'm taking a break from everything, so I'm gonna run in the morning."

"You feeling okay?"

"Just peachy. Look, I invited you here for an on-the-record convo, and no camera, just to clear up a few things."

"Okay."

"At first, I didn't come forward to back up William Rocker because I was being blackmailed. All of us were. Me, Ken Capilon, Aldon and Landale.

We got some pretty strong emails from somewhere, we couldn't figure that out. I've done some shady shit back in the day and I didn't want it to come out. What I didn't know is that the blackmailers were my so-called friends, Aldon and Landale. I found out much later they were behind all of it. I'm guessing when Ken told one of them he was going to tell the truth, well, he was killed. And yes, those same two were responsible for running me off the road, but that will come out through police. We all let William down. All of us. Ken and I were going to make it right."

Booker watched her stretching. "And you thought Aldon and Landale were victims like you?"

"Yep. Boy was I wrong. So now you know. If Ken and I testified, they were afraid the investigation would somehow turn toward them. All this to frame Rocker and keep attention away from themselves. You go do what you have to do and me, I'm gonna start running and ease my mind from all this. Thanks, Booker."

He turned to leave, set to get into the office early. Mercedes Campana took off toward the hiking trail. Her smooth easy gait took her past the nature-made rows of palmetto palms where she disappeared down the path, among the tall Banyan trees.

Just after noon, Booker stood in front of the house on Willdrift Lane, on the edge of the yard full of rocks. Near the house, there was a line of overgrown oak trees, their branches nearly touching the ground from years of no maintenance. The house looked like it was begging to be torn down. Off to the far right, there was a For Sale sign.

Coffee zoomed in on Booker's face. He was thirty seconds from his live spot. In his ear, the words of the anchor, "A week after the stunning threat to Channel 27's Booker Johnson, we have several major breaks in the story. Booker?"

"Thank you. This is the house where Shanice Rocker was tortured and murdered. All, police say, because her attackers thought she knew the whereabouts of incriminating videos. Shanice didn't know anything about them. She was lured here, authorities say, by someone claiming they had information about the death of her daughter, Fila Mackee. Now, the men responsible for the death of Rocker have been arrested. In an attempt to avoid the death penalty both men will be pleading guilty next month. They were in court this morning, where they indicated they do not want to go to trial."

Booker's videotaped story included video of Aldon and Landale in court, clean-shaven and dressed in new suits. Neither man wanted to look back toward William Rocker, who was seated four rows behind the defense tables.

On tape, Booker's narration continued, "Police say the men will be cooperating in a growing investigation involving the former mayor of Everpalm who stepped down three days ago." Booker's story cut to Detective Jensen. "A statewide grand jury has handed up an indictment against Munis Grant, former mayor of Everpalm. This is a RICO indictment alleging Grant and three others conspired in a scheme to funnel bribe money to Grant by way of six shell companies. Our investigation will prove the men, including Ray Aldon and Branson Landale organized the scheme and pushed more than three million dollars into the hands of Grant. And with Grant's assistance, Aldon and Landale secured votes on a number of projects. The Racketeering, Influence and Corrupt Organizations or R.I.C.O. investigation has been ongoing since the death of Shanice Rocker. We have also reopened the overdose death investigation of Rocker's daughter, Fila Mackee, as we now suspect she was a victim of murder, forced to overdose. Part of the R.I.C.O. investigation has uncovered that these men were so confident they could get away with anything, they came up with something for kicks. According to one of the defendants, they wanted to hire unknowing drivers as money mules to transport some of the cash. Now, we have some of that money, along with fingerprints. And we have the full cooperation of Aldon and Landale."

The video went back to Johnson, live in front of the house. "Mayor Grant has not spoken to Channel 27. We have reached out to him and his attorney and, so far, no comment. We do know Grant is working out a date soon to turn himself in. There is one other part of this still-developing story and other arrests are expected. Days ago, we brought you the interview of Mercedes Campana. She is the one who was just about to come forward and speak with detectives. She says she was the target of an attack and escaped. She told her story to Channel 27, then her car was run off the road. She told me this morning she was being blackmailed and that's why she didn't come forward at the time. She also implicated Landale and Aldon in forcing her off the road. Police did find a burned-out car near Alligator Alley. A car police believe was the one that slammed into Campana's car. Even though the car was burned, they were able to collect paint samplings and match them to the collision. A search warrant at a warehouse also turned up most of the cars used in the scheme. A money mule scheme started for kicks on top of the bribery through wired payments and shell companies. I want to make it clear, this whole investigation started because of Fila Mackee. In the thumb-drive she gave her friend, there were several photographs showing herself and Aldon and Landale at the various charity functions. They clearly knew her. She saw something wrong and tried to do something about it. Booker Johnson, Channel 27 news."

Booker gave the wireless microphone back to Coffee. She usually ended a live broadcast with a question. Today would be the same. "So, if those two plead guilty, that means you don't have to testify?"

"Looks that way. The guilty charges also include my involvement."

Booker looked beyond their SUV and saw a gleaming, two-door, convertible Ford that looked like a roadster from the 1930s. All teal with wide whitewalls. Next to the car was a tall, slender woman. Her hair had been kicked about all over the place, yet she probably didn't care. She held her hand out ten feet before she reached Booker.

"I just want to thank you. I saw you on social media. Booker, I thought those two were going to kill you."

"Salanna. Salanna Stock. Antique car president."

"Yep. That's me. I managed to pull it out of your station, and they told me where you were. I just wanted to drive over in my other favorite car and say thank you for showing people what idiots these guys were."

"It's up to the justice system now. They need to be sentenced."

"At least you got'em caught and they're off the street. Thanks." She jammed her hands through her hair in a vain attempt to straighten out the locks. "I'm headed back. Please stop by anytime. You and Coffee." Stock turned to the photographer. "See, I remembered your name. You two stop on by and I'll give you a ride you'll never forget."

"Thanks."

53

Booker was wearing a suit for the first time in months. He had avoided time in the studio which would have required a shirt and tie. He stood next to the person who resembled him. Demetrious Moreland refused the suit and wore a long-sleeved black dress shirt and black pants. Demetrious wiped lint off his sleeve. "Hate wearing ties."

"So, is there anything you want to tell me?" Booker had his hands in his pockets.

"No."

"About the person who saved you that night? From what I'm hearing he was armed. And came to your rescue. That was the night, rather early morning, I helped you move in."

"Yeah, we had a dust-up."

"Sounded like it was more than a dust-up. They were going to kill you. Let me guess. It was your father, and he was armed."

"I really don't—"

"I know, you don't want to talk about it. But it had to be Roland Caston. Man-on-the-run."

"Not anymore."

Booker's hands shot out of the pockets. "What? He was arrested?"

"Not exactly. That's why I can't talk about it. He is no longer a wanted man. He worked it out and now, well, he's a good guy."

"Your father? A good guy?" Booker couldn't hide his disbelief. For the next few seconds, Booker put together everything connected to the words 'now he's a good guy.' And then thought about why Demetrious didn't want to say anything publicly. "I'll tell you what, I won't bring it up again. If I can read what you're saying, it's better for me to leave it alone."

"Thanks, Book."

"You ready to go in?"

Booker and Demetrious entered the cemetery. Booker already knew the path leading to the graves of Shanice Rocker and Fila Mackee. Before them, a large gathering was already in place. Many held flowers in their hands. Booker took up a spot near the back. In the middle of the crowd was B.B., dressed in a black dress. To her right was William Rocker. There were some faces Booker did not recognize. A wall of clouds had moved in front of the sun, blocking off any direct heat from above. For some reason, the cemetery always had the wind breezes gliding across the headstones.

B.B.'s face beamed. "Thank you all for coming. I am wearing an exact copy of the dress my best friend planned to wear. This black dress was going to be worn at a party. I know now this was going to be a special night. I think she was about to announce to me and the world she had found her biological mother, Shanice. She was so happy." B.B. paused. She gripped and regripped the flowers in her hands, then turned to the headstone. "Fila, we are here for you today in numbers to say we love you, we miss you." B.B. placed the flowers on the grave and stepped away.

William Rocker took a step forward. "I never got a chance to meet Fila. I never got a chance to know my stepdaughter. I saw the pictures of her, and she looked just like Shanice. I'm glad they got a chance to meet. Their time together was so short. Fila spent her adult life looking for her natural mother. After her death, Shanice spent the rest of her life trying to find the truth. And we know the truth. Someone took the life of Fila. I want to acknowledge the Mackees, who are here from Chicago. I promised them we would find out the facts and we did thanks to Booker Johnson and his team. Many thanks to them. We lost Fila and Shanice four and five years ago, but the pain of those losses is here with us. I want to thank everyone for taking a moment to remember them."

Rocker stepped back and, one by one, person after person placed flowers on the graves. Booker watched an older couple, him with all gray hair and her wearing a long black dress. They stood in front of Fila's gravesite. The only sounds came from the rustling of the wind cascading through nearby magnolia branches. Everyone stood there, in place, until finally Rocker said thanks. There were hugs.

Booker stepped toward Rocker. "There's something I need to return to you." Booker pulled out the set of house keys. "I never went inside your house. Just stood outside and tried to connect the dots."

Rocker took the keys. "I'm renovating my house and moving back in. You are welcome anytime."

"Thank you."

B.B. walked over to Booker. "Thank you for shining the light on Fila's life."

"No problem. It was my brother Demetrious who first brought some attention to her job. And my colleague Lacie Grandhouse who uncovered the first facts behind her death." Booker had one last question for her. "Five years ago when Fila died, did Shanice ever show up to your apartment? If she got any facts from police at the time, the address would be listed in the information."

"I think she did. I really don't know. My neighbor told me a woman stopped by twice, but I was out of town for several days. Then, nothing. I'm guessing it must have been Shanice."

"Understood. Thanks for everything you did."

"Well, welcome. I'm still reeling from all the attention that showed up at my door. First two crews from your station, recording everything the police did. They still have my car. And I was able to send you copies of the thumb-drive like you asked. Thanks for coming."

"I had to be here for Fila and Shanice."

54

Misha Falone stood in the shallow waters of the Atlantic and looked out over the ocean. Each incoming wave kicked at her legs. She dug her toes down deep into the sand. Booker joined her. When he moved in next to her, he kissed her on the forehead.

She kissed him back, on the lips. In doing so, she brushed up against his now-healed shoulder. Booker still massaged it. "I have to be careful. Some of my parts are out of warranty." Booker let out a laugh.

Misha wasn't smiling. "You have to be careful, Booker. I watched that video once and I had to close my eyes."

"I'm okay."

Another wave smacked up against her shins. "When I stand in the sand and the ocean, I feel connected to the whole world. I love it here."

"What we need is a vacation."

A grin spread across her face. "I know the place. We talked about it."

"If it's where I think, let's go. I'll set it up."

"Then, let's go. We're off to Key West."

Investigation Con
Book #1 of the Frank Tower Mystery Series

They thought he'd be an easy mark. They were wrong...

A con gone wrong sends two women running for their lives in this sizzling thriller about lust and power.

After meeting in domestic violence therapy, two women decide to change their lives in a radical way. Reinventing themselves as the Pearls, they establish their con. Flirting with single men in bars. Slipping drugs into their drinks. Stealing valuables from their unconscious bodies. They won't be victims anymore.

Until they steal a locked briefcase from the wrong man.

Now the girls are running from a trail of death following them across South Florida. A private investigator by the name of Frank Tower is their last hope for survival.

As you follow the Pearls through a "Fugitive" style chase, you'll be desperate to uncover the dark secrets behind the briefcase...and you will never believe what's inside.

Get your copy today at
severnriverbooks.com

AUTHOR'S NOTE

Please know the county of Apton, Florida, and the Crummick app are the creation of the writer.

I want to thank the always-hardworking team at Severn River Publishing. From building the plot to release day, they have been there, supporting and helping me put together *The Disclosure*.

I also wanted to celebrate the memory of one of my beta readers, Ron Larkin. Ron made it his mission to give me excellent feedback on my writing and offered valued opinions on the development of the characters. Ron's passion was he loved to read books.

ABOUT MEL TAYLOR

For many years, Mel Taylor watched history unfold as he covered news stories in the streets of Miami and Fort Lauderdale. A graduate of Southern Illinois University, Mel writes the Frank Tower Private Investigator series. He lives in a community close to one of his favorite places – The Florida Everglades. South Florida is the backdrop for his series.

Sign up for the reader list at
severnriverbooks.com

Printed in the United States
by Baker & Taylor Publisher Services